Yorkshire Lass

J. Carol Nemeth

Copyright 2016
Written by: J. Carol Nemeth
Published by: Forget Me Not Romances, a division of Winged
Publications

Cover Design: Cynthia Hickey

ISBN-10:1-944203-26-5
ISBN-13:978-1-944203-26-9

J. Carol Nemeth

Southampton, England
September 1918
Near the End of World War I

Chapter One

"*E*xcuse me, Miss. Hello! Excuse me! Gotta get through."

As she stood by the ship's railing, a firm tap on Jessica Montgomery's shoulder tugged her attention from the bustling port's activity. "Excuse me, Miss, but I gotta get this luggage to the quay right away. I'd love to stop and watch the view with you, but there'll be angry passengers if I don't get this luggage moving."

Turning, Jess realized she blocked a young porter struggling to push his loaded luggage dolly through the tide of moving passengers. "I'm terribly sorry." She stepped closer to the rail. "My mind was elsewhere."

"You're an American! Welcome to England." He smiled, tipping his cap. "It's difficult to move about on this deck, but I must press on. Have a pleasant stay."

"Thank you." Jess turned to join the masses disembarking, her stomach fluttering excitedly. England! She'd only ever dreamed of coming here. Despite the circumstances she was excited to see Mother's homeland.

5

After catching a taxi to the train station, Jess boarded the northbound train to Harrogate, settled into her seat and thought of her mother. They had planned to visit England, but Mother had become deathly ill, forcing Jess to quit teaching to care for her. After Mother's death, Jess was at a loss and felt very alone. Father had died in a train crash during a business trip three years earlier, and she had no close relatives... in America.

After writing her grandmother in England to tell of Mother's death, Jess received her letter expressing great sorrow and urging Jess to come to England. Jess had prayed for guidance. Was this an answer to prayer? Grandmother had written often through the years, and she'd visited when Jess was ten. They'd played games, gone for walks, and she'd taught Jess to bake her delicious scones while Jess listened to Grandmother's childhood stories. Oh, the memories of that visit!

Grandmother's invitation had spurred Jess to come. And here she was...in England. Mother had told her so much about this country that Jess felt she was coming home.

As the train rumbled along she leaned her head back, closing her eyes. Grandfather McDonald died before Jess was born, and with Mother in America, Grandmother had no one. Grandfather left a substantial estate, which Grandmother put to good use. At the beginning of the Great War, she opened an orphanage on her North Yorkshire farm, housing war orphans. With emotional wounds, they needed love and personal attention, which Grandmother had plenty to give. Devastated by the war, children were brought to her, where she loved them, helped them to accept their loses, and introduced them to her Heavenly Father.

Jess watched the landscape speeding by. What lay ahead? Until Grandmother's letter arrived she'd planned to return to teaching. One thing was certain. She knew she needed to trust God to guide her steps.

Swirling steam hissed from the train's brakes as Jess stepped onto the Harrogate station platform. Other passengers, mostly locals, headed home from work, purpose in their stride. Soon she was the only passenger left. She glanced at the watch pinned to her jacket. Four-thirty. Grandmother's telegram said someone would meet her, but she saw no one. Perhaps he'd be here soon. Collecting her trunk, she pulled it to a nearby bench to wait.

At five o'clock, Jess decided no one was coming. She approached the information window where a gray mustached gentleman sat reading the evening paper. She noticed the bold headlines: "Homeless Man Found Dead in Knaresborough Alleyway".

She shuddered at the headline. "Excuse me."

Laying down the paper, the man shifted his glasses up onto his nose. "Can I help ya, Lass?"

"I thought someone was meeting my train, but apparently he's been delayed. I'm going to Hope Orphanage, near Pateley Bridge. Do buses run there?"

"No, but the Nidd Valley Light Railway train departs tomorrow morning to Pateley Bridge. Have you considered a taxi?"

Before Jess could answer, a voice spoke from behind her. "Sorry for interruptin', lass, but I couldn't help hearin' ya say ya need to get to Hope Orphanage."

Turning, Jess found an older gentleman, possibly in his seventies. A tweed cap covered his silver hair; his dark green corduroy trousers tucked into his knee-hi boots. A tweed jacket topped his green sweater.

"That's right." She smiled at his deep Yorkshire accent.

"No need for ya to be waitin' for the train or payin' taxi fare when I'm headin' out that way meself. I come into town to pick up farm supplies what's come in on the train. If ya don't mind waitin' a bit, you're welcome to ride along. I drive right past your Grandmum's place. Me farm's just past hers. By the way, me name's George Higgins. Morag said you'd be comin'." He extended a work worn but clean hand. Jess took it, only to have hers shaken vigorously. She glanced at the man behind the window, uncertainty in her eyes.

"Seems things have worked out nicely, Lass. George here's a fine fellow. Don't worry. He'll get ya there right enough. I'll vouch for him any day."

"Thank ya much, Pete." George bowed grandly. "Will do me utmost to see that Morag's granddaughter arrives safely." He turned to Jess. "I'll fetch me things and we'll be gettin' ya home." Tipping his cap, he walked down the platform to retrieve his packages.

"Still concerned, lass? Ya needn't be," Pete reassured. "George is as fine a fellow as you'll find."

"I'm sure you're right. Thank you for your help."

"I didn't do anything. It was George there. Enjoy your visit with your grandmother."

George hefted Jess's trunk into his horse-drawn wagon alongside his packages then helped her onto the seat. Turning, she waved to Pete who returned her wave.

As George guided his wagon through Harrogate, Jess looked around the town, noting its Edwardian and Victorian architecture. They passed several large gardens where the early fall flowers bloomed profusely in shades of crimson, gold and amethyst.

"Your Grandmum's sure happy you're comin'." George said. "She misses her daughter somethin' fierce. She was a sweet, beautiful lass. All the young lads came a courtin', but none caught her eye 'til your dad come along. You look like her when she was your age." George paused thoughtfully. "Don't understand why Old Charlie didn't come out to meet ya. He's a do-it-all fellow on Morag's farm. Somethin' real important must've happened for him not to show up."

"I hope nothing's wrong. How much farther?"

Leaving the city, they traveled through the countryside past drystone rock walls, built decades ago, enclosing fields where sheep and cattle grazed contentedly. More stonewalls surrounded other fields and pastures, looking like a huge patchwork quilt pieced together and spread across the gentle slopes of the hills and valleys. The grass was the greenest Jess had ever seen. Patches of trees displayed early fall colors. Occasionally they passed a gritstone farmhouse built near the road, some so close they touched it. Aged green moss covered the slate roofs while ivy clung to the walls and attached barns.

"Not much further now. We're almost to Pateley Bridge, and your Grandmum's farm is t'other side."

The village of Pateley Bridge draped down the side of a hill that ended by the Nidd River. Mr. Higgins explained that in the early 1800's lead mining and textiles were the local industries, but the mines and most of the mills had long since closed, leaving the area to farming. The village's High Street buildings would've looked dreary except for the scattering of flowers in window boxes and gardens. Arched alleyways between buildings hinted at the courtyards and dwellings hidden behind them. They passed The Old Bakehouse, its window filled with delicious breads and pastries, reminding Jess that she hadn't eaten since breakfast on the ship that morning. Hopefully Grandmother would have something waiting for her.

The road from Harrogate was curvy and narrow, but the road to Grandmother's was even more so, climbing higher than before. The Yorkshire Dales were known for ruggedly beautiful green hills, valleys and purple moors. Jess had never imagined the sheer wild beauty of the landscape spread before her as they reached the top. The western sky was bright with the evening sun shining from behind golden clouds, lighting the hilltops while the valleys lay in purple shadow. The drystone walls surrounding the pastures were topped by a golden reflection making the "quilt" appear to be stitched with golden threads. Farmhouses and cottages settled in for the evening; the chimney smoke indicating the chilly air.

Jess fell in love with the beautiful countryside where time seemed to stand still. Mother had told her about the many moods of the Dales and how the weather could change quickly, about the treacherous winds that often swept over the hills and into the valleys and of the rains that followed. Jess was glad the sun was shining, welcoming her to the Dales.

George turned the wagon down a dirt lane where a sign stood with bold letters: HOPE ORPHANAGE. A drystone wall lined each side of the lane, black-faced sheep grazing in pastures on either side. As they approached the farmhouse, butterflies danced excitedly in Jess's stomach.

The two-story gritstone farmhouse with an attached barn was large compared to the ones on the road from Harrogate. Curtains in the windows of the barn indicated it had been converted into living space. The front of the house was covered with ivy, only the windows showing through. Moss covered the slate roof while a low stone wall enclosed the front garden where an open black iron gate beckoned visitors up the stone footpath to the front door. The neatly trimmed garden flaunted a colorful array of roses: pink, yellow, peach and crimson. Yellow and purple pansies grew by the borders while colorful trailing blooms crept over the wall waving a welcome to visitors.

Jess wondered how such beautiful flowers bloomed in the chilly fall air, but she knew the British took great pride in their gardens, keeping them blooming for months.

Halting the wagon by the front gate, George helped Jess down then unloaded her trunk. The front door opened and a white and liver English springer spaniel bounded down the path, running straight to Jess and jumping up on her. If a dog could smile, this one did, her tail wagging excitedly.

"Down, Jossie!" a voice called as Jess spotted Grandmother hurrying down the front path, leaving the door open in her excitement. Jess ran straight into her arms. Tears streamed down Grandmother's cheeks as she held Jess back for a good look.

"My lands, luv, how you've changed! Where's the little girl who helped me bake tarts?"

"Well, you haven't changed a bit, Grandmother. You look just like you did when we baked those tarts. I haven't tasted any as good since."

"Then we'll have to bake some." She turned as George arrived with Jess's trunk.

"What happened, George? Garth Samuels drove into Harrogate to fetch Jess. Charlie was supposed to go, but this afternoon the tractor fell on him while he worked on it and broke his collarbone, a couple of ribs, and his right arm. Garth came and patched him up. He's one of our local doctors," she explained to

Jess. "Since Charlie couldn't go, Garth volunteered to fetch you. We knew he wouldn't make it in time to meet the train but hoped you'd still be waiting. But, you're here, and that's the important thing."

"And very well she might be, too, I might add," piped in George. He'd talked the whole ride out from Harrogate, was silent while Grandmother greeted Jess but was ready to go again. "I heard yer granddaughter askin' Pete at the station how to get here. I step up and says I'm headin' out this way meself and would be happy to give her a ride. Pete vouched for me."

"Mr. Higgins has been very kind, Grandmother. He's told me a lot about Harrogate and the Dales." She smiled covertly at Grandmother.

"I'm sure he did," Grandmother nodded. This was lost on George who carried the trunk into the house, talking to whoever was inclined to listen.

"Come inside, luv." Grandmother linked her arm through Jess's.

The front door opened into a large living room, the lower half of the walls oak paneled, the upper half cream painted plaster. Thick, aged oak beams crossed the ceiling while a large stone fireplace stood at the far end of the room, a huge oaken mantel above holding brass candlesticks and gilt picture frames. An overstuffed couch and armchairs and antique side tables surrounded a blue and cream woven rug. Blue curtains framed the windows while watercolor paintings, mostly of the English countryside, graced the walls. Jossie, the spaniel, curled up by the fire, keeping an eye on things.

"Have a seat, luv. I'll call the children." Grandmother turned to George who stood by the door, twisting his cap in his hands. "Won't you stay for tea, George? I've the kettle on."

"Thank ya, Miz Morag, but me missuz will be waitin' me tea." He turned to Jess. "It were a real pleasure to meet ya, Miz Jess. If there's anythin' I can do for ya whilst you're here, just give a shout."

"Thank you for driving me out, Mr. Higgins, and for telling me about the Dales. It was fascinating."

After George left, Jess sat in an overstuffed chair. Realizing how tired she felt and how comfortable the chair was, she doubted she'd be getting up soon, but as the children filed in, she sat up, forgetting her fatigue.

Grandmother introduced the eleven children, each by name and age. "Jess, this is Claire, who is sixteen. Jason is fifteen. Paul and Paula, our twins, are eleven. Neil is nine. Kevin and Geoffrey are both eight. Jeannie is six. Tommy is five. Billy and Katie are both three." The children stood straight, a couple giggling when introduced. Little Katie approached Jess.

"Will you be staying wif us, Miss Jess? You're pretty." She reached up, touching Jess's cheek.

"For a while, Katie." Jess lifted the child onto her lap. She looked smaller than her three years and weighed nothing. Jess turned to smile at Grandmother over the child's blond head but instead looked straight into a pair of unfamiliar gray eyes. For a moment, she couldn't look away. The smile in the gray eyes brought a flush to her cheeks, causing instant annoyance with herself.

"Garth! I didn't hear you come in." Grandmother saw the young man standing in the doorway. "Have you been there long?"

Reluctantly pulling his gaze from Jess, he turned to Grandmother. "Not long. Gwen let me in the back. I didn't want to interrupt your introductions." He smiled as the children gathering around him, the little ones pulling at his jacket. Picking up Billy, he reached over and rumpled Neil's hair. Clearly the children adored him.

"Let me introduce my granddaughter, Jessica Montgomery. Jess, this is Dr. Garth Samuels, the man who tried to meet your train."

Jess stood as Garth put Billy down and extended his hand.

"It's a pleasure to meet you at last, Miss Montgomery. Your grandmother speaks of you often. She's really looked forward to your visit."

The deep tones of his voice struck a chord somewhere inside

of Jess. Accepting his outstretched hand, hers was swallowed by his large one. Tall with broad shoulders, Jess had to look up to meet his smiling gray eyes. Set in a ruggedly handsome face, they seemed to penetrate right into her soul, making her self-conscious.

To her dismay the direct look from his penetrating eyes made her cheeks burn. Never self-conscious with other young men, what made this one so different?

"It's nice to meet you, Dr. Samuels. I'm sorry for the inconvenience I caused you." Jess gently but pointedly pulled her hand from his. "I'm sorry you made a wasted trip."

"Not at all. Pete said George gave you a ride, so I came straight back. I knew you were in good hands."

He ran a quick hand through his dark hair, only to have it fall forward again. Jess had an unexplainable desire to reach up and push it back. *How ridiculous!* she thought.

"I must add my thanks to Jess's," said Grandmother. "Both for going to the station and for treating Charlie. He was still sleeping when I checked on him."

"The medicine I gave him will help him sleep, but ensure he stays in bed for a few days. He has some pretty bad breaks. He can't do anything for a while."

"Don't worry. We'll see he gets plenty of rest. Now, how about some tea? I'm sure Jess is hungry after her long journey. Won't you stay, Garth?"

Grandmother's inviting smile contrasted with Jess's fixed one. For some reason he'd made a bad start with her and didn't understand why.

"Thanks, Mrs. McDonald. There's nothing I'd rather do than enjoy Gwen's wonderful cooking, but I must go. I've some house calls to make before heading home, but I'll check on Charlie first." Garth turned to Jess. "I hope you enjoy your stay, Miss Montgomery. I'm sure we'll see each other again." The look in his eyes carried a promise.

Jess sighed deeply as the doctor left. She had a funny feeling he just might be right.

Chapter Two

Gwen was a plump Scottish lady with rosy cheeks that reminded Jess of newly ripened apples. She wiped her hands on a flour sack towel as grandmother introduced Jess. A large white apron covered her gray ankle-length dress from her ample bosom to below her knees while a white cap perched on her head, springy tendrils of steel-gray hair escaping from under it. She smiled and laughed easily.

Grandmother called the children to supper, the younger ones sitting at the long table while the older ones brought in the food. Having decided to wait for Jess before eating, they said the blessing and dug in hungrily. Glancing around, Jess noticed the children talking in turn, except Billy, the three year old. When spoken to, he merely nodded or shook his head. Jess guessed he was shy.

Grandmother encouraged a family atmosphere so she, Gwen and, usually Charlie, ate with the children.

"This is delicious, Gwen," Jess said. "I don't think I've ever had it before. What's it called?"

"Shepherd's Pie, lass. Quick ta make and vera fillin'. Me own dear mither made it when I was a wee lassie."

Filled with beef, potatoes, mushrooms and gravy, the pie was topped with a thick flour crust. Brussels sprouts, homemade bread with butter and milk provided by the farm's cows were followed by custard cream pie. Jess watched delightedly as the children devoured it.

After supper, the older children washed the dishes while the younger ones went upstairs to prepare for bed. With the kitchen in capable hands, Jess helped pull pajamas and gowns over heads and brushed teeth. Everyone gathered in the living room around Grandmother's chair by the fire, Katie on her lap. Billy sat in Claire's lap. As the oldest, she helped out like a little mother. Grandmother turned on the big floor radio. The children became engrossed in the serial story while Gwen pulled out her knitting, her clicking needles making the only sound besides the radio. Jess watched the children, wondering what circumstances brought each one to Grandmother's home.

As her mind wandered she relaxed, her long day catching up with her. Leaning against the soft cushions, her eyes drifted shut. She didn't realize she'd fallen asleep until she was suddenly awakened by a vigorous hug. Tommy, the five-year-old, jumped onto her lap, hugging her before Grandmother could stop him.

"Tommy, dear! Jess was resting! She's had a very tiring day, and you shouldn't have disturbed her."

One glance at the little boy's repentant face tugged at Jess's heart. "It's alright. Tommy did me a favor. I should've been listening to the story." She suddenly realized the radio was off.

Grandmother's old worn Bible lay open in her lap. "Every night we read the Bible together and pray, luv. Whoever wants to pray may do so." Grandmother looked questioningly at Jess. "Would you join us?"

"I'd love to. We always had devotions at home."

Grandmother was glad she wanted to participate. She knew how Jess was raised but didn't know if she'd put her trust in Christ. Jess's mother often wrote requesting prayer for Jess and over the years Grandmother had bowed her knees, praying for the granddaughter whom she rarely saw.

She read from Philippians, a passage expressing Paul's encouragement to the church of Philippi during his imprisonment. Having recently had their lives torn apart, these children needed this encouragement. As Grandmother read, the older ones drank in the words. While not understanding the meaning, the little ones still sensed the importance. Grandmother stopped to answer their questions with the wisdom that comes from years of trials, hardships and searching the scriptures. Having seen the pain and bitterness come through her door when children were brought to her, she spent time on her knees and in the Word, looking for the only cure that could heal these young lives.

When Grandmother closed her Bible, everyone knelt for prayer. She began, followed by several of the children, most saying a simple "thank you" for something special to them. Jess was glad this was a nightly occurrence. These children needed the hope only the Lord could give.

When the children were in bed, Jess joined Grandmother in the kitchen for a cup of tea while Gwen took Charlie tea and scones. When she returned, Gwen said goodnight and turned in. Tomorrow would start earlier than usual. With Charlie laid up, she'd do the milking. Jess offered to get up and help, but Gwen wouldn't hear of it.

"There'll be plenty o' time for that, lass. You need to rest up from your lang journey, so sleep in. I'll milk the wee cows with young Jason's help. He's a grand laddie, he is."

As Grandmother filled their cups, Jess asked, "Grandmother, why doesn't Billy talk? I noticed when the others speak to him, he only nods or shakes his head."

"He's never spoken since being here." Grandmother sipped her tea. "Billy came from London after both parents and his older brother were killed in a bombing raid last year. If you notice, he's closer to Neil than any of the others, and Neil treats him like a little brother. If anyone picks on Billy, Neil always defends him."

"He needs someone to stick up for him. But do you think he'll ever learn to stick up for himself?"

"Aye, in time. At least he responds. If not by word, then in other ways."

"What about the others? Were all of their parents killed?"

"No. Some were so severely injured they've no memory of their children and couldn't care for them. Paul and Paula, the twins, were found rummaging through rubbish bins. It was later discovered that their mother lost her mind due to shock from the bombings. These children have no other family or else they're not wanted. England's been hard hit by this war, and recovery will be a long time in coming. Most folk have enough difficulty feeding their own families without taking on more mouths to feed. Even little ones."

"Could those parents with memory loss still recover and come looking for their children?"

"Anything's possible," Grandmother sighed. "But that's not the case so far." She often wished they would so hope would return to the hearts of these young ones. But remembering the real Hope she could help them find, she was happy they stayed with her. Grandmother wiped a hand across her misty eyes. "It's late, luv. I'll show you to your room, and you can sleep as late as you like."

Jess's room was located farthest from the converted barn containing the children's rooms, giving her privacy. A large, antique four-poster bed with a cream ruffled duvet stood between two windows. The antique dresser was polished to a shine, and a spacious wardrobe stood opposite. Rose print curtains graced the windows, with throw pillows and lampshade matching them. Tiny pink rosebuds covered the wallpaper, and the polished wood floor boasted a light green rug. A vase of wildflowers was thoughtfully placed on the bedside table. Charming! Jess knew she'd be comfortable here.

"If you need anything, just call." Grandmother hugged Jess. "You're being here means so much."

After Grandmother left, Jess unpacked a few things from the trunk, planning to unpack the rest tomorrow. Settling into the cloud-soft mattress, Jess reflected on her exciting day, wondering what tomorrow would bring.

~

Ten o'clock found Garth Samuels driving home after his house calls. What a busy night! After leaving Hope Orphanage, Garth called on another patient. While there, Bob Hartley came to get him as his wife, Ruth, was about to deliver their first child, two weeks early. Garth followed Bob home and, within an hour, delivered a baby boy. Garth smiled, recalling the proud, new father walking through the house, newborn in his arms and a wide grin on his face. Temporarily forgotten, Ruth hadn't minded. She simply rested, smiling each time her husband passed by, baby in tow.

After Hartley's, Garth stopped by Caleb Daniel's farm. Caleb had bronchitis but tonight when Garth listened to his chest, he found less congestion. Soon he'd be out and about again, he'd told Caleb. And Caleb, in his easy way, said he'd known all along that he would. Caleb was a patient Garth never minded seeing. Taking everything in stride, never complaining. At seventy-five, surely there was something to complain about. Garth hoped he could take life so steadily at that age.

Having completely missed tea and supper, Garth longed to get home. Mrs. Sixsmith, the landlady at his boarding house, would leave a plate for him. She was good about that; looking out for him like his own mother had.

Garth's thoughts returned to the afternoon at Hope Orphanage after arriving from the train station. He'd often seen Jess's childhood and school photographs in Mrs. McDonald's home and had always thought her lovely, but he wasn't prepared for the beautiful woman sitting with Katie on her lap. He'd observed her for a few minutes before she saw him. Her honey-colored hair was pinned up in a braided twist, loose tendrils framing her oval face. A small dimple creased her right cheek as she smiled at the children.

Garth's heart skipped when remembering her deep brown eyes. When they'd suddenly met his, her cheeks flushed, causing him to smile, but as he'd taken her hand, she quickly withdrew it, turning cool towards him. Thinking back, he didn't know what had happened. Could he have offended her? He couldn't think how. Perhaps she just wasn't as lovely on the inside as she was on the outside. No, he didn't believe that. Her smile for the children was genuine.

Parking behind the boarding house, Garth went inside to find Mrs. Sixsmith had indeed left him a plate in the warming oven. Eating quickly, he went up to his room to retire, his thoughts on Jess. Why had she become so aloof? Well, he'd find out. She'd be in England for a while, and he'd see her again soon. He'd make sure of it.

~

Exhausted the night before, Jess had slept soundly and felt refreshed when she awoke. Excited about her first day in England, she quickly bathed at the washstand, and after searching in her trunk, she dressed in the least wrinkled blouse and skirt she could find. Then brushing her long hair, she wound it into a loose chignon.

In the kitchen she found the children leaving for school, all except Katie and Billy, who were too young. The children walked to Pateley Bridge where a two room stone building held the various combined grades.

Gwen was attacking the mound of breakfast dishes left by the departing troop. Katie and Billy sat finishing their milk and sausages.

"Mornin', lass!" greeted Gwen. "Did ya sleep well?"

"Very well, thank you."

"Grand. Now, how aboot some breakfast? There're eggs, sausages, grilled tomatoes, scones, marmalade and butter. Tea or coffee?"

"It smells delicious." Jess breathed in the heavenly aroma. "Coffee, please. Tell me where everything is, and I'll help myself."

"The food's warmin' in the oven, and the coffee's on top of the cooker. Thank ya, lass. If ya can serve yourself, I'll finish the dishes."

"Good morning," Jess greeted the children. "How are you today?"

"Biwwy an' me's doin' fine, Miss Jess," said Katie. "We was awful hungwy."

Billy merely glanced at Jess before taking another bite of sausage.

"I'm pretty hungry myself. I'll fix a plate and join you, alright?"

"Biwwy and me gotta make our beds," informed Katie importantly. "But we'll see ya later." Both children ate the last bite then, carrying their plates to the kitchen, ran upstairs to do their chores.

Jess poured her coffee, filled a plate and sat at the kitchen table. Humming loudly, Gwen scrubbed away at the mountain of dishes.

"Morning, luv." Grandmother carried in a wicker basket of wet clothes which she set by the back door and then joined Jess. "Did you sleep well?"

"Like the proverbial log. I haven't slept that well in ages. I'm sure the bed had something to do with it. It's like sleeping on a cloud."

"That was your mother's room. She chose the wallpaper and the fabric when she was a girl. I made the curtains, the pillow covers and the lamp shade for her fifteenth birthday." Grandmother smiled, reminiscing. "Your grandfather refinished that old bed and dresser for her. She was so happy when that room was finished."

"It's beautiful, and I'll enjoy it as much as she did." Jess glanced at the basket of clothes. "Are you going to hang those outside?"

"Yes. It's sunny with a bit of wind, so they should dry quickly."

"I'll do that while you do something else you need to do. I'm helping while I'm here, and with eleven children and an injured man to care for, you and Gwen can use some help."

"You're right." Grandmother sighed heavily. "I've thought about hiring more help, even before Charlie's accident. I'm thinking about hiring someone to do the laundry and the cleaning.

Both take so much time, and although I can still work, I'm not as young as I was. The children keep up their rooms and help with farm chores, but during school, they can't do much. Charlie will be a while in healing, and Gwen has her hands full in the kitchen. She used to help with the housework, but the more mouths there are to feed the more time she spends preparing meals."

"Then it's settled. I'll help out, and we'll advertise for more help, too."

With that, Jess added her dishes to the pile and picked up the laundry basket. "Just tell me where the clothes pins are."

~

Jess was hanging the last of the clothes when Garth walked into the backyard. She didn't see him until he was almost upon her.

"Good morning, Miss Montgomery." He carried the ever-present black "doctor's" bag.

"Good morning, Dr. Samuels. Are you here to see Charlie?" Jess asked brightly, refusing to think about her response to him the night before. She wouldn't respond to that smile any way but casually.

"Yes. How is he this morning?"

"I don't know. This may sound strange," she said sheepishly, "but I haven't met him yet. After a cup of tea with Grandmother, I fell into bed and didn't wake until about an hour ago. I feel like such a lazybones."

"You're entitled," he chuckled. "I'm sure you needed the rest after your trip. Come and I'll introduce you. Has he had his breakfast?"

"Probably. Gwen doesn't let anyone go hungry around here."

Leaving the clothesbasket by the clothesline, Jess walked with Garth to Charlie's bungalow near the barn. When he came to work at the farm years earlier, Grandfather had converted the old wagon shed for Charlie. Taking his meals with the family, he only had a small sitting room, a bedroom and a bath. A flower border bloomed on either side of the door, giving the little house a cheerful look.

"Come in," came a response to Garth's knock.

Charlie was a stocky little man in his late fifties, his once pepper black hair now more salt than pepper. He was propped up in bed, his right arm and shoulder encased in plaster, his chest and midriff bandaged tightly. A pajama top hung loosely around his shoulders. An empty breakfast tray sat on the table by his bed.

"Good morning, Charlie," greeted Garth. "This is Mrs. McDonald's granddaughter, Jessica Montgomery."

"A pleasure to meet you, Miss Montgomery. I'm dreadfully sorry I couldn' meet your train yesterday." He put out his left hand to grasp Jess's.

"Don't worry, Charlie. I was well taken care of. You just take care of yourself and get well." Jess patted his hand. "I'll be helping out around here, so you needn't worry about getting things done. We'll manage."

"I hate bein' a burden to your Gran'mother. She's such a sweet lady, an' there's so much to do 'round here."

"Well, you must get well before you can return to work," reminded Garth. "The only way to do that is to rest and take it easy. That was a nasty accident yesterday. The injuries you suffered won't heal overnight. I know you hate being laid up, but as your doctor I order you to rest." He smiled, taking the edge off his words. "And," he grinned at Jess with a sidelong look, "there are plenty of ladies here to see you do just that. I don't think you have a choice."

Charlie groaned and sank further into his pillow.

"Don't worry, Charlie," Jess chuckled, picking up the breakfast tray, "we'll take good care of you. I'll take this and leave so the good doctor can get down to business. See you later." Glancing at Garth, she added with a nod, "Doctor."

Katie and Billy were bouncing a ball around the back yard as Jess walked to the house. Katie replaced Neil as Billy's companion when Neil was at school. Katie, of course, chattered away endlessly, never expecting a response.

Jess sat the breakfast tray by the sink then found Grandmother sorting laundry in the washroom just off the kitchen.

"What's next? More clothes to hang out?"

"Not yet. We need some things from the market, but Charlie's the only one who drives. There's an old bike in the shed, but I haven't ridden in years. I suppose I depend on Charlie too much."

"I'll go. Just give me a list of what you need."

Jess followed Grandmother into the kitchen where she was handed a shopping list and some money. "This should cover it. Here's the ration book. We've used them throughout the war, and I'm afraid we'll have to for a good while." She pulled a large, handled basket from a low cupboard. "This will strap to the bike rack to put the groceries in. Do you need help finding it?"

"I'll manage." Jess took the basket.

"Oh, and here." Grandmother handed her a piece of paper. "Here's a notice for Mr. Phillips' shop window advertising for help. Since you're going, will you ask him to display it for us?"

"Certainly." Jess planted a kiss on Grandmother's cheek. "Now, tell me how to find this shop."

Chapter Three

*T*ess coasted downhill toward Pateley Bridge, her chest swelling with exhilaration as the crisp air whisked by. It was a beautiful, early fall day, and according to Grandmother, probably one of the last nice days they'd have until spring. She passed sheep grazing in the pastures beyond the stone walls. Cows meditated in the sun, their warm vaporous breath rising in the cool morning air. She passed folks working in their gardens, hanging laundry or cutting wood for winter. A huge lake lay between the hills reflecting the bright blue sky and white clouds. A lady on a bike passed Jess on the road, calling a cheery "Good morning."

Jess quickly found Mr. Phillips' shop. Parking the bike out front, she carried the basket inside.

"Good mornin', luv." An elderly man behind the counter turned from stacking goods on the shelves. "Can I help you?"

Jess was surprised when he called her "luv". She'd thought Grandmother called her that out of affection, and although she was sure that she did, Jess soon realized Yorkshire folk called everyone "luv".

"Good morning. My grandmother, Morag McDonald, asked me to pick up a few things."

"Ol' Morag's granddaughter, eh? Well, welcome to England. Me name's Sam Phillips. I heard you was comin'. Have you a shopping list?"

"Yes." Jess handed him the list then browsed the shop while he filled her order.

Two other customers also browsed: an elderly woman and a young lady examining scented soaps near the register. Both glanced up when she introduced herself. Jess noticed the shop shelves were sparsely stocked. Although America hadn't been in the war as long as England, Americans still dealt with rationing. Meals were difficult to prepare because items were scarce, but she and Mother had managed. It must be harder for Grandmother to feed the children, although their rations were greater than most.

Glancing at the newspaper laying on the counter, Jess read the bold lettered headlines: "Young Woman's Body Found in Harrogate Alleyway". Where had she seen something similar recently? She read on until Mr. Phillips placed her basket of groceries on the counter. After he stamped the rations card, she handed him Grandmother's advertisement.

"Grandmother asked if you would place this ad in your shop window. She's advertising for help out at the orphanage."

"Certainly, luv. Just tell Morag I put it right up." Turning to the window, he did just that. "Now Charlie's laid up, she'll be needin' help. She's got lots to do around there with all those little uns."

"And without Charlie, she and Gwen just can't manage. I'm helping out but even that won't be enough."

"With times as they are, she won't have difficulty finding help," Sam smiled broadly.

"Thank you, Mr. Phillips. Have a good day."

"Good day, luv, and give me best to your Grandmum."

"I certainly will." Outside Jess tied the basket to the bicycle rack. While leaning over, she heard someone exit the shop and stop beside her.

"Excuse me, Miss Montgomery," said a soft, well-educated

voice. Jess looked up to see the young lady from the shop. She wore a beautifully tailored gray, tweed coat and an expensive but simple gray hat.

"May I introduce myself?" She extended a gloved hand. "I'm Constance Cameron. I overheard your conversation with Mr. Phillips about your Grandmother's need for help at the orphanage. Do you think she would consider me for the position?" she asked hesitantly.

"Well, I don't know, Miss Cameron, but you're welcome to ask her. I'll tell her you're interested then maybe you could come by this afternoon to speak with her."

"I will and thank you. Perhaps I'll see you this afternoon. Goodbye." With a genteel nod, she turned and walked up the street.

Jess mounted the bike and rode toward home, her thoughts on the young woman. Why would an obviously well off young lady pursue work at an orphanage doing manual labor? She'd soon find out.

When Jess mentioned Constance Cameron to Grandmother, the older woman paused from folding clothes at the kitchen table.

"Constance Cameron? Now why on earth would she want to work here?"

"Is she from a wealthy family? Her clothes were expensive looking."

"Oh my, yes!" Grandmother said vehemently. "Her father's one of the great shipping magnates in Hull. They've a country home here in Nidderdale, a huge manor house called Cameron Hall. Said to be magnificent! Constance was at boarding school for many years and just recently made her social debut. Which returns me to my original question, why would she want to work here?"

Reaching into the laundry basket, Jess started folding clothes. "Well, she'd like to visit this afternoon."

"Alright." Grandmother shook her head. "I'm sure she has her reasons."~

That afternoon a large shiny, black car parked in front of the orphanage. Jess was in the kitchen attacking the wrinkled clothes from her steamer trunk with Grandmother's heavy iron when she heard the car. Heading to the living room, she looked out to see a chauffeur in dark gray livery opening the back door of the car. Constance Cameron stepped out and approached the house. Grandmother had heard the car as well and came downstairs to answer the door.

"Hello, again," Jess greeted with a smile.

"Hello, Mrs McDonald. Miss Montgomery. Your front garden is simply lovely. The flowers are still beautiful despite the cooler weather."

"Thank you, Miss Cameron. Won't you have a seat?" offered Grandmother. "Would you care for tea?"

"Yes, thank you."

"I'll get it, Grandmother." Jess waved her back as she headed to the kitchen.

Gwen was setting out a tray with the special china. Iced cookies lined a plate painted with dainty roses, and she poured hot water into the matching teapot.

"These aren't used often, are they," Jess smiled.

"No, lass. Just when the vicar comes to visit. They don't usually see such aristocracy."

"Well, if the king himself were served from this tray he wouldn't have anything to complain about." Jess carried it into the living room where she set it on the table beside Grandmother's chair.

"Miss Cameron, I'm a bit puzzled by your interest in the position we have open here," Grandmother said, pouring the tea. "I expected someone more...well...domestic to apply. Please don't take offense. You just don't seem like the domestic type. Why are you interested in the position?"

Constance smiled warmly. "I'm not offended, Mrs. McDonald. I know I'm a most unlikely prospect for the position, but I'm perfectly serious in my desire to volunteer to work for you. I don't need the money, and I certainly won't allow you to pay me. I simply want to help." She hesitated before continuing. "I've never done housework before, so you'd have to teach me what to do. Not that I can't," she added hastily, "I've just never had the opportunity. There was always someone to do the work for me. Please don't think I'm boasting because, honestly, I've been miserable these last few years. As a child I didn't know better, but as I've grown older I realize there's a simpler way of life, and I long for it. I'm quite bored with my current lifestyle, and this is an opportunity to escape it, if only for a bit."

"I see." Grandmother nodded. "Well, if you're willing to work, and I mean work hard, then I suppose you can help us. I certainly appreciate your willingness to volunteer. I'm happy to pay for help, but truthfully, money is stretched to its limits around here. We'll all pitch in and help you learn the ropes. You'll have to be here early morning to start the day's work but it won't be a strict schedule, and some days you mightn't be needed at all. Hopefully you're flexible because with eleven children, you'll have to be."

"I won't pretend it will come easily, but I promise to do my best."

"That's all I can ask." Reaching across, Grandmother refilled Constance's teacup. "When can you start?"

"Tomorrow morning?"

"Lovely. Be here at six o'clock, and dress comfortably and nothing that matters if it's soiled. Use the back door. Gwen will be preparing the children's breakfast. You're welcome to eat with us, if you like, and of course you'll have lunch here."

"Thank you, but I'll eat before I come," replied Constance. She didn't want to burden these people, only to be a part of their lives. She would soon learn that it wasn't as simple as she thought it would be.

~

Jess woke early the next morning and, looking out her window, was surprised when she couldn't see anything. Was she that bleary-eyed from sleep? After rubbing her eyes, she looked again and knew she wasn't mistaken. A fog so thick she could barely see the gate at the end of the front walkway hung like a heavy cloak around the farm. And after the beautiful sunshine of the day before.

Dressing quickly, she ran downstairs as the children prepared for school. With all that noise she wondered how she'd slept the morning before. As she entered the kitchen, Constance walked through the back door.

"Good morning, Constance. How are you this morning?" She reached into the cupboard for a cup and saucer. "Cup of coffee or tea?"

"Yes, thank you. Tea, please." Constance hung her coat and hat on the peg rack by the door. "Please, call me Connie. My family refuses to indulge me, and Constance is so…stand-offish."

"Certainly, if that's what you like." Jess poured the tea and coffee then glanced out the window over the sink. "I've never seen fog this thick. Does it happen often?"

"It's foggier in the winter and early spring, but it's unusual for early fall. It's heavier than usual making driving difficult this morning. I could barely see the front of the car, and I'm always afraid I'll hit a biker on these narrow roads. Most local folk bike everywhere since they don't have cars."

Glancing at Connie, Jess found no disdain on her face or in her voice. Recalling yesterday when Connie had first spoken to her, Jess had been on a bike. She knew Connie didn't understand the culture of those without the money her family had.

"Morning, girls!" Grandmother entered the kitchen cheerily. "Goodness, but its foggy this morning."

"We were just discussing that," said Jess. "Where's Gwen?"

"Taking Charlie's breakfast to him." Grandmother filled a cup with tea. "Jess, after you eat, please show Constance around. The children will be at breakfast and you can show her upstairs. There's the dusting along with cleaning the bathrooms. The laundry will wait. It'll never dry in this fog. I'm sure Gwen could use help, but we'll see how things go."

"Alright, but first, Constance wants to be called Connie."

"Certainly." She smiled at Constance. "Connie it shall be."

Gwen entered just then, and after introducing Connie to her, Jess ate breakfast. Gwen asked Connie to set the long dining room table for the children's breakfast, and so the morning began.

While the children ate, Jess introduced Connie to them. Except for Billy, each said a quick hello and continued devouring their pancakes. "Let's introduce to you Charlie."

~

"Come in," Charlie called when Jess knocked on his door.

"Good morning, Charlie. How are you feeling today?" asked Jess, smiling.

"Not bad, luv. Not bad. Better than yesterday." He looked at Connie. "And who might this young lady be?"

"Charlie, this is Connie Cameron. She's come to help us out. See, I told you we'd be able to handle the farm while you're recovering."

"Connie Cameron." Charlie repeated the name slowly, trying to remember where he'd heard the name. Then it hit him. "Not Cyril Cameron's daughter!"

"That's right," said Connie. "It's nice to meet you, Charlie. Jess explained about your accident. I'm sorry to hear about that, but you've lots of people who are happy to care for you."

"What? Oh, yeah. Right, luv." Charlie quickly recovered from his surprise. "And they be doin' a bang-up job, too." Surprised, he wondered why Cyril Cameron's daughter was working here.

"I'll take your breakfast tray if you're finished," said Jess.

"I'm done, luv. Tell Gwen she's the best. Couldn't get through the day without her cookin'."

"I'll tell her," Jess smiled. "If you need anything, just yell. But yell loudly. The fog's pretty thick out there."

"Get on with ya, luv."

"It was nice meeting you," said Connie.

"Nice meetin' you, too." Charlie lay back on his pillows, pondering why a rich girl would come to work at an orphanage.

~

Jess showed Connie around the house then set her to dusting upstairs while Jess dusted downstairs. In the living room, Jess found Billy curled up in an over-stuffed armchair, Jossie lying on the floor by his chair watching him.

"Hello, Billy. Did Katie decide to play alone today or have you two had a falling out?" Kneeling by the chair, she reached up and rumpled his hair, realizing his forehead was warm. She felt his flushed, warm cheeks.

"Billy, you have a fever," she said gently. "Do you hurt anywhere?"

Billy nodded, pointing to his head.

"Okay, little man, let's get you into bed, and I'll tell Grandmother."

She carried him to his room where she removed his shoes and tucked him into bed.

"You stay right there while I get Grandmother." Jess gently smoothed his hair. "She'll know how to make you feel better, okay?"

After checking on Billy, Grandmother called Garth's office.

"Where's Biwwy, Gran'muver," Katie tugged on Grandmother's skirt. "We wanted ta pway out in da fog. I went to da lew, an' when I got back, Biwwy was gone."

"Katie, luv, Billy's running a fever. Doctor Samuels is coming to see him." Grandmother hugged the little girl. "Billy won't be playing today, luv. He'll have to stay in bed and rest."

"Like Charwie?" asked Katie, her forehead scrunched up.

"Like Charlie," nodded Grandmother.

Hanging her head, Katie walked away scuffing her feet on the floor. Finding some picture books, she climbed into a chair in the living room and slowly turned the pages.

~

"His fever's a bit high and his glands are swollen." Garth shook down the glass thermometer he'd removed from Billy's mouth. "Most likely a viral infection. Keep him in bed and force the liquids. He'll be fine in a few days, but if there's any change for the worse, give me a ring."

"Thanks for coming," said Grandmother. "You know I always appreciate your quick response. Can you stay for tea?"

"I don't usually have the time, but I think I will today," he smiled. "It's been a rather hectic day and a cup of tea would hit the spot."

Jess had put the kettle on when Garth arrived knowing Grandmother would ask the good doctor to stay for tea.

As they entered the kitchen, she heard Grandmother say, "Jess! You've already put the kettle on."

"Well, I couldn't let the good doctor leave without a cup of tea." Jess smiled as she set two cups on the kitchen table, placing cream and sugar beside them. "Enjoy!" She picked up her dust cloth and left the room.

She missed Garth's wry expression as he realized she wouldn't be joining them. He'd hoped to chat with her a bit before heading back to work. *She's either very busy or she's avoiding me. Hmmm. We'll see.*

~

Finished downstairs, Jess was heading upstairs to help Connie just as Garth rounded the corner from the kitchen. She stopped on the third step as he approached.

"I'm just letting myself out," he said, taking his coat from the coat tree. "Thanks for the tea. It was just what I needed."

"I'm glad you enjoyed it," smiled Jess. "You always seem to be running from here to there, caring for patients and answering calls. You probably don't sit down to a leisurely cup of tea very often."

"You're right, I don't," Garth sighed dramatically. "Or leisurely meals either," he added sadly. Then, as if a thought suddenly popped into his head, he snapped his fingers. "I've a wonderful idea! Why don't you join me for a leisurely dinner one evening? I'm sure we can find a nice restaurant where the atmosphere would help me forget for a while the daily grind that inundates me." He paused for effect, and then asked, "Well, what do you say? Will you?"

Jess couldn't help but smile at his contrived drama and laughed softly. "Somehow I think you're exaggerating a bit, but," and this time it was her turn to pause, "I could probably tear myself away from my busy schedule for a while. All in the course of helping you relax, of course," she added quickly.

"Oh, of course," agreed Garth in mock seriousness that never quite reached his gray eyes. "How about Saturday evening?"

"Are you sure you won't be neglecting your patients in order to have this leisurely meal?" Jess's eyebrows rose suspiciously.

"Absolutely not. I'm in partnership with my father, and although we stay busy, we manage the occasional day or evening off."

"I didn't know you were in a partnership!"

"I'm sure there's a lot more you don't know about me." Garth flashed a crooked smile. Before she could reply, he added, "I'll see you Saturday at six. Then you can learn more." He flashed his brightest smile as he left.

Jess stood on the steps, cheeks burning, as the door closed behind him. *Of all the arrogant…. As if I wanted to know more,* she thought indignantly. *I certainly don't.* But as she climbed the stairs she knew she really did.

Chapter Four

*T*he next day the fog was gone, leaving a sunny, if windy, day. Grandmother decided it was time to do some heavy cleaning before winter set in, so all available hands pitched in, except Charlie, who was still confined to bed. Garth said he could get up in a day or two but couldn't return to work for a long while yet. Billy's fever had remained constant the previous day. Jess and Grandmother took turns sponging him down throughout the day and night. It finally broke in the early morning hours. With its departure the little boy wanted to get up and play but was made to stay in bed to ensure it didn't spike again. Poor Katie was lost without her playmate. Jess and Connie scrubbed and polished everything in sight, while Gwen, on her hands and knees, scrubbed the floors. The older children were thankful they were in school all day.

At noon they stopped for a well-deserved lunch and talked about what was still left to do.

"I never realized what it really takes to clean a house." Connie rubbed her aching neck.

"Do you regret volunteering, luv?"

"Not at all. For the first time in my life I'm doing something worthwhile for others instead of others doing for me." She smiled. `"It's a nice feeling actually."

"Mother used to knit sweaters and scarves for the servicemen," said Jess. "Since she was sick so much, it was her way to help with the war effort. She enjoyed it. Her items were shipped overseas with those knitted by other volunteers, so the soldiers never knew who'd made them. She never expected a thank you, but she knew she was doing something helpful for others."

"That's why we should remember what our Lord did for us on the cross," said Grandmother. "He made the ultimate sacrifice." Glancing at Connie, she prayed she'd come to understand what that sacrifice was.

Looking thoughtful, Connie said nothing.

Before leaving that afternoon, she approached Jess as she tucked the last of the linens into the cupboard.

"Jess, my family's having a formal dinner party next weekend, and although I'm not looking forward to it, I'm expected to be there. I wondered if you'd come as my guest. I'd love for my family to meet you."

"A formal dinner party? Goodness! I've never been to one before. I don't have anything to wear! I wouldn't know how to act! What would I say? All those society people would take one look at me and laugh." She laughed herself. "I'm sure I'd embarrass you to no end."

"You wouldn't embarrass me at all. You'd be your own sweet self, and if those snobs can't accept that, then I pity them. They don't know what they're missing. Listen to me, a snob calling them snobs."

"You're not a snob, Constance Cameron." Jess indignantly planted her fists on her hips. "You're just the opposite. But getting back to the party, what would I wear? I don't have formal clothes."

"No problem," Connie waved a dismissive hand. "We're about the same size. I've plenty of clothes, and you could wear something of mine. If it doesn't fit, I'll have it altered for you.

Please say you'll come."

Jess felt torn. Imagine. A formal dinner party! But she'd feel so out of place. Connie was raised in a sophisticated home where formal dinner parties were the norm. She wasn't. She was bound to make a social blunder. Perhaps Grandmother would have the right advice

"Can I think about it? I'll let you know in a day or two, if that's alright."

"Of course. There's no hurry, as long as I can let Mother know in time to plan accordingly. And don't worry. Everything will be fine. If you decide to go, I'll be glad. If not, that's fine, too. I won't pressure you into something you're uncomfortable with."

"Thanks. I'll let you know."

~

When the children were in bed and Jess and Grandmother were reading by the fire, Jess broached the subject of the dinner party.

"Grandmother, can I ask you something?"

Grandmother closed her book. "Of course, luv. What is it?"

"Connie's invited me to a formal dinner party at Cameron Hall next weekend. She's not looking forward to it, but she's expected to be there."

"What will you wear, luv?"

"Connie offered one of her evening gowns. She doesn't want to pressure me but really hopes I'll attend."

"What do you want to do?" Grandmother asked quietly.

"I don't know." Jess shook her head helplessly. "On one hand I feel like I'd make a grand fool of myself, but on the other I feel like, well, why not? I've never been to one before and will probably never have the opportunity again. Connie would be there to help me along. I just don't know what to do."

"Well, you must remember that most, if not all, of those society folk have different values and morals than you. Many of the principles you were raised to believe in are foreign to them. You've nothing in common."

"I know, but would it be so wrong to go? Knowing they won't

change my principles and values?"

Grandmother hesitated. What should she say? If she agreed to Jess going, she might be swayed by the lure of the social crowd. But if she suggested she not go, Jess might hold that against her. "We should pray about it. When I'm torn over a decision, I ask for the Heavenly Father's guidance. He always comes through. I can't tell you what you should or shouldn't do. Only He can guide you. But you must ask with an open heart and an open mind, willing to accept however He leads. Truly seek His will, and He'll guide you."

"Thanks, Grandmother." Jess got up and kissed her cheek. "I'll pray about it."

As she watched Jess go upstairs to bed, Grandmother prayed that her precious granddaughter would make the right decision.

~

Friday as Jess weeded the front garden, she heard a car stop in front of the house. Standing, she stepped outside the gate to find a tall sandy-haired young man exiting the car.

"Good morning," she greeted him. "Can I help you?"

He doffed his hat as he approached. "Good morning. I'm Robert Kilpatrick, the supply pastor for Rock of Ages Church in Pateley Bridge. I'm substituting for Pastor Wright while he's out of the country. And you are…?"

"Jessica Montgomery. My grandmother mentioned her pastor was going away for a while. I've newly arrived myself."

"Your grandmother must be Morag McDonald."

"Yes. Please come in. I'll get her for you." Inside Jess offered him a chair then went in search of Grandmother.

Jess found her in the back yard removing clothes from the line.

"Robert Kilpatrick's here to see you."

Grandmother looked momentarily perplexed, and then replied, "Oh yes, Robert Kilpatrick. I remember the name now. He'll be preaching at church while Pastor Wright's in America. He's gone to visit some relative or other. I don't remember exactly. Oh well, let's not keep him waiting."

Robert stood as the women entered the living room.

"Pastor Kilpatrick." Grandmother offered her hand. "I'm very happy to meet you. Please, won't you sit down? Would you like some tea?"

"Yes, thank you."

"I'll get it, Grandmother. You just sit and visit with your guest."

Returning with the tea tray, she heard Grandmother asking, "How long will Pastor Wright be away?"

"He wasn't sure, but thought possibly for several months. He hasn't seen his brother in years, and with the long journey there and back, he thought he'd stay a while."

"We'll miss him while he's away," said Grandmother, pouring the tea. "However, I'm looking forward to hearing your messages. I do hope you'll feel at home while you're here. Are you staying at the parsonage?"

"Yes. Pastor Wright felt I should be located where folks are used to finding their pastor when they need him. I'll keep an eye on the property as well."

Although not handsome in an exceptional way, Robert was pleasant with a quiet demeanor. His sandy hair was cut in a clean no-nonsense fashion, while his blue eyes were kind. His less-than-fashionable suit was clean and well pressed.

"I hope you'll join your grandmother in church Sunday," he addressed Jess.

"Yes, I'm looking forward to joining her and the children in church. I imagine we'll fill a whole pew, maybe two."

Robert chuckled pleasantly. "Now if we can just fill the rest as easily." Then he added, "Your accent indicates you're American. I attended seminary there before the war. Then, like most young men in England, I fought in France. A battle injury brought me home in February." His voice sobered but he continued, "I like America better, but then France is ravaged by the war, and America, although at war, has been spared the battle on the home front."

"Yes, we've been very fortunate. I'm sorry you were injured. I hope you've recovered completely."

"For the most part, thank you." Robert set his cup on the table and stood. "I must be going. Pastor Wright mentioned several of his faithful members to me, and I just wanted to stop and introduce myself."

"I'm glad you did." Grandmother walked him to the door. "If you need anything while you're here, please let us know. We'd be happy to help out. And drop in for tea anytime."

"Thank you. I may just do that. We'll see you all on Sunday then." He placed his hat on his head as he stepped outside.

"We'll be there. Thanks for stopping by." Jess and Grandmother waited by the door until Robert turned his car into the lane.

"He seems like a fine young man." Grandmother closed the door.

"Yes, he does," agreed Jess, picking up the tea tray and walking toward the kitchen. "It should be interesting to hear him speak on Sunday."

~

"Connie," Jess stopped her friend later that day as she prepared to leave. "I wanted to tell you I've been thinking about your invitation, and I'd love to go. That is, if the offer of a gown is still good?"

"Of course it is!" exclaimed Connie. "I'm so happy you're coming. It'll be much more enjoyable with you there. I'll pick some gowns for you to try on. If the one you pick needs altering, I'll have it done in time for the party." She impulsively reached out and hugged Jess. "I'm so glad."

"Connie," Jess began hesitantly as Connie stepped back, "We're going to church in Pateley Bridge Sunday. Rock of Ages Church behind the bakery shop. I wondered if you'd join us then come for Sunday dinner afterward. I promise not to make you wash dishes or dust anything."

Connie laughed. "Even if you did, I'd still come. Is it alright if I meet you there?"

"Absolutely," agreed Jess, holding the front door open.

"Your grandmother told me you're going out with Dr.

Samuels tomorrow night," Connie said, walking out to her car. "Have a wonderful time!"

~

As Jess prepared for her evening with Garth, she heard a timid knock on her door. Opening it, she was surprised to find Billy standing in the doorway, hands behind his back.

"Billy! What brings you up here? Shouldn't you be washing up for supper?" Jess asked, smiling.

Billy nodded sheepishly then thrust out a handful of flowers he'd picked from the garden. Jess supposed he'd picked them when Grandmother wasn't looking.

"Oh, Billy! They're beautiful!" Jess accepted the simple bouquet. "The most beautiful flowers I've ever received! Are they for my dinner date tonight?" *Date?* Jess thought. *Is this really a date? With the handsome Dr. Samuels?*

Shuffling his feet, Billy nodded shyly.

"How thoughtful! Thank you." Jess dropped a kiss on the boy's cheek, causing him to shuffle harder.

"Run wash up now. I'll be sure to take these with me tonight, okay?"

Billy, relieved to get away, nodded and ran down the hallway.

Jess looked at the flowers in her hand. How sweet of Billy! He'd risked picking Grandmother's flowers for her. She certainly wouldn't disappoint him.

Grandmother, who was watching for Garth, opened the door when he arrived.

"Come in, Garth. Jess is almost ready. I'll run up and let her know you're here."

As she walked to the stairs, Jess appeared on the landing. "It's alright, Grandmother. I'm ready." She smiled as she descended the stairs. "Good evening, Dr. Samuels."

Jess wore a long-sleeved, ankle-length, cornflower blue silk dress with pin tucks across the loose bodice. A wide white silk sash hugged her waist. She'd borrowed Grandmother's cashmere shawl and wore the pearl necklace her parents had given her for graduation. Her honey-colored hair was arranged in the latest

Gibson girl style and crowned with a simple navy wide-brimmed beribboned hat. She had tied Billy's flowers with a ribbon and pinned them to her bodice. She thought she looked rather plain.

Garth, however, had never seen anyone lovelier than Jess was at that moment. He suddenly found it difficult to breath.

"Good evening, Miss Montgomery." His voice sounded husky. "You look lovely. And someone has given you flowers. A secret admirer, perhaps?"

"Thank you. And no, it's no secret at all." She smiled, winking at Billy, who'd slipped into the room quietly.

"Where are you going for dinner?" asked Grandmother.

"We have reservations at the Royal Hotel Restaurant. It's supposed to be quite good," said Garth.

"And posh," added Grandmother. "It's quite splendid, so I've heard."

Jess caught her lip between her teeth doubtfully. Hopefully she wasn't underdressed. Garth wore an informal dark gray suit, a white shirt and burgundy tie. Perhaps she'd be alright.

"Shall we go?" Garth asked. "Our reservations are for seven."

"Of course. Goodbye, Grandmother." She gave her a hug, and then turning, blew Billy a kiss. "Goodnight, Billy."

He blushed, again shuffling his feet. Grandmother laid her arm around his shoulders as they walked toward the dining room where everyone was gathering for supper.

Chapter Five

*T*he Royal Hotel was a large establishment catering to England's wealthy. Surrounded by beautiful gardens and stretches of green lawn broken only by meandering footpaths where guests could wander at their leisure, the hotel itself was built of the gritstone so prevalent in the Dales. Ivy grew in lush green splendor across the walls of the building. Crystal chandeliers lit the huge windows. With a two-hundred year history, it had seen many celebrity visitors throughout the years. When Harrogate was a busy resort, visitors flocked from around the world to enjoy the mineral waters at the Royal Baths. Many stayed at the Royal Hotel, playing away their days in leisure and comfort. Although the war had affected business, the Royal Baths were still used by those who could afford it's diversion from the horrors of war.

As Garth stopped the car at the entrance, a uniformed valet opened Jess's door. After she and Garth got out, he drove the car into the valet parking. The doorman tipped his hat, greeting them as they entered the large revolving glass doors.

The hotel lobby was more spectacular than Jess had imagined. Crystal chandeliers hung from the carved ceiling. Tan and dark green velvet couches were scattered around the room while matching drapes graced the long windows across the front of the building. Huge pillars rose from the richly patterned carpet to the intricately carved ceiling. To the right was a row of shiny brass elevator doors, and straight ahead was the reception desk. People milled about leisurely; some in eveningwear, others dressed casually. Porters and bellhops rushed about, delivering messages, carting luggage, and ringing elevators for guests.

With his hand at Jess's back, Garth led her through a large entryway to the left, past the hotel bar and into the elegant dining room with dimmed lights and soft music, where the atmosphere was quieter and more relaxed. The maitre'd led them to an intimate table for two in the corner of the room.

Jess was enthralled. Garth watched with growing pleasure at the awe in her shining eyes.

"Well, what do you think? Will it do?"

"Will it do?" Jess exclaimed softly, taking the seat he held for her. "I'll say! The only thing keeping me from total embarrassment in this glamorous setting is the fact that others are dressed almost as plainly as I am." She looked at their fellow diners dressed in everything from travel clothes to exotic evening dress.

Garth took his seat. "You've nothing to worry about. You're the loveliest woman in the room." He forced his husky voice to a lighter tone. "Besides, that dress is far from plain. It's really very lovely. You can hold your own anywhere."

"Why, thank you, kind sir." Jess tilted her head in a slight bow. "You're the answer to a maiden's prayer."

"One can only hope," Garth muttered quietly, then added normally, "Chivalry isn't dead yet."

Jess looked at her menu to escape the light in his gray eyes. *Concentrate on the menu. He's only teasing.*

Garth noticed the color invading her cheeks at his words. She was unlike any woman he'd ever known. Most girls played up to men these days, but Jess was different and he was intrigued. Immensely.

After the waiter took their order, Garth leaned his forearms on the table. "I hope you know how much your visit means to your Grandmother. You've taken some of the burden from her shoulders."

"I'm glad." Jess relaxed a bit. "She should take things easier, but I don't think she's slowed down much physically."

"Perhaps not, but she's certainly more lighthearted than I've seen her in a long time."

"How long have you known her?"

"Most of my life, I suppose. She hasn't changed much. Still gives as much love and attention to whoever comes through her door." He paused before asking, "You didn't see much of her when you were growing up, did you?"

"No, I didn't. She visited once when I was ten. We had such a wonderful time baking, playing games and hiking in the woods. Looking back, I'm sure she was making up for the time we'd missed not being together." Jess's eyes grew misty at the memory. Then she smiled. "But the short time we had was precious. And now we can enjoy each other again for a while."

"Your mother must have loved your father very much to leave her home and family to move to America."

"She did, and they were happy, too. But she and Grandmother always corresponded. Mother read her letters to me, and I felt like I knew Grandmother before she ever came to visit." She paused. "And now she's the only family I have."

"I was sorry to hear that your mother passed away," Garth said sincerely.

"Did you know her?" asked Jess, surprised.

Garth caught himself before he said how sorry he'd felt for the girl in the picture frame sitting on her grandmother's mantel. "Some, but I know that your grandmother mourns her daughter."

"Yes. Sometimes I forget I'm not the only one who hurts because of her death."

"You know, I lost my mother several years ago. I'd just finished school and was entering medical school when she suddenly became ill and died within a week. I wanted to give up on everything, including medical school, but Dad reminded me that she would've wanted me to continue with my plans and not give up. I realized I wouldn't be any good to anyone if I quit, so I determined to practice medicine. The thought of my mother encouraged me through many hard times in medical school. She was a very strong woman and never gave up on anything. She was quite a lady."

"I'd love to have known her."

"She'd have liked you, and even though you can't meet her, you can meet Dad. He's a grand fellow. I'm sure he'll be out to the orphanage soon. We're both called out sooner or later. There's usually one child or the other becoming ill or getting hurt somehow. The orphanage gives us the most business in the whole of the Dales."

Jess laughed. "So I've noticed. But how is it that I haven't met your father before now? So far you've been the only doctor to come when Grandmother calls."

"Well, umm...just fortunate, I suppose." He wouldn't tell her that since her arrival he'd made every effort to come to the farm. He quickly changed the subject. "By the way, how is Constance Cameron working out?"

"Connie, as she prefers to be called, is working out nicely. She works hard and learns quickly. It doesn't seem like she comes from an aristocratic family. She's very sweet and fun and the children love her."

Just then the waiter brought their dinner. After they were served, Garth asked, "Have you been to her home yet? It's quite grand."

"No, I haven't." Jess sliced the tender lamb cutlet on her plate. "I've heard it's beautiful. I guess I'll find out soon enough. I'm invited to a formal dinner party next weekend. I'm a little nervous though. I've never been to one before. Have you been there?"

Garth didn't care for the idea of her attending the party, but he was in no position to say anything. "Only as a doctor. Connie seems amiable, and I'm sure you'll enjoy yourself. Her father is reputably a fair businessman. He started at the bottom and worked hard all his life to get where he is today. Connie's brother, Ian, has recently returned from France. Apparently because of his moneyed family, he obtained a commission that kept him behind the battle lines." His voice was edged with disapproval.

"Connie says little about her family and has never mentioned her brother. Your voice suggests you dislike him."

"You're rather perceptive, aren't you?" Admiration slipped into Garth's voice. "I don't care for him much. I have my reasons, but I don't want to bias your opinion before you've met him for yourself. Besides, my reasons are based on the past, and who knows, but the war may have changed him."

"I'm interested to meet this heir to the Cameron riches," Jess flashed a teasing smile. "Maybe he has a colorful past worth investigating."

"Nothing as romantic as that," Garth said wryly. *Now you've done it. She wants to meet Ian, and he can be rather charming when he chooses. Way to go, chump.* Aloud he added, "Just don't forget your lowly doctor friend, will you?"

"Of course not, doctor," said Jess happily.

"Which reminds me." Garth laid down his fork, looking into her smiling eyes. "Please call me Garth. I think you're the only one in the Dales who doesn't."

"I suppose I could, if you like."

"I do like." Garth flashed his own charming smile. "When you call me 'doctor', I feel like you're talking to my father."

"Oh, no!" Jess exclaimed in mock horror. "Not at all. Just showing respect for your profession."

"Thanks, but I prefer being called by my name and not my profession."

"Very well then... Garth." Jess paused before asking quietly, "Weren't you in France as well? Grandmother mentioned it."

Garth sipped his water before answering. "Yes, I served in France, like so many other Englishmen."

"If I'm not being too nosey, what did you do there?"

"I was a captain in the medical corp. I saw more horrors of war than I care to recall," he said gruffly, reminded of the death and destruction he'd witnessed on the battlefield.

Jess instantly regretted her question. "I'm sorry I reminded you of those horrors. I'm afraid my curiosity gets the better of me sometimes."

Garth smiled into her troubled eyes. "Curiosity can be a good thing at times. At least you're interested in knowing more about me."

Jess remembered his arrogant statement from a few days before when he'd asked her out. *I'm sure there's a lot you don't know about me,* he'd said. *I'll see you Saturday at six. Then you can find out more.* She was definitely finding out just how arrogant he could be. What a shame. She was just starting to like him.

"I'm afraid I'm not that curious." Jess glanced at the big wall clock at the far end of the room. "It's getting late and Grandmother won't settle down until I'm home. Besides, there's church in the morning. She'll need a hand getting the children ready."

"I suppose you're right," Garth agreed wryly. *You've done it again, Chump.* "I should get you home." He signaled the waiter for their bill.

The trip home was mostly quiet; Garth regretting his arrogant statement halting their pleasant evening and Jess fusing at herself for letting him get to her. She'd have to be more indifferent in the future. After parking in front of the old farmhouse, Garth helped Jess out, walking her to the door.

She turned to say good night. "I had a very nice evening. Thank you for asking me."

"I'm glad. I did as well. Perhaps we can do it again. That is, if you have the time. After next weekend's dinner party, your calendar will be full." He smiled faintly then squeezed her hand. "Good night, Jess." Then he was gone.

As she prepared for bed Jess thought back over the evening. Had she enjoyed herself? Of course she had. Garth was interesting to talk to, and he'd made her feel at ease in the elegant atmosphere of the restaurant. So why did he have to spoil the evening by commenting on her curiosity about him? Was she really upset with him? As she crawled into bed she knew the answer was no. In truth, she'd never met a man like Garth before and wanted to know more about him. No, she wasn't upset with Garth. It was only a front to hide her interest in the young doctor with the smiling gray eyes.

~

The next morning Jess sat between Connie and Billy, looking around as the congregation gathered inside the little church. They were mostly farmers and shopkeepers from and around Pateley Bridge. She'd met a few of them. She recognized Sam Phillips from the corner grocery store and George Higgins and his wife, with whom they'd ridden to church. When everyone stood to greet one another before the hymn preceding the message, Jess turned to greet those behind her. As she did, she looked straight into a pair of now familiar gray eyes. Garth stood two rows back, smiling and nodding before turning to greet those around him. Jess shook hands with the little lady behind her and then turned around. Her hands trembled slightly as she shook hands with a gentleman in front of her. She couldn't remember afterward what people had said as they welcomed her to the Dales. Or for that matter what the next hymn was.

When Robert Kilpatrick stood to deliver his message, Jess forced herself to concentrate on his words.

"Joseph's brothers sold him into slavery then lied to their father and turned their backs on him. After he was brought to Egypt as a slave, Joseph faced more hardships. His master's wife had him imprisoned because he refused to bend to her will. In prison, he was placed over other prisoners, and after he interpreted correctly the dreams of Pharaoh's butler and his baker, they promised to remember him and have him released from prison. But again, he was betrayed and forgotten. Forgotten by men but not by God. God remembered Joseph, and through all the years of enslavement, Joseph never forgot God. He was faithful no matter how difficult the trial or how great the temptation, and God rewarded Joseph for his faithfulness. He caused the men to remember him in that prison, and Joseph was brought out to interpret Pharaoh's dream, too. Pharaoh was so pleased with Joseph he lifted him up to the second highest position in the land, giving him his ring and the daughter of one of his priests to marry. Do you think that once Joseph was set up and his problems solved that he forgot God? When men become self sufficient, many times they do forget Him. Life becomes easy and they forget their need for Him. But not Joseph. Even when he had everything, he still remembered God. His two sons were named in remembrance of God. Manasseh, because God helped him forget the pain of his hardships, and Ephraim, because God had made him fruitful. He had blessed him."

Glancing at Connie, Jess saw that she was absorbing every word of the sermon. *Lord, help her see Your love and want to become Your child.*

After the sermon, as Robert shook hands at the front door, Grandmother approached him. "What a wonderful Message, Mr. Kilpatrick."

"Why, thank you, Mrs. McDonald." He extended his hand, shaking hers.

"Please join us for dinner, if you've no other plans? We'd love to have you."

"I'd enjoy that. I'll come as soon as everyone's gone and I can close up."

"Wonderful!" Grandmother exclaimed. She turned to find Kevin and Geoffrey exchanging punches. "If you'll excuse me, I've a fight to stop."

Holding Katie and Billy's hands, Jess walked toward George's wagon. As she approached, she saw Garth leaning against the tailgate, hands in his pants pockets.

"Hello, Billy! Katie!" He ruffled the head of the first and tweaked the cheek of the second then looked directly into Jess's eyes. "Hello, Jess."

"Hello. You never mentioned you attend church here."

"Well, I've been occasionally," Garth evaded. "Sometimes I attend St. Cuthbert's up on the hill." He nodded toward Robert standing at the front door of the church. "But that was a very good sermon this morning. You don't usually hear that kind up on the hill."

"Then why go there?" Jess asked simply.

Garth smiled. "Well, that's a good point. I'll have to think about that. When I heard there was a new pastor speaking here this morning, I thought I'd give him a try. I'm glad I did."

Jess nodded. "It was a good message." She paused, looking hesitant. "Would you like to come to Sunday dinner? Grandmother asked Mr. Kilpatrick to come and... Connie is coming, and well... I thought maybe you'd like to come, too," she finished lamely.

Garth's eyes lit up as he flashed his smile. "Nothing would please me more." Then he added quickly, "It would give me an opportunity to ask Mr. Kilpatrick some questions I've been thinking about."

"Of course." Jess spotted Grandmother approaching with Kevin and Geoffrey, held by their ears, firmly in tow. The other children followed her and the Higgins'. "I'd better get Katie and Billy loaded up. The others are coming."

"I'll help." Garth lifted Katie and Billy into the back of the wagon then, placing his hands around Jess's slender waist, he lifted her, setting her on the tailgate.

Her breath caught as her cheeks stained crimson. "Oh!" She quickly scrambled up onto the wooden bench, mumbling "Thank you".

Garth, delighted at her confusion, chuckled and turned, helping everyone else into the wagon. As George snapped the reins to start the horses moving, Garth slammed the tailgate shut and waved. "See you shortly."

Jess pretended to be busy with the children as she tried to still her erratic heartbeat.

Chapter Six

The crisp, fall days, intermingled with warmer ones, came to an end; winter had arrived in the Dales. The flowers faded, while the sky turned a bleak gray that hid the sun's rays. The winds blew relentlessly bringing rain and occasionally sleet. Smoke billowed from chimneys across the Dales.

The children bundled up for the cold walk to school, happy that yesterday's rain had ended. Geoffrey and Jeannie had colds, and Grandmother refused to allow them out into the chilling wind, which they didn't mind. The other children envied them as they snuggled into their warm beds.

Although Charlie couldn't yet work, he came to the kitchen to eat once the breakfast rush ended.

"Charlie!" exclaimed Gwen as he entered the back door. "What on earth are ya doin' here? Ya should'na be out in this cold. I was just fixin' to bring breakfast to ya." She clucked around him like a mother hen. "Since ya're here, sit ya down and eat whilst it's hot. Here's some coffee."

"Thank you, Gwen. I knew you'd not disappoint me." Charlie gingerly removed his coat to prevent aggravating his sore ribs, hanging it by the door. Sitting at the kitchen table, he grinned at the good-natured cook. "I couldn' stand bein' in that house another minute. I had to get out a bit and you're cookin's worth comin' out in the cold for."

"Oh, ye do go on, Charlie. Now eat up," Gwen scolded happily, pleased with his compliment about her cooking.

"Good morning, Charlie." Grandmother entered the kitchen. "It's good to see you up and around. How are you feeling?"

"A bit sore yet but happy to be up an' about."

"Well, don't over-do. Remember what Garth said. You've still got bandages to be careful of."

"Aye, that I do," sighed Charlie. "It's been hard this last two weeks. I'll be glad to return to work. Where's Miss Jess this mornin'?"

"She's with Geoffrey and Jeannie. They're terribly congested. I've called the doctor, but he can't come until later. Seems the colder weather's brought on a lot of illness." She poured herself some tea. "Gwen, I called Connie to tell her not to come today. We'll manage, don't you think?"

"Well, an' sure, Mrs. Morag. I've just some bakin' to do. Nothin' I can't handle." Gwen finished the last of the dishes before bringing out her mixing bowls.

~

Charlie was reading the paper by the fire when Jess skipped down the stairs. "Hello, Charlie. I thought I heard your voice. How do you feel? You're looking better."

"Much better, thank ya kindly. How're the young'uns doin'?"

"Geoffrey's not too bad, but Jeannie's feverish, coughing and very congested. I hope the doctor arrives soon." She wondered if Garth's father would come as he had yesterday for Charlie's check-up. Garth hadn't been to the farm since Sunday dinner. She liked the elder Dr. Samuels though. A tall, slim man in his mid-sixties, his thick iron-gray hair was streaked with white, as was his "handle-bar" mustache. His perpetual smile and charm put people at ease and Jess liked that.

As if on cue, there was a knock at the front door. Answering it, Jess found the very subject of her thoughts standing in the doorway.

"Hello, Miss Montgomery." He removed his hat. "Your grandmother called and said some of the children are ill."

"Good morning, Dr. Samuels. Please come in." Grandmother came into the room as Jess closed the door.

"Thanks for coming, Neville. I know you're very busy, but I really felt the children should be seen."

"Well, that's why I'm busy. There are a lot of germs scurrying about the Dales. It's the season for it." He spotted Charlie reading his paper. "Good morning, Charlie. I'm see you're up and about. Couldn't stand your cottage any longer, eh?"

"Got that right, Doc. I was goin' bonkers out there."

"Well, just take it easy. You're not healed yet, you know. I'm sure these ladies will see you don't overdo. Now, let's have a look at those children?"

Half an hour later, Connie entered in the kitchen door, arms filled with bundles.

Gwen saw her struggling to get in. "Here, lass, let me hold the door."

"Thanks, Gwen. Is Jess around?"

"She's upstairs with Jeannie and Geoffrey, who're down with colds."

Connie found Jess sitting against Jeannie's headboard, the sick girl leaning against her shoulder. Geoffrey lay across the foot of the bed, listening as she read to them. Jess looked up when Connie entered.

"What're you doing here? You have the day off."

"I do." Connie dropped her bundles on another bed. "Gracious, those are heavy."

"What are they?" Jeannie asked, her words followed by coughing.

"I've some dresses for Jess to try on. Want to have a fashion show?"

"Oh, yes, please." The girl brightened at the prospect.

Geoffrey groaned, rolling his eyes. "I'll be in my room."

As he left, Connie pulled Jess to her feet. "Come, try these on.

You can model them for Jeannie. Your grandmother can sit and watch, too!"

"Alright." Jess curiously eyeing the heap on the bed.

Grandmother was called, and she and Jeannie watched as Jess modeled one dress after another. There were so many to choose from and most fit well. Jeannie ooh-ed and ahh-ed at them all. Grandmother gave her opinion on each. Some were too low in the front. Some were too low in the back. A few were altogether too immodest for her tastes. But one was simply stunning on Jess. A full-skirted cream gown with elbow length sleeves. Cream lace edged the modest neckline and the gathered edge of the sleeves while a burgundy sash hugged the waist. A pair of burgundy silk pumps perfectly matched the sash. Grandmother nodded with approval. Looking in the full-length cheval mirror Jess was amazed at the transformation. Never had she worn anything so beautiful.

"That's very lovely, Jess." Grandmother nodded with approval.

"She'll be the belle of the ball." Connie sighed happily. "It fits perfectly. How do the slippers feel?"

"Just fine." Jess stared at her reflection. "I feel like Cinderella minus the glass slippers. I'm glad these aren't made of glass."

"Well, the dress doesn't need altering." Connie glanced at her watch. "Gracious! I must run." She repacked the remaining dresses and shoes. "I'll send my hairdresser over Saturday afternoon to style your hair then a car will pick you up at 6:30." From another box she withdrew a fur trimmed evening cloak. "You'll need this."

Jess gaped at the cloak then gave her friend a quick hug. "You've thought of everything. I wouldn't know where to begin, but you've planned it all out. Thank you."

Connie smiled. "Perhaps I can't plan a meal or clean without instructions, but I do know what's fashionable for a formal dinner party." Her expression turned wry. "Not that it's an important ability."

"It's all in what you've been taught," Grandmother said

kindly. "In your home it's important."

"Well, I'm finding there are far more important things in life," Connie sighed.

~

Saturday morning while enjoying her coffee, Jess scanned the morning newspaper. She'd missed the news all week while nursing the children. Geoffrey had returned to school, but Jeannie was still sick. Her fever and congestion had worsened until Thursday, when her fever finally broke. If things weren't hectic enough, on Wednesday, Gwen received a letter from her sister in Scotland who was very sick and wanting Gwen to come. After packing her bag Gwen was on the next train to Edinburgh. Jess and Grandmother prepared meals while Connie completed Gwen's other duties.

One headline in the paper caught Jess's eye: "Local Police Find the Body of an Old Age Pensioner." She remembered the headlines she'd seen at the train station and also in Mr. Phillips' shop. Reading further, she was shocked to learn that not just two, but four bodies were found in various places throughout the Dales in the past few weeks, perplexing authorities. Nothing like this had happened in England since Jack the Ripper's reign of terror in 1888.

"Have you read this article?" she asked Grandmother as she entered the kitchen. Handing her the paper, Jess waited as she perused the article.

"Yes, luv." Grandmother shook her head sadly, laid the paper on the table and reached to fill the tea kettle. "I read it this morning. I was talking with Martha Higgins yesterday. Dale folk are generally superstitious, and there are some strange speculations passing about. Personally I don't believe in such nonsense, but I don't have a better explanation."

"According to the article, all the victims were loners with no family or friends. That's sad. You know, it might be a good idea if I walked the children to and from school. Or better yet, I'll drive the truck. I drove at home and even though they drive on the other side of the road here, it shouldn't be too hard to adjust."

"Well, I don't know," said Grandmother doubtfully. "I wouldn't want you driving unless someone can help you practice a bit first. You know . . . to ride in the truck while you're drive."

"Well, I suppose . . ."

A knock sounded on the back door just before Garth sauntered in. "Good morning. I hope I'm not interrupting anything."

"Certainly not." Grandmother filled a cup with coffee for him. "Come in and warm yourself."

"Thank you. It's rather cold out." Removing his jacket, he hung it by the door.

"Not working today?" Jess noticed how tired he looked. She filled a plate with muffins she'd baked that morning.

"No, I'm taking the day off. It's been a very hectic week with very little let up. Dad and I have both been on more calls than I care to remember." He looked up as Jess set the plate on the table. She wanted to reach out and gently smooth back the wave of hair falling over his forehead and ease away his strain and fatigue. His eyes flashed understanding, curving his lips into a slight grin. One eyebrow rose questioningly.

Her cheeks flaming, she quickly turned to the sink. What had come over her, thinking such things? "So that's why you haven't been by in a while," she said as casually as possible.

"Have you missed me?" he asked just as casually, not letting on that he was thrilled she'd noticed his absence the past week.

"Well, your father's regularly checked on Charlie and the children," she evaded. "He's been very helpful."

"Yes, he usually is."

"Garth," said Grandmother, having unobtrusively followed their prevaricating exchange. "I need a favor, if possible."

Garth's attention turned to Grandmother. "Certainly. If I can, it'd be my pleasure."

"Jess and I were just discussing this week's newspaper article before you arrived. We're concerned about the children walking unsupervised to and from school each day. I've never felt it necessary until these awful murders started happening. Jess suggested she walk with the children." Jess knew what was coming, but was helpless to stop it. She swallowed hard, keeping her back to them as she listened.

Having read the papers, Garth didn't like this idea. Jess would be in as much danger as the children. "How can I help?" he asked gravely.

"Well, Jess wants to drive the children to school until Charlie's able to drive again, and it would save her biking in the cold to the village. Would you ride with her while she practices driving on the 'wrong' side of the road?" Grandmother asked, chuckling. "She drove at home so it should just be a matter of practice."

Mortified, Jess felt heat flooding her cheeks. Grandmother hadn't said anything about this idea beforehand! She wasn't prepared for this!

"I'd be happy to," Garth replied. It would be safer than Jess walking to and from school twice a day. That wasn't going to happen. He was horrified at the thought of her or the children running into the murderer who was still on the loose.

"Wonderful!" exclaimed Grandmother. She turned to Jess. "There, luv. That problem's solved."

"Yes….well…. I…."

"I've an idea," Garth spoke before she could say more. "I've the day off. Let's go now. Greenhow Hill would be a good place to practice with very little traffic and lots of open road. That is unless you've other plans."

Before Jess could speak, Grandmother answered, "She just needs to return by 3:30 to prepare for her dinner engagement this evening."

"Dinner engagement?" Garth glanced intently into his coffee cup.

"Connie's dinner party." Jess turned from the sink.

"Oh, yes, I remember. I'm sure you'll enjoy it. And I'm sure you'll be the loveliest woman there." His gaze locked onto hers. Then more casually he asked, "So, how about that driving lesson? Are you ready?"

Jess tried not to think about how Garth's presence always made her self-conscious, something she'd never experienced before meeting him, but she needed to drive the children to school, and he was the logical one to help.

"I suppose so." She turned to Grandmother. "Are you sure you don't need my help with anything?"

"Not at all, luv. You've been busy since you arrived, and this is an opportunity for you to see something of the Dales while you're driving. So take your time. You needn't be back for hours."

"Then I'll get my coat and the truck keys," said Jess.

~

Seated in the truck beside Garth, Jess realized her first problem was the awkwardness of sitting on the opposite side of the truck, the gear stick on her left instead of her right. Starting the engine, she managed to shift into first gear. Driving slowly around the house, she reached to shift into second. *It's on the left, it's on the left.* She managed second gear and drove down the lane. So far Garth had merely commented on the weather. Concentrating on driving, Jess didn't respond. At the end of the lane, she asked, "Which way to Greenhow Hill?"

Garth gave directions as she managed to turn the truck, progressing through the gears with a minimum of grinding. Noticing when she relaxed a bit, Garth began talking about the Dales.

The road to Greenhow Hill wound steadily upward, passing sheep grazing in rocky pastures that looked no different than any other Dales' landscape Jess had seen so far. But then the scenery began to change. Pastures became barren moors, covered with heather and bog moss. Only the sheep scattered over the rough terrain remained the same. Overlooking Nidderdale and the surrounding moorlands, the view was magnificent. Garth told how the moors were mined from Roman time's right up until the last century. The hills still bore the scars and pockmarks from mining. Occasionally an old sealed mine shaft entrance could be seen, but the once-thriving industry was now remembered only in legend and history books. It reminded Jess of the old ghost towns scattered across western America. The sky was its usual mid-October gray, adding a mysterious touch to the bleakness of the moors. They passed a few scattered farmhouses and The Miners Arms Pub where miners had once gathered, but was now frequented by local farmers. The houses and the pub, looking much as they had for centuries, were built to withstand the gale force winds that often blew across the moors. The weather up here could change quickly, and the inhabitants were always prepared for the worse.

Fascinated, Jess drove slowly so as not to miss anything as Garth talked about the area's history. They passed Stump Cross Caverns, a natural underground cavern system discovered during the mining era. Garth suggested she visit it sometime. Continuing down the other side of Greenhow Hill, they reached Hebdon where they turned and headed back toward home.

At Pateley Bridge, Garth said, "It's still early. Care to see more of the Dales before we head back?"

"I'd love to!" Jess exclaimed, her eyes shining. Garth was happy she'd forgotten her self-consciousness and enjoyed watching her pleasure and interest in his little part of the world.

"There's so much to see in the Dales because they stretch for many miles, but there certainly isn't time to explore it all today."

"So how did I do, Doctor?"

"Driving? You've done great! You'll have no problem getting where you need to go. But we're not going back to being formal now, are we? I thought we were past all that."

"Oh, we are," Jess flashed an impish grin. "I was only teasing." The look in the gray eyes that met hers made her quickly look forward and change the subject. "Why don't you drive now? I've practiced enough for today."

She pulled the truck over, and after exchanging seats, Garth pointed the truck in the opposite direction from where they'd come.

The road meandered through the valley, past Gouthwaite Reservoir and through several small hamlets. They passed the Foster Beck Flax Mill, one of the surviving textile mills that once thrived in the area. Still in use, the two-story gritstone building's huge waterwheel reached from the top of the second story and dropped below the surface of the ground. Water from a stream on the hill behind the building fed the wheel's slow rotation.

At Lofthouse, a small farming village, they took a narrower road in desperate need of repair. It began a steady and sometimes steep ascent through pastures where more sheep grazed contently. They passed the occasional beck, which Garth explained, was a small brook. Here the vast expanse of bleak moorlands stretched as far as the eye could see, meeting the steely gray sky. No longer driving, Jess saw more than she had on Greenhow Hill. In the distance she spotted a large lake lying between the hills of the grassier lowland dales.

"That's Roundhill Reservoir," Garth explained. "Just above it in that forest is an old druid circle called Megalithic Folly."

"A druid circle? You mean like Stonehenge?"

"Something like that," Garth smiled. "Stonehenge was built centuries ago. Megalithic Folly was built less than a hundred years ago in the 1820's. Hence, the name, Folly."

"But, why?"

"Who knows? Probably because it's builder was eccentric. Want to see it?"

"Can we? I've never seen a druid circle, real or not. Do we have time?"

Garth glanced at his watch. "Plenty of time."

As they drove down from the moors and once again entered grassy pasturelands, Garth turned down a small dirt road that ended at a clearing in the woods. Parking the truck, he came around to help Jess out.

Placing a hand beneath her elbow, Garth led her down a wide path into the heart of the forest where the trees grew thick and the forest was eerily quiet. Jess shivered.

"Are you cold? We'll head back if you like." Garth stopped and pulled her coat collar closer beneath her chin, observing her closely.

"No, I'm not cold." Jess looked anywhere but into the gray

eyes gazing intently at her. "The forest is so quiet it made me shiver. I'm okay, really. Let's go on."

Shortly, they entered a large clearing that sloped uphill. In the middle of the clearing a series of huge boulders stood in an oval; the far end built into the side of the hill. Jess followed Garth inside the oval where several elongated boulders stood on end in symmetrical positions. One flat rock lay in the center, waist high and about seven feet long. Jess guessed it represented a sacrificial altar.

"I don't know much about the druids. Did they really make human sacrifices or is that merely fiction?"

"I don't know much about them myself, but folks say they did back when Britain was a barbaric land. Druid cults still meet and carry out their nature worship, but they don't sacrifice humans." Garth glanced at his pocket watch. "We need to get you home so you can prepare for your evening."

Back at the orphanage, he parked behind the house. As they walked to the kitchen door, Jess said, "Thanks for going with me to practice driving. Do you really think I'll be alright on my own?"

Garth stopped by the door. "You'll be fine. Just remember to drive on the left."

"When I go home I'll have to get used to driving on the right all over again," she laughed lightly.

Nodding grimly Garth didn't want to think about her going home. "Hopefully, you'll love it here so much you'll want to stay. We can hope anyway," he added gruffly.

Suddenly, Jess thought that was a good possibility. Then she mentally shook herself. Of course she had to go back. It was home; all she'd ever known. "Thanks for the tour of the Dales. I enjoyed seeing the countryside."

"I'm glad. Perhaps we'll do it again soon. Like I said earlier, it'll take a long time to see it all, but we could make a start anyway."

"I'd like that."

Garth flashed a smile. "Enjoy your evening, but don't get too used to the aristocratic social life."

Jess laughed softly. "I won't.

Garth reached for her hand and placed a quick kiss at her temple. "Take care," he spoke huskily and returned to his car.

Chapter Seven

*T*he sleek, black luxury sedan stopped beneath the portico in front of the huge manor house. The uniformed doorman opened the car door, offering his gloved hand to Jess. As she alighted, she gazed up at the magnificent white house, vines adorning its stone facade. Ivy entwined the columns supporting the portico as sparkling chandeliers lit the house, welcoming guests. Situated on a huge estate, the house was surrounded by manicured gardens with fountains that, in summer, sent plumes of water into the air. Paths meandered through the gardens and under trees where the occasional bench beckoned invitingly.

As the doorman opened the front door, Jess glanced down at her borrowed dress. She looked like she belonged here. Why didn't she feel like it? As promised, the hairdresser had expertly arranged her hair, and after donning Connie's dress, shoes, and cloak, she'd gazed at her reflection, unable to believe her eyes. She didn't look like herself, and now as she stepped into the grand entrance hall, she certainly didn't feel like herself as butterflies romped wildly in her stomach.

As she hesitated, Connie suddenly appeared, giving Jess a quick hug. "I'm pleased you're here. I was afraid you wouldn't come."

"The thought crossed my mind," Jess nervously looked around the front hall, feeling overwhelmed. The two-story ceiling displayed artistically painted carvings. A huge crystal chandelier hung from the center as carved mahogany banisters decorated the grand staircases ascending from both sides of the hall. Old family portraits abounded. Jess was almost afraid to see the rest of the house.

Connie led her through a large archway into the large living room redundant with a high ceiling, and on the far wall a huge fireplace burned brightly. Everything here was on a grand scale! Sofas and chairs lined the walls and surrounded the fireplace. Smaller chandeliers and wall sconces sparkled brightly. Expensive paintings of the English countryside and more old family portraits adorned the walls.

"Who are they?" Jess whispered.

"Just some ancestors," replied Connie offhandedly. "I couldn't tell you who they are. My father, on the other hand, can name them all." She looked up as an older gentleman approached them. "Speaking of whom....."

"Constance, dear." The man dropped a kiss on her cheek. "Is this your guest you were telling me about?"

"Yes. Jess this is my father, Cyril Cameron. Father, my good friend, Jessica Montgomery."

"It's indeed a pleasure for you to join us, my dear. Constance tells me you're American." Cyril held out his hand to take hers.

"Thank you for having me, Mr. Cameron." She shook his hand. "Yes, I'm American."

"I've been to America many times. Business, you know. But I always stop to see a bit of your country while I'm there." He smiled politely. "Well, I must mingle with my guests. Please make yourself at home and enjoy yourself."

"Thank you." Jess nodded as he bowed slightly before joining another group of guests.

"Come." Connie took Jess's hand. "I want to introduce you around."

"Do we have to?" Jess held back. "I mean, it doesn't matter to them who I am."

"No, but it does to me. Don't worry; I'm right here. You'll be fine."

Connie introduced Jess to several people, talking with each briefly and trying to help Jess relax. Some were curious about this American who'd joined their circle, but most didn't care. Jess decided they'd either vacationed in America or done business there, so this insignificant American girl wasn't worth their interest.

As they talked with an interesting older couple, a young man stopped by Connie and draped his arm across her shoulders. "Well, there's my favorite sister." He glanced at Jess, flashing a charming and debonair smile. "Well, Constance. Who's this little treasure?"

Connie smiled at him. "Ian, this is my friend, Jessica. Jess, this dashing young man is Ian, my older brother. Pay him no mind. He tries to charm all the girls."

"Tries!" Ian exclaimed, sighing dramatically. "You wound me, Sis! I always thought I succeeded."

"Only in your dreams. Most girls see right through you."

Jess looked up, finding Ian's gaze on her. His dark blond hair was cut in the latest fashion while his formal evening attire was impeccable. Not a wrinkle or a hair out of place, she observed with amusement. As he drew her hand to his lips, she noticed his were well manicured. Hands that didn't know manual labor. His icy blue eyes glittered brightly. Jess had never seen such eyes. She was fascinated.

"I'm sure Jessica doesn't believe that. Do you?" he asked innocently.

"I'll withhold judgment. I haven't known you long enough to make a sound decision."

"We'll remedy that. Why not sit beside me at dinner so we can talk?" Seeing the look on Connie's face, he added, "And Constance can sit on my other side. Although," he noticed a young man approaching, "she may have her own invitation."

As Connie spotted the young man, Jess saw her expression harden. "Constance, darling, I've looked everywhere for you. I thought you'd try and avoid this little gathering."

"Hello, Reginald," Connie spoke without enthusiasm. "I'd like to have done just that." Because manners demanded it, she introduced Jess. "Reginald, this is Jessica Montgomery, my good friend." Jess noticed an emphasis on "good". "Jess, Reginald Haley."

The young man looked down his long nose at Jess. "How do you do?" he said in a bored tone. "Now, Constance...."

"Reginald," Connie interrupted, "My guest is new to Nidderdale. I'd like to introduce her around. If you'll excuse us?"

Before she could move, Ian pulled Jess's hand through the crook of his arm. "I'll do that, Sis. I'd enjoy escorting this lovely creature around." Before she could respond, he swept Jess away, leaving Connie with the unwanted suitor. Connie vowed to have words with Ian later.

Intending to stay by Connie's side all evening, Jess was surprised at Ian's move. Glancing back, she lost sight of her as guests closed the gap between them. Eyeing her captor warily, she noticed the satisfied smile on his face.

"Connie won't be happy with this move. I don't think she likes Reginald."

"I'm well aware of that," Ian responded pleasantly, "but I couldn't let her monopolize the loveliest girl in the room, could I?"

Jess was pleased at the compliment, but everything seemed surreal. Her appearance, the atmosphere and Ian's solicitous attitude combined, made her feel like someone else.

As Ian introduced her, Jess relaxed, enjoying herself. Never leaving her side, he showed her every possible attention. When the dinner gong sounded, he escorted her into the dining room where two long tables were graced with the finest china and crystal. The silver cutlery reflected the sparkling light from the two chandeliers hanging gracefully above the tables.

Ian seated Jess then sat beside her. Connie appeared behind the chair next to Ian's, looking none too happy.

As Reginald seated Connie, she caught Ian's eye, glaring at him. Unfazed, he simply turned back to Jess.

"Please allow me to show you around while you're here. I know several terrific night spots I'm sure you'd enjoy."

Jess felt like a lead weight hit her. What was she doing here? She didn't fit in. Why was she pretending to? Her world was far removed from this one. She looked at the guests seated around the table. Comfortable in this atmosphere, they knew what was socially acceptable, and she wasn't it. Her appearance may have changed, but she hadn't. As God's child, she didn't belong here, but she wouldn't think about that now. Besides, it was just for tonight. It would be over tomorrow . . . just a memory. She forced her attention back to Ian's words.

After dinner, Connie invited Jess to follow her. She sent Ian a warning look, preventing a repeat of his earlier maneuver.

As guests returned to the living room to mingle, Connie led Jess up the grand staircase to a long hallway extending the length of the house. Once inside her room, she locked the door. Leaning against it, she sighed heavily.

"What's wrong, Connie? Are you alright?"

"I'm fine now that I'm away from that boorish Reginald. When he attends these parties, he shadows me." She flung herself onto the large, antique canopy bed. Jess sat beside her.

"I'm sorry. I felt I'd abandoned you, but Ian was rather insistent. I couldn't stop him without making a scene."

Connie's frown disappeared as she smiled at Jess. "I know. He can be domineering sometimes, but don't let him push you around. If I thought making a scene would have changed anything, I'd have made one. Nothing affects Ian unless he wants it to." She frowned. "Reginald's like that, too. No matter how much I discourage him, he won't give up. He's never interested in my thoughts, only in himself." She paused momentarily. "You know, Sunday at your grandmother's, I talked with someone who was interested in what I had to say."

"You mean Robert Kilpatrick?" Jess grinned. "I noticed you two had a lot to talk about."

"Well, he answered some questions I've had," Connie evaded. Getting up, she walked to the dressing table, gazing at her reflection in the mirror. Jess knew she wasn't seeing her reflection. "He was very interesting to talk to, and I enjoyed his sermon, too. I've never heard anything like that before."

"Then come with me again tomorrow morning."

Connie turned to Jess. "I think I will. I'd like to hear what else he has to say." Then she changed the subject. "What do you think of Ian?"

Jess considered before answering. "He's charming and debonairly handsome, but as I told him, it's too soon for an opinion." She suddenly remembered Garth didn't like Ian, but she didn't know why. "Tell me about him. Wasn't he in the war? What did he do?"

Connie sat on the bed, shrugging her shoulders slightly. "He served in France for a year but never saw battle. As captain of a supply company, he and his men supplied the soldiers at the front. He doesn't talk about it much. He came home a few months ago. Father was so proud of him. His son, the officer. I wasn't impressed, because I know several young officers who weren't so fortunate. So many are still on the battlefield. Others will never return home. I wish this war would end so the rest can come home. I'm sure the Americans feel the same, don't they?"

"Yes, we feel the same." Jess remembered her conversation with Garth. "You know, Garth Samuels served in France as a medic. He saw terrible things on the battlefield."

"Poor man! He must've been through so much. He's a good doctor, so he must've been a good medic."

Jess noticed the clock on the bedside table. "I should be going. It's late, and I have to prepare breakfast in the morning and help the children get ready for church. With Gwen gone, Grandmother and I share kitchen duty." She smiled wryly.

Downstairs, she turned to Connie. "Thanks for inviting me."

Before Connie could answer, a middle-aged woman in an elegant gold gown approached. Jess remembered seeing her during the evening, but hadn't met her.

"Constance, darling, I've waited all evening for you to introduce your little friend to me." Looking down her patrician nose, she eyed Jess coldly.

"Sorry, Mother. I was taking her around when Ian took over, leaving me behind. Jess, this is my mother, Valerie Cameron. Mother, Jessica Montgomery."

"Miss Montgomery. I've heard about you. You're assisting your grandmother at the orphanage, I understand." She frowned. "I'm sure your grandmother is doing a good thing, but I disapprove of Constance working there. I wish you would help me dissuade her. It isn't what she should be doing at all."

"I'm sorry, Mrs. Cameron, but I can't dissuade Connie from doing something she wants to do."

"Mother," Connie said firmly, "let's talk about this later."

Mrs. Cameron looked reproachfully at Jess then severely at Connie. "Yes, Constance, you can rest assured we shall. Miss Montgomery." With her head held high, she stalked away.

"I'm sorry, Jess. She shouldn't have said that."

"It's alright." Jess squeezed Connie's hand. "I'm fine, but I have to be going."

"I'll get the cloak and send the car around for you. Wait here. I'll be right back."

As Connie left, Jess heard Ian say her name. She turned, finding him right behind her.

"A beautiful girl like you shouldn't be all alone." He flashed his charming smile. "Come back inside, or better yet, let's go out to the veranda. We'll stroll for a bit."

"Thank you, but Connie's getting my cloak."

"Your cloak! Surely you're not leaving!"

"Yes, I have to go."

Connie returned with the fur-trimmed cloak. Ian took it from her, settling it around Jess's shoulders, his hands lingering momentarily.

"Thank you for coming, Jess. I'm happy you did." Connie said.

"Me, too. Thanks for inviting me." Giving Connie a hug Jess whispered, "See you at church?"

Connie nodded. "Good night."

Ian took Jess's hand, squeezing it possessively. "Good night, sweet Jessica. I'll see you soon. I promise."

"Good night, Connie. Good night, Ian."

Settling into the darkness of the luxury car, Jess's thoughts and emotions vied for attention. Between her drive through the Dales with Garth and the dinner party, it had been an unusual day, but she was too tired to examine it all tonight.

When the driver dropped her at the orphanage, Jess paused at the front gate. Grandmother would be waiting up to hear about her evening. Not wanting to discuss her thoughts and feelings tonight, she did owe Grandmother a description of the party. Sighing heavily, she opened the gate, walking to the front door.

As she reached for the doorknob, her foot bumped something on the front stoop. Opening the door to let out some light, she found a large basket. She carried it inside where, as she'd expected, Grandmother waited up. Closing the door, Jess pulled back some rags that filled the basket.

"What have you got there, Luv?" Grandmother rose from her chair.

"I just found it on the front stoop. It's filled with rags." Pulling back another, she gasped.

In the basket lay a tiny, newborn baby wrapped in a clean white sheet. Jess stroked its cool cheek, anxiety gripping her heart. "I'm going to call Garth. There's no telling how long this baby's been outside." Setting the basket on the sofa, she hurried to the phone.

Grandmother reached into the basket, pulling the baby into her arms.

"You poor thing," she crooned. The baby stirred as she unwound the sheet binding the tiny arms. Carrying the infant nearer the fire, she rubbed its arms and legs trying to warm it.

"Mrs. Sixsmith? This is Jessica Montgomery. May I speak with Dr. Samuels please? It's urgent."

"I'm sorry, Miss Montgomery, but he's not here. He's at his office unless he's been called out. Can I call him for you?" the landlady offered.

"Yes, please. Tell him there's a baby here and he needs to come quickly. Thank you. Good-bye." In her haste she didn't realize the vagueness of the message. After hanging up, she filled a pan with warm water to bath the baby in, hoping to warm him up. Oh, she prayed Garth would come quickly!

Chapter Eight

Garth tried reading but couldn't move past the first page. Distracted, all he thought of was Jess attending that ridiculous dinner party. After pacing and occasionally staring out the window, he decided to drive to his office, hoping to find something to occupy his mind. It didn't help. Sitting at his desk, he stared out the window, unable to concentrate. Part of him hoped she'd have a wonderful time; another part hoped she hated it. Remembering their outing that afternoon, he'd enjoyed Jess's reaction to the scenic countryside. Bright eyed and pink cheeked her excitement was evident. Nervous with him beside her, she'd done well driving, and then she'd relaxed, truly enjoying herself.

Determined to show her more of his Dales, he hoped she'd fall in love with them and want to stay. Better yet, perhaps she'd fall in love with.... *Not a chance,* he scolded himself. Running fingers roughly through his hair, he paced some more. Once across the floor and back again, he stopped at the window. Again. She wouldn't be interested in him with Ian Cameron around. She'd be set for life married to a man like him. A real charmer when he wanted to be, and she was with him tonight. Or she might have some lucky fellow waiting in America. A girl like her wouldn't be left alone for long. And what about him? Just a country doctor. What could he offer her? His patients led simple lives, most living on meager incomes. Sometimes his only payment was a loaf of homemade bread, vegetables or a block of cheese. Jess deserved better.

Recalling their walk to the druid circle, he'd wanted to pull her into his arms, to be the one to protect her, to be by her side day and night. Shaking his head, he knew he had to stop thinking this way.

The desk phone rang loudly, jarring him from his thoughts. As Mrs. Sixsmith relayed Jess's message, his heart skipped at the mention of her. What did she say? A baby? After Mrs. Sixsmith repeated the message, Garth hung up and grabbed his jacket. Running to his car, he drove as fast as he could toward the orphanage.

~

By the fire, Jess rocked the infant and stroked his downy soft head. Having bathed him in warm water and dried him with a soft towel, she'd bundled him in a soft blanket Grandmother had found. He now slept quietly in Jess's arms. They'd determined he was only a few days old. Jess was in awe at this tiny life. How could anyone abandon such a precious one?

As Grandmother returned to the living room after making tea, a knock sounded at the door. When she opened it, Jess heard Garth before she saw him, thrilling at the sound of his voice.

"Good evening, Mrs. McDonald. Mrs. Sixsmith said you needed me here urgently. Something about a baby?"

"Yes, yes. Thank goodness you're here." Grandmother pulled him into the room. "The child is right over here."

Garth saw Jess sitting on an ottoman by the fire holding the infant. His breath lodged in his throat. She still wore Connie's evening gown, the firelight reflecting off the gauzy fabric and her hair giving her an ethereal appearance. Her eyes were wide with concern, her lower lip caught between her teeth. He forced his gaze to the baby in her arms, but not before Jess saw the admiration in his eyes. She lowered her own gaze to the baby's face.

Kneeling beside Jess, Garth pulled his instruments from his

bag, examining the baby thoroughly. Draping the stethoscope around his neck, he leaned back on his heels.

"He seems fine. What have you done for him?"

Jess told him everything. "But I didn't want to feed him until you made sure he was okay."

"That's good. And the bath was a wonderful idea. He probably wasn't outside long enough to cause problems, but I'd keep him in for a while just in case. You can offer him some warm milk. He's quiet now, but that won't last long."

"I'll fetch it." Grandmother hurried to the kitchen.

"Thanks for coming so quickly." Jess kept her gaze on the baby's face. "I guess it wasn't that urgent, but its cold out, and I didn't know how long he'd been out there. My first thought was to have you examine him."

"Me and not my father?" Garth's voice was husky.

Jess, refusing to look at him, busily arranged the baby's blanket. "You came to mind first," she said with forced casualness.

"I see." A slight smile lifted the corners of Garth's mouth. He watched her momentarily. "You look natural with a baby in your arms. Ever thought of having a family of your own?" he asked, his casual tone matching hers.

"Occasionally." Jess stood up. She had to put distance between them. "Maybe someday," she added evasively.

Rising, he came to where she stood. "You'll make a wonderful mother. It's obvious from the way you care for the orphans." He gently stroked the baby's head. Then before he could stop himself, reached up, intending to push a tendril of Jess's hair away from her temple, but instead found her check. He stroked it tenderly, in awe of the warmth and softness beneath his fingers. His gaze dropped to her parted lips. More than anything he wanted to pull her into his arms and savor her lips beneath his own. Sliding his hand behind her neck, he felt the silky tendrils escaping her chignon. He wanted to pull the pins and combs from her hair, allowing it to tumble around her shoulders. Tugging her toward him, he lifted his gaze from her lips to find her watching him uncertainly. Her breathing was more rapid indicating her awareness of him. She caught her lip between her teeth as he'd seen her do when she was uncertain.

Forcibly slowing his own breathing, Garth dropped his hand, reluctantly stepping back. Jess's vulnerable gaze told him she wasn't ready for this. As much as he wanted to kiss her senseless, he didn't want to scare her away. He jammed his hands into his pants pockets. *They're safer there.*

Moving to the fireplace, he leaned against the mantle. "Was there a note in the basket?"

Jess gasped. "Oh, gracious! I was so concerned with the baby I didn't think to look." Reaching into the basket she rummaged through the rags. "Look at this." She held up a scrap of paper.

Garth turned from the fire, and reaching for it, read it aloud: *"Can't take care of me baby. Please feed and care fer him. I have to go away. We ain't got nobody else."*

Jess hugged the baby gently. "Well, now he has us."

Grandmother returned with a bottle of warm milk. "I thought I had some old baby bottles somewhere. Here, luv. I've already made sure it isn't too hot for the little one."

Sitting in the overstuffed armchair, Jess put the bottle to the baby's lips. Latching on, he suckled hungrily. Jess smiled at Garth. "You were right; he's hungry. I don't think he realized it until now."

Garth smiled slightly before turning to Grandmother. "If there's nothing more, I'll be going." He picked up his bag. "My day off is almost over, and I'm on duty in the morning."

Jess looked up quickly. "You mean your father's on duty tonight?" At his nod, she paled. "Oh, Garth, I'm so sorry. I forgot it was your day off. If I'd remembered I'd have called your father."

Garth knelt by her chair watching as the baby drank hungrily. Then he looked into her dark eyes, glanced at her lips then back into her eyes. "I'm not sorry in the least. Call me anytime you need me. And I mean that."

After letting him out, Grandmother returned to Jess. She hadn't even asked about the dinner party. Concern for the baby eclipsed everything. She looked at the clock on the mantel -- one am. Talk of the party would wait until tomorrow.

"Jess luv, why don't you head up to bed?"

Having finished the bottle, the baby slept against her shoulder. She yawned wearily. "I'm more tired than I realized." She gazed at the sleeping infant. "I'll help you settle the baby first."

"I've a cradle in the upstairs store room. Just hold him while I fetch it."

Jess leaned her head back and closed her eyes. The evening had ended differently than she'd expected. Once the baby was discovered the dinner party was forgotten, and she certainly hadn't expected to see Garth tonight.

Remembering the look in his eyes as he'd pulled her closer, her heart raced. Had he almost kissed her? She admitted she'd been glad to see him and wished he had. She'd enjoyed their drive through the Dales. Then she realized she just plain enjoyed spending time with him. She drifted off thinking about a pair of gray eyes and a smile that did amazing things to her heart.

~

Sunday morning Grandmother gathered the children in the living room, most still in pajamas and nightgowns. The baby, dressed in a blue cotton gown, lay in the basket covered with a soft blanket on the sofa.

"Children, God has brought a tiny baby into our home. I suppose He thought the baby would find a lot of love here, and that's just what we'll do. Love and care for him just like we love and care for each other. But first we need to give him a name."

"How about George?" came one suggestion.

"I like Bud," came another.

"Well, let's consider for moment," Grandmother said patiently. "Since God sent him to us, he needs a good Bible name."

"Adam."

"Gabriel."

"Moses. He's like baby Moses in the basket."

Grandmother held up her hand. "This isn't working. There

are too many good Bible names." She looked at Jess watching in amusement. "Since Jess found the baby she should name him. Jess, what do you think?"

Reaching into the basket Jess picked up the sleeping infant. He stirred but continued sleeping. She stroked his tiny fisted fingers thoughtfully. The children grew restless, wanting the baby named now. "We'll name him Michael. Michael McDonald."

"Michael?" the children asked in unison.

"Is Michael a Bible name?" asked Tommy.

"Absolutely." Jess smiled. "He's an archangel. There's only one archangel in the Bible, and his name is Michael. Like Grandmother said, God sent this baby for us to love and to care for. He's brought joy into this home, just like the archangel Michael will bring joy to God's children when he steps out and blows the trumpet of God, calling His children home."

"Splendid, luv," agreed Grandmother. "Michael it shall be."

The children all immediately addressed him by his new name.

"Children," reminded Grandmother, "you must hurry and prepare for church. Jess will drive you. Dr. Samuels thought Michael should stay in for a few days, so he doesn't get sick. I'll stay with him, but you must listen to Jess and do as she says."

Several of the children hugged Jess, agreeing they would.

~

Three weeks had passed since Michael arrived. He'd remained healthy, and the children all loved him and pitched in, helping Jess and Grandmother. When news of his arrival spread, neighbors dropped in with baked and canned goods. Grandmother gently reminded them it would be a while before the baby could eat solid foods, but they insisted on leaving the gifts.

Jess helped Charlie, now able to work, bring the sheep from pasture for the local veterinarian to check. Found to be healthy, they were returned to pasture. She and Jason alternated milking the cows. Jess had become quite good at it

Garth occasionally stopped in to check Michael, but never stayed long. He attended church every Sunday possible, but always left immediately after. Was he avoiding her? Even though she stayed busy, her mind often wondered to that moment when he'd almost kissed her. Or had he? Was it just wishful thinking?

Jess was cleaning upstairs when she heard the telephone ring then Grandmother calling her name. Hurrying downstairs, she noticed Grandmother's slight frown as she waited for her.

"It's for you, luv." She turned, leaving the room.

Jess picked up the receiver, never guessing who the caller would be.

"Hello. This is Jessica."

"Hello, sweet Jessica," greeted a cheery male voice. "Haven't forgotten me, have you?"

Jess started to reply "yes" since she didn't at first recognize the voice.

"Ian?"

"Yes, my sweet. Tis I, your ever adoring admirer."

"I haven't heard from you since your father's dinner party. How are you?"

"Sorry about that. I was in Hull for two weeks on business. Father runs a large ship yard there, you know." With an almost pleading voice he added, "You understand, don't you?"

"Of course," Jess replied easily. She'd been so busy around the orphanage and the farm that she hadn't given him much thought and was surprised to hear from him.

"I knew you would," Ian said confidently. "I called to ask you to dine with me tomorrow night. Then we'll see a play. Will you?"

Flattered by his invitation, Jess wasn't sure what to do. Should she go out with this high society man? She realized at his father's party that she didn't fit in with his crowd, but she loved plays. Having attended a few with her parents, she'd always enjoyed them. Would it hurt to go with him? She probably wouldn't have many opportunities like this.

Before she could change her mind, she accepted. "That would be fun, Ian!"

"Then I'll pick you up at six. Be ready to have a good time." With a quick "good bye" he was gone.

As she hung up, Jess started having second thoughts. *Should she go with him? What would Grandmother say?*

"Jess, are you alright?" asked Connie from behind her.

Jess turned to find Connie, bucket and mop in hand.

"I'm fine; just thinking. That was Ian on the phone."

"Oh? What did he want?" Connie asked warily.

"He invited me to dinner and a play tomorrow night."

"And . . .?" Connie prompted.

"And I accepted. I haven't attended a play in years and thought it'd be fun."

Connie paused before speaking cautiously. "Jess, as your friend, I want to say something, but I don't want to upset you."

Jess drew Connie's arm through her own in a comradely manner. "Constance Cameron, you're my friend, and as such, you can say whatever you need to say to me. What's up?"

"Be careful of Ian. He's my brother, but he's very worldly-wise. He's known as a . . . well . . as a bit of a charmer, if you know what I mean."

"Yes," smiled Jess, patting Connie's hand. "I picked up on that, but don't worry. I'm only interested in Ian as a friend. Besides, it's only dinner and a play. It'll be fun."

"I hope so," sighed Connie.

~

Glancing at her shopping list as she left Sam Phillip's shop, Connie saw the bakery was her next stop. Turning in that direction, she ran right into another pedestrian. He reached out to steady her as she dropped the shopping basket, groceries tumbling across the sidewalk. Looking up, she met Robert Kilpatrick's concerned gaze.

"I'm so sorry! How silly of me! I wasn't watching where I was going," Connie smiled awkwardly.

"Are you alright? I'm afraid we collided rather hard. You're just a bit of a thing. I'm surprised I didn't knock the wind out of you."

"Oh, no, I'm fine." Connie, suddenly aware he still held her arms, gently withdrew and stepped back. "But I can't say the same for the groceries. They're everywhere." Stooping, she began putting them back in the basket.

Robert knelt beside her. "Here, I'll help with that." As they reached for the same package, their fingers touched. Connie looked up into blue eyes still filled with concern. Glancing down quickly, she grabbed another package.

They remained silent until the basket was refilled and they stood facing each other.

"I haven't seen you at church lately," began Robert. "We've missed you."

"I didn't think anyone had noticed whether I was there or not," Connie replied shyly. "Mother asked me to attend St. Cuthbert's with her, but I must say I rather enjoy the services at Rock of Ages Church. The people sing from their hearts, and I've learned a lot from your sermons."

Robert's smile widened. "I'm glad. It means a lot to know they're being heard. A pastor sometimes wonders. I hope you'll come again soon."

Connie decided then and there. "Yes, I will. This Sunday."

"I'll look forward to seeing you then." Tipping his hat, he entered the shop.

Connie walked toward the bakery, thinking how nice Pastor Kilpatrick was. His messages were interesting and enlightening, like she'd never heard before. Her parents attended St. Cuthbert's when their schedules allowed. Their minister spoke to soothe the consciences of his congregation, words to encourage giving from the well-to-do congregation who came out of duty, and to appease God for their lack of commitment to Him throughout the week. But since visiting Rock of Ages and seeing the sincerity and love on the faces of that congregation, Connie realized they were committed to something, and she wanted to know what it was. She'd ask Pastor Kilpatrick the next chance she had.

~

While glancing over the shelves in Sam Phillip's shop, Robert's thoughts were on Connie Cameron. After meeting her several weeks ago at Hope Orphanage for Sunday dinner, she'd attended services a few times. She listened attentively to his sermons, but when she hadn't returned, he'd begun praying for her. Perhaps God intended for them to run into each other. Literally, he smiled to himself.

Chapter Nine

All day Jess wondered how to tell Grandmother about Ian's invitation. Not once had she asked about the phone call, but then, they *had* been busy. Putting away the last of the supper dishes, she hung the dishtowel up to dry. Looking through the kitchen window, she spotted Jason and Geoffrey pitching hay in the barn under Charlie's supervision. Donning an old heavy coat from the rack by the door and wrapping a wool scarf around her head, Jess walked out to the barn.

"Hello," Charlie greeted. "Come in out o' the cold. That winds pickin' up a bit."

"Yes, it is." Jess shut the big wooden door behind her. "Poor Daisy and Belle. I don't envy them. Living in a drafty old barn isn't my idea of a pleasant life."

"The likes of them don' know no better. Their hides are tough," smiled Charlie.

"I suppose you're right." She looked at the boys as they finished feeding the cows. "You two have been a big help since Charlie's injury. It means a lot to Grandmother, you know."

Jason leaned on his pitchfork, scuffing a toe in the dirt. "I suppose, but Geoffrey and me agree that Grandmother's done a lot for us. We'll do whatever we can for her. Right, Geoffrey?"

The younger boy nodded eagerly. "Yeah! She always takes real good care of us."

"I know." Jess ruffled his hair. "She takes good care of all of us. Why don't you head inside if you're finished? The others are playing games in the living room."

As they stowed their pitchforks and left, Charlie sat down on a bale of hay. "You look like somethin's botherin' ya, lass. Why not tell ol' Charlie here what's wrong?"

Cramming her hands into her coat pockets, Jess sat on another bale. "I must talk to Grandmother about something, and I'm not exactly sure how to begin."

"Is it somethin' you think she won' like to hear?"

Jess smiled at Charlie's perception. "That may just be it, Charlie."

"Well, when something needs doing, just do it. Get it behind you. No finer lady ever lived than your Grandmum. She mightn't like what you've got to say, but she'll try to understand, and she won' judge you none, either. Give her a chance."

"Thanks, Charlie. I will." Standing, she tightened her scarf. "And now's as good a time as any."

"You'll see, lass. It'll work out." He reached for the lantern by the door.

"Good night, Charlie."

"Night, lass."

Jess glanced at the night sky as she walked to the house. Not a star in sight, and the moon was a mere pale glow behind the clouds. The wind had grown stronger, pushing her as she opened the door and stepped inside.

After the children were in bed, Grandmother and Jess enjoyed tea by the fire while listening to news on the radio.

"Yorkshire police continue their investigation into the murders of five people," informed the newscaster. "Each has been identified as a loner or a vagrant, with no family claiming them. All were murdered in the same manner, connecting all to the same perpetrator. Experts believe the murders may be connected to a cult group that's formed in the area. Officials won't release further information. In a moment, the weather." A commercial jingle for tooth powder began as Grandmother turned the volume down.

"I can't believe this is happening in our Dales." She shook her head sadly. "England's history is full of tales of mystery, murder and intrigue, and yet it's hard to believe it's happening so close to home."

"The sad part is that none of the victims had anyone who cared. No one to mourn them or miss them."

"Ah, but our Heavenly Father knew them and cared. Hopefully they knew Him. I pray they find the culprits soon. I'm fearful for the children's safety. Everyone knows they're orphans."

"But everyone also knows they have family and are dearly loved. They'd be missed."

"I know, and all we can do is trust them to the Father's care. They're His children, and when I can't watch them constantly, He can." She turned the volume up as the newscaster returned.

"Forecasters predict a winter storm over most of England, Scotland and Wales. Across the northern part of the country, temperatures will plummet as winds gust to 65 mph. Snow is expected in the higher elevations with freezing rain and sleet in the lower. It's expected tomorrow night and all day Sunday. This broadcast is sponsored by...." Click.

Grandmother turned the radio off. "The news certainly left much to be desired tonight. I should be used to this weather, but I don't think one ever adjusts to it. Winter in the Dales can be treacherous, but each year I hope and pray for a mild one."

Jess wasn't listening to the forecast. She wanted to talk with Grandmother but how to begin? Setting her cup on the table, she decided to just start.

"Grandmother, about my phone call today...."

"Yes, luv?" Grandmother sipped her tea.

"Ian Cameron invited me to dinner and a play tomorrow night."

"Did you accept?" Grandmother feigned interest in her tea.

Standing, Jess walked to the fireplace, picked up the poker, and stirred the glowing embers. "Yes, I did. Mother, Father and I occasionally attended plays and always enjoyed them. It's been years since I've been to a one, and this is a great opportunity. It'll be fun!"

Grandmother gazed tenderly at Jess. Once again she was tiptoeing through a discussion with her. "Jess, you hardly know this young man. Consider his lifestyle and upbringing. He moves in a different social circle and has a reputation of being, for want of a better word, a philanderer."

Jess slowly turned from the fire. "He was a gentleman at the dinner party, and as for knowing him, I hardly knew Garth when I went out with him. Anyway, going to dinner and a play doesn't commit me to him. How can I get to know him if I don't spend time with him?" She knew she sounded peevish.

Grandmother heard the irritation in Jess's voice and decided to let it go. She'd leave it in the Father's hands and pray Jess would make the right decision.

"I hope you have a wonderful time, luv." She held out her arms toward Jess. "But, please, promise you'll pray about it and trust God's guidance."

Kneeling beside her chair, Jess gave her a hug. "I promise."

As will I, Grandmother thought emphatically.

~

The restaurant was near the theater in downtown Harrogate. Looking around, Jess compared it to the one Garth had taken her to. This was an exclusive restaurant for an exclusive clientele. Darker and smaller, oil lamps on the tables and sconces on the walls were the only lighting. Jess wore the same blue silk dress, only this time she was underdressed. A piano played quietly in the background as couples, dressed in expensive eveningwear, danced in the middle of the room. Jess met Ian's thoughtful gaze watching her.

"What's wrong? Did my face turn green?"

"What do you mean?" He flashed a lopsided grin.

"Well, you were staring right through me."

Leaning forward, Ian took her hand. "I was thinking how truly beautiful you are," he crooned.

Jess recognized his compliment as simple flattery. Retrieving her hand, she smiled. "I bet you say that to every girl you meet."

Ian crossed his fingers over his heart. "Cross my heart, I don't. Only to the ones who truly are, and you are, my sweet."

Uncomfortable under his gaze, Jess changed the subject. "Ian, tell me about the play."

Holding up his hands defensively, he leaned back in his chair. "Alright. I know when I've been thwarted. We'll talk about the play. It's a mystery, full of intrigue and suspense. Of course, you should know I chose such a play so when you become weak-kneed and afraid, I'll hold you close and comfort your fears."

"You should be on stage," laughed Jess. "I hope you won't be disappointed. I love mysteries, and I'm not the swooning type."

"A man can always hope." Ian sighed dramatically.

As they ate, Jess overheard the conversation at the next table, realizing the patrons were discussing the recent murders.

"It's simply horrid how they continue bringing up these murders in the news," said one older lady in a haughty voice. "That's all one hears about these days. It's terribly frightening."

"Yes, my dear, it is," replied her companion. "Now they're talking about cults and druids and such. It's simply preposterous. No one would think of following such ancient practices these days. The police are looking in the wrong place. It's some lunatic with a sad childhood, if you ask me."

"I'm sure you're right, Agatha, dear, but I do hope the police find the culprit soon. I can't rest at night for fear of being murdered in my sleep." The lady snapped open her fan, waving it frantically.

"There, there, dear," replied Agatha soothingly. "You needn't worry. You've lots of family and friends. The victims are only vagrants and orphans, and no one really cares about them anyway."

Jess's anger grew at the conversation she couldn't help overhearing. She was on the verge of speaking to them when Ian put his hand on her arm.

"Forget them, Jess. They're not worth your time."

"Just like those poor souls who were murdered? They weren't worth anyone's time either." She spoke in a low voice. "But there is One who cares, Ian, and He's grieved when people like . . like . . . that," she nodded toward the next table, "don't care."

"Hey, settle down, firebrand. They're just a couple of old fussbudgets."

Jess shook her head slowly. "I'm sorry, Ian. I didn't mean to spoil dinner by jumping on my soapbox. I just get upset when I hear such selfish and uncaring remarks. But for the grace of God, we'd all be in the same place as those poor souls who were killed."

Jess saw a fleeting cold expression cross Ian's face then it was gone, leaving her wondering if she'd actually seen it. "We wouldn't be in the same place as they are, Jess. We each make our own way in the world. If we work hard and make good, we succeed. If not, we fail and are nothing. God doesn't care about us. Remember the saying, 'God's in His heaven and all's right with the world'?"

"But Ian, all's not right with the world. It's full of sin. That's not the way God wanted it. Man made it that way. Man chose to sin. Each of us would've had to pay a penalty for our sin, but Jesus, God's son, paid that penalty for us. All we have to do is trust Him. He already did all the work."

A frown formed on Ian's handsome face. "I don't care to continue this discussion. If you're finished let's head to the theater and find our seats."

Putting her fork down, Jess reached for her purse. As he held her coat for her, she prayed for him. He was spiritually blind to Christ's love and His gift of forgiveness and salvation.

As they strolled toward the theatre, Ian talked about the play, speaking as if the tension over dinner had never happened.

Their seats were in the dress circle. Jess had never sat this close to a stage before and was thrilled how skillfully the actors and actresses drew the audience into the mystery. Not until intermission did she realize how engrossed she was.

In the lobby, Ian asked, "Well? Feel like swooning anytime soon?"

Jess laughed. "Not a chance. I don't want to miss a single minute of it."

"Have you ever been to a play before?" Ian ordered two cups of coffee from the refreshment bar.

"My parents took me when I was young. Father loved Shakespeare, but Mother and I preferred comedies and mysteries."

"How about a good romance?" Ian wiggled his eyebrows as he handed her the coffee.

Jess ignored his grin. "Occasionally, but not often."

Ian suddenly spotted someone he knew on the other side of the room and seemed displeased at the discovery. "Excuse me a moment. I must speak with someone. If the gong sounds before I return, go on in. I'll return shortly." Without waiting for her response, he left.

Jess noticed the man who'd captured Ian's attention wasn't dressed for the theater. Maybe there was an emergency, and he'd come to tell Ian. As she watched however, she saw Ian speaking angrily to the man who merely shrugged his shoulders, nodding. Jess quickly looked away as both men looked in her direction. The gong sounded the end of intermission, and without looking their way, Jess hurried to her seat.

Shortly after the play resumed, Ian slipped into his seat. Leaning toward him Jess whispered, "Is anything wrong?"

"Everything's fine. Just some business." He seemed distracted, but Jess was soon engrossed in the play and forgot the incident.

On the way home, Jess attempted conversation but realized Ian still seemed distracted. Settling into her seat she stared out the window. Snow started falling while they were in the theatre, and the closer to home they got, the heavier it fell. Remembering the forecast, Jess hoped for little accumulation.

Pulling up to the orphanage, Ian came around, helping Jess

out.

"Will you come in and meet Grandmother, Ian?"

"Not this time, my sweet," the regret in his voice exaggerated. "Perhaps another time. I hope you enjoyed yourself."

"I had a very nice time. Thank you."

Reaching for Jess's hand he removed her glove, touching his lips tenderly to her fingers. "Goodnight, my sweet."

Jess watched him drive quickly away.

Gazing at the dark sky, Jess felt snowflakes falling gently against her face. What an unusual evening. Sometimes Ian was cheerful and lighthearted while other times he seemed distracted and brooding. Puzzled, she shook her head as she went inside. Ian's behavior certainly was odd.

Chapter Ten

*J*ess expected to find Grandmother waiting in the living room, but she wasn't. The fire had burned low and only one lamp was lit. Maybe she'd gone to bed.

At the foot of the stairs, she heard faint voices coming from the kitchen. Who was Grandmother talking to this hour? Following the voices, she opened the kitchen door, surprised to find Grandmother and Garth at the table drinking coffee and munching cookies. Grandmother saw Jess first.

"Jess, luv, we didn't hear you come in." She patted the chair beside her. "Come have some coffee with us."

Garth started to rise from his chair.

"No, don't get up." Jess waved for him to remain seated. "I'll get a cup and join you."

As Jess sat beside Grandmother and across from Garth, he seemed subdued. She looked up, right into his deep gray eyes and immediately dropped her gaze.

"How was the play?" Grandmother asked cheerily.

"Wonderful! The actors and actresses drew you right into the plot. And the suspense was thrilling."

"I'm glad you enjoyed yourself," Garth said quietly. "They

have some very good performances at the Harrogate Theatre. I haven't been recently, but I've always enjoyed their productions."

"Oh my," said Grandmother. "The last time I attended a play was many years ago."

They listened to the wind howling around the house and the old clock ticking on the shelf by the door.

"Is it still snowing, luv?"

"Yes and the temperature's dropping." Jess asked Garth teasingly, "How is it you can actually sit and relax, doctor? I thought on such a cold night you'd be in demand."

Garth's eyes lit at her teasing. "It was one of those days, believe me. Dad and I were both in demand. I stopped by to check on things, and your grandmother's invitation was too good to pass up."

The phone rang in the living room. Jess started to rise, but Grandmother gently stopped her. "Enjoy your coffee, Luv. I'll answer it."

Silence followed her departure as Jess sipped her coffee and nibbled a cookie. Garth wasn't very talkative; only refilled his cup and remained silent. After several uncomfortable moments, Jess asked. "So, what's the local news? Anything exciting happened lately?"

Garth set his cup down. "Well, I delivered twins to Mrs. Frymont over in Bewerly this morning. A boy and a girl with red hair like Mr. Frymont."

"Twins!" Jess exclaimed. "With six children already, where will they put them?"

Garth chuckled. "Coat pegs in the hall are an option. Their house is small, you know."

"I'm sure they have lots of love to make up for the lack of room. Anything else?"

"Well, let's see," Garth thought. "Friday I helped George Higgins deliver a litter of piglets. That was an experience!"

Jess laughed. "I'm sure. Have you delivered animals before?"

"Well, I'm not a vet and don't pretend to be, but I've delivered the odd calf or sheep. These were my first piglets." He grinned at the memory. "Human babies are by far better."

"And how many have you delivered?"

"I've lost count, but I'd say a good hundred or so."

"Really? But you haven't been in practice very long."

"If I can't say anything else about Dale folk, they do enjoy large families," he grinned.

"I understand why. They'd always be surrounded by love, fun and laughter, no matter how hard times get. Maybe that's why I've enjoyed being here so much. The children are fun, and they keep you on your toes. You never know what to expect from them."

Garth looked into Jess's eyes. "And don't you want those things for yourself?"

"Children, you mean?" She sipped her coffee. "As I've said before, someday, in God's time."

Garth leaned forward, arms resting on the table. "You really believe He controls everything, don't you? Just as your Grandmother does."

"Yes, I do. My mother taught me from the time I was very young that God cares about the details in our lives and guides us. When I was small my father lost his job when his employer went bankrupt. It took time to find another job, and until he did, finances were tight. Mother stretched pennies thinner than paper, Father used to say. My parents never told anyone but God about our situation. Mother took in sewing, but it didn't help much. Down to our last can of beans, Mother prepared them. We said grace, and as we began to eat, someone knocked on our door."

Garth watched tenderly as Jess wiped moisture from her eyes. He imagined the precious little girl and what she must've experienced. Reaching over, he gently covered her hand with his own.

"I clearly remember the delivery wagon driver at the door. A carriage had pulled in front of him. Trying to avoid hitting it, he ran into a ditch and overturned his wagon, his load of food spilling everywhere. It was impossible to sell in stores, so he asked if we could use some of it. He even helped carry it into the house. There were tinned goods and some jars that hadn't broken. Fresh fruit and vegetables that would spoil if they weren't used soon. Even some dry goods. Some neighbors took food home, too. After he left, we bowed down, right there in the kitchen in the middle of all that food and thanked God for what He'd done. Mother and I canned most of the fresh foods. Soon after, Father got another job." Jess added with deep conviction, "No one in this world can convince me that God doesn't take a personal interest in our lives."

Garth saw how deeply she believed what she was saying, and for the first time in his life, he wanted that same peace and assurance.

"I wish I could be as certain of Him as you are. You've a peace about you that most people I know don't have."

"But you can," Jess replied eagerly. "Just trust in Him. He's holding out His gift of salvation to you. Just reach out and accept it. As for my peace, it comes from Him. Sometimes the situations and problems I find myself in are my own doing. When I'm not at peace, it's not because He's taken it away, but because I've turned from Him. His peace is always there."

Garth nodded slowly. "I'll think about it. You'll be in church tomorrow?"

"Yes," Jess smiled, "if the weather holds." She suddenly noticed Grandmother leaning on the kitchen doorframe.

"Grandmother! How long have you been there? Why didn't you come in?"

Approaching, Grandmother gently lifted Jess's chin. "Long enough to hear what my daughter never told me. But I'm happy that she and her family had faith in the One who cares."

"Mother never told you?"

"No, I never knew your father was out of work or that you all nearly went hungry." Tears filled her eyes. "If only I'd known . . . "

Standing, Jess hugged her. "If you'd known, you would've helped us, and maybe prevented God from getting the glory and me from learning a valuable lesson that will stay with me as long as I live."

Grandmother patted her cheek. "You're probably right, luv. So we'll just thank God for His blessings." She started suddenly, "Oh! I nearly forgot. Garth, that phone call was your father. He needs you at the clinic. Something about someone going to the hospital. I'm so sorry! I was caught up in Jess's story."

Standing, Garth placed his arm around Grandmother's shoulders and looked straight into Jess's eyes. "Not to worry. I wouldn't have missed it for the world. It's given me food for thought. Jess, would you walk me to the door?"

At the front door, Jess waited as Garth donned his coat and scarf.

"I've Thursday afternoon off. Want to go for a drive? I'd like to show you something."

"I'd love to".

"Thank you," said Garth after a pause.

"For what?"

"For sharing a very special time in your life." Leaning over, he kissed her cheek then hurried out the door before he planted one soundly on her lips.

~

Glancing out her bedroom window, Connie saw a fine layer of snow blanketing the ground; the heavy, gray sky promising more. Heading down to the breakfast room, she hoped that Mother wasn't yet awake. She wanted to eat quickly and leave before Mother stirred, but upon entering the breakfast room, she found Mother sitting at the carefully appointed table, determination on her face. Connie had avoided a confrontation with her for weeks, but knew it was inevitable.

"Good morning, Mother." She cheerily dropped a kiss on Mother's cheek. "Have you seen the snow this morning? The first of the season." Sitting down, she reached for the silver coffeepot, filling her china cup and spooning in sugar. Glancing at Mother's expression, she groaned inwardly.

"Constance, dear," Valerie Cameron began firmly, "we must talk. I've been meaning to speak to you about something important, but with my schedule lately, there's been no opportunity. However, we shall settle this once and for all."

"Settle what, Mother?" Connie knew exactly what she referred to.

"Constance, I won't sit by any longer while you waste your time at that orphanage. They're common people who are accustomed to hard work and difficulties. You, however, were born for a refined and sophisticated life. I cannot allow you to return there and continue to waste your life. How can you do this to your father and me? Don't you realize how embarrassing it is for us?" She dabbed her eyes with a delicate hanky.

Mr. Cameron came in and sat at the head of the table. "Good morning, my dears. Who's embarrassed about what?" He began filling his plate.

"Cyril, darling," Valerie pleaded, "please speak to Constance about this silly volunteer work she's doing. She's wasting her life, not to mention ruining her hands with all that manual labor." She shuddered distastefully.

Constance laid down her fork. "I'm not wasting my life at Hope Orphanage. For the first time I'm actually doing something worthwhile. Those precious children have no families of their own. They've been through terrible things no human, much less a child, should endure. Mrs. McDonald dedicates her life to making a home for them. I enjoy working there. And yes, I even enjoy getting my hands dirty." Pausing for effect, she was rewarded with a gasp. "And I'll continue to help as long as they need me."

"Cyril," Valerie implored, "please talk sense into your daughter." She looked at Constance. "It's that American girl you brought to the dinner party, isn't it? She's corrupted you. I forbid you to set foot in that place ever again. And I forbid you to see her again."

"Now, Valerie dearest, that's a bit harsh." Cyril replied. "Constance is helping where help is needed. Surely things will improve, and she can move on to bigger and better things. Let's not over-react," he soothed.

Valerie tried a new tactic. "Constance, you know Reginald

wants to marry you. He won't wait forever, and when he finds another girl who will marry him, you'll regret it for the rest of your life. You'll never find another young man with the prestige and promise that young Reginald has."

"Mother, Reginald is the biggest bore that ever lived. I'd rather be a spinster for life than to spend five minutes with him. He thinks only of himself and could care less what I think."

"That's not true. He often calls for you, and you're never around to see what a fine young man he is."

Connie dropped her napkin beside her plate, pushed her chair back and stood. "Mother, I love you very much, and I won't argue with you over Reginald or Hope Orphanage. I'm not a little girl anymore. I'm a grown woman with hopes and dreams of my own. Please leave me to get on with my life as I see fit." With head high, Connie left to gather her coat.

Valerie buried her face in her hands and sobbed. Cyril came to her, patting her shoulder gently. "She's right, dear. You must let her go. She has her own way to make in the world. Neither you nor I have the right to plan her life for her. The greatest gift we can give her is to stand aside and let her go."

"But Cyril," Valerie raised red-rimmed eyes, "she's too good for that. There are better things for her than she's willing to give herself."

"We can't make that decision. We can only hope she does the right thing."

~

When Connie arrived that morning, Jess immediately saw she was upset, but waited until the children left for school to approach her. Jess found her in the upstairs bathroom scrubbing the big porcelain, claw-foot tub.

"If you scrub any harder, we'll have to refinish it," Jess teased. "Either it's very dirty or something on your mind. Want to share?"

Connie recounted the conversation with her mother. "She'll never understand."

"You're probably right, but she loves you and only wants the best for you. What mother wouldn't want her daughter to marry a rich young man? She'd be set for life."

"Would she? Then I don't want to be set for life." She looked at Jess, her heart in her eyes. "I just want to live a simple, meaningful life. I know girls who live solely for fun and pleasure, floating from one social event to another, never accomplishing anything with their lives. I won't spend the rest of my life like that."

Jess thought momentarily then smiled. "I know someone who might be able to help you."

Connie asked warily, "Who?"

"Robert Kilpatrick."

Connie's cheeks flamed. "Robert Kilpatrick? How can he help?"

Jess chuckled. Connie's reddened cheeks confirmed her suspicion that she was interested in the young pastor. "Well, he's throughout the community a lot. Suppose you broaden your horizons and help out more than just here."

"But I enjoy working here."

"You still can, but when you're not needed you could help out elsewhere. Why not ask him? See what he says."

"If my mother found out I was not only helping here, but all over the Dales, she'd disown me." She paused thoughtfully. "But I'll risk it and pay him a visit first chance I get."

The front door bell rang sending Jess to the bathroom window. She smiled. "I think your first chance is here. Come on." Connie hesitated before following Jess downstairs. Grandmother was inviting the young minister into the living room.

"Pastor Kilpatrick, please come in. Jess, Connie . . . see who's here."

"Thank you, Mrs. McDonald." Removing his hat, he turned as the young women came in. "Good morning, Miss Cameron. I hope you're well."

"Yes, thank you."

"And you, Miss Montgomery," he added hastily.

"Good morning, Pastor Kilpatrick. Please sit down." For once

Jess didn't mind being an afterthought.

"I can't stay long, but I've been out visiting and thought I'd drop by to see how everyone's doing."

"For the moment all is fine," replied Grandmother. "All the children are in school again, and no one's ill."

"I'm pleased to hear that."

"Grandmother," said Jess, "would you help me in the kitchen please?"

Grandmother looked quizzical as Jess nodded imperceptibly toward the kitchen. "Certainly. Excuse us."

As she left the room, Jess winked at Connie. She almost laughed at Connie's expression.

In the kitchen Grandmother asked, "What was that all about?"

Jess explained Connie's interest in becoming involved in the community. "She planned to call on Pastor Kilpatrick the first chance she got. Neither of us expected it would come so soon. I thought it would be easier to ask him without us around."

"It's wonderful she's so eager to help others. She's certainly been a God-send here. Hopefully she won't leave us altogether."

"She won't." Jess filled the teapot with hot water from the stove. "She's family now."

~

"Do you enjoy working here?" Robert asked the young woman sitting across from him. "Mrs. McDonald has mentioned how valuable you are. She appreciates your volunteered time."

"I love it here. I'm actually doing something worthwhile for the first time in my life. I never knew that dusting, sweeping, and cleaning could hold such purpose." She laughed lightly, never realizing its effect on the young man's heartbeat. "Which brings me to something I wanted to ask you."

"Yes?" He noticed her hesitation. "How can I help?"

"Well, I'd like to become involved in the community somehow, but I've no idea how. Perhaps you could suggest something?"

A slow smile crossed Robert's face. "Actually I've been

brainstorming over an idea recently. Perhaps you'd be interested. Many of the Dale families are hard-hit by this war, and this Christmas will be difficult for them. I've been searching for a way to involve the whole community to help them. Do you have any ideas?"

Connie thought momentarily. "Perhaps we could organize a Christmas fund raiser. If someone would donate the use of a building and folk could donate food and the things we need, we could have a fair. The proceeds would purchase gifts for the needy families."

"That's a wonderful idea!" Pulling a notepad from his coat pocket, Robert jotted down ideas as they brainstormed. When Jess and Grandmother returned with refreshments, they found them deep in discussion.

"Whatever you two are discussing sounds big to me." Jess teased as she set the tray beside Grandmother's chair.

"Jess, Robert has proposed the most wonderful idea: a Christmas fund-raiser to help the needy in the Dales. The proceeds will purchase gifts for them."

Robert raised his hand. "Now just a moment. I can't take the credit. This young lady is full of ideas. All she needs is an outlet for them, and I can help with that." He looked at Connie appreciatively.

"What a lovely idea!" Grandmother exclaimed. "We can help, too."

"Absolutely." Connie, seeing Jess's knowing smile, felt her cheeks burn. She'd explain to Jess that this was nothing but a simple desire to help the community. Then why did her heart race as she met the young pastor's gaze?

Chapter Eleven

As she entered the kitchen to start supper, Jess noticed the snow falling quite heavily out the window. She was glad Charlie would return with the children soon and that Connie had left early.

Grandmother brought Michael into the kitchen. "This young man just woke from his nap. He's changed and ready for a bottle. Do you want to feed him while I make the biscuits?"

"Certainly." Jess reached into the icebox for a bottle of milk, and placed it in a pan of water on the hot stove.

"Come here, little man." Reaching for the infant, she was again amazed at this little life. He curled his tiny fingers around one of hers, gripping tightly. Kissing him on the head, she tucked his blanket closer around him.

"It's getting colder." She shivered slightly.

"The wind's up, and the snow's falling heavier. I'll have Charlie bring in more wood and stoke the fires when he returns."

Just then Charlie entered the back door followed by the younger children. The older ones headed to the barn for their afternoon chores.

"Charlie!" Grandmother exclaimed in relief. "I'm glad you're back safely.

"Yes, Ma'am, but it's turnin' bad out there. And quickly, too."

"The house has become chilly. Would you please bring in more wood and stoke the fires?"

"For certain. The temperature's droppin'. Felt bad about the young'un's havin' ta sit in the back o' the truck, but naught could be done about it."

"They'll warm up shortly, Charlie," Jess replied.

Tightening his scarf, he plunked his hat back on as he headed out the door. A chilly wind surged in before the door closed behind him.

"I'll check the radio for weather news." Grabbing Michael's bottle Jess tested the temperature before heading to the living room.

As she listened to the forecast, her heart sank. A huge winter storm was moving across Northern England and Scotland with high winds and temperatures dropping well below freezing. Holding Michael, Jess walked to the front window to watch the rapidly accumulating snow just as a car's headlights swept the front yard.

Jess opened the front door as the driver ran up the front steps.

Robert Kilpatrick removed his hat, shaking off snow as Jess closed the door.

"Mr. Kilpatrick!" Jess noted his grim expression, disheveled hair and dark streaks of grease and dirt marring his face. "What's happened?"

"An accident at the flax mill. The freezing temperatures caused the water wheel to seize up. Some men were working on it when a rod splintered, injuring three of them. One's caught in the machinery, and they're trying to free him. I've come to see if you've extra blankets and sheets we can use for bandages."

Grandmother entered as Robert spoke. "Certainly! We'll round up those things and more." Turning to Jess, she reached for Michael. "Jess, the blankets and sheets are in the upstairs storage room. I'll get coffee going."

"I'll go with Mr. Kilpatrick. Send Charlie with the coffee and some sandwiches. Claire, Paula and Jason can help make them."

As she hurried upstairs Robert called after her. "Miss Montgomery, are you sure you should brave this storm? We could be there for hours."

"I know, but maybe I can help. Will you come help with the blankets?"

Ten minutes later they drove down the lane. Jess had changed into warmer clothes, topping them with a wool coat, a felt hat, a scarf, warm gloves and an old pair of Grandmother's boots. The blankets and sheets sat on the back seat. As Robert drove, he noticed the road had become slippery. Despite their rush, he drove only as fast as he dared. To Jess, it seemed they were crawling. The three miles to the mill felt like thirty. Straining to see as the windshield wipers swiped frantically at the heavy snow, they were relieved when the mill finally came into view. Jess hadn't realized she'd been holding her breath.

Carrying the supplies through the blinding snow, they hurried into the large factory. Jess followed Robert up wooden stairs to the machine room. Outside, the water wheel reached the highest point of the roof. The machinery at the center of the wheel operated the gadgets that ran the mill. Entering the large room, they passed large equipment and stacked crates. Robert stopped and turned to her, blocking her view.

"You should stop here. It's not a pleasant sight."

"I didn't come just to bring blankets. I came to help." Hearing moans of pain and agony, Jess stepped around Robert to see Garth Samuels treating an injured man. She stifled a gasp as she saw the man's mangled leg. Swallowing the bile filling her throat, she approached the crates where Garth worked. Two other men lay on crates nearby. Robert and Jess covered them with blankets, making them more comfortable as another worker clumsily applied a dirty rag to an open gash on his head.

Tearing a sheet into strips, Jess bandaged the man's head. Placing a folded blanket beneath his head she washed blood from his face from a nearby bucket as she quietly reassured him. Several men worked on the machinery, trying to break it free.

Soon Charlie appeared beside her with a large thermos of coffee, another of hot water and a food hamper.

"What should I do with these, Miss Jess?"

"I'm glad you're here. Set it on that empty crate. Are there cups?"

"But, of course. Your Grandmum wouldn't forget 'em. They're in the hamper."

"Please pour coffee for the men. They need the warmth to prevent shock." She tucked the blanket around the man before pouring a cup of coffee for Garth. He glanced up as she approached then back to the man's leg.

"What are you doing here?" he asked gruffly.

"Robert came for blankets and sheets for bandages. I thought I could help somehow."

"Didn't the good minister tell you it might be dangerous?" he asked angrily without looking up. "Not to mention very cold. You could catch your death in here."

Jess felt both hurt and anger. "As could you." She sat the cup beside his instruments and walked away. Hearing a yell, she watched in horror as one of the machinists was pulled into the gears. The equipment groaned to a halt pinning the man's arm. The others worked frantically to release him. Helpless, Jess prayed.

Garth pushed her aside as he ran to help. Turning to the man whose leg Garth was working on, Jess tucked a blanket around him, watching the men's struggle to free the machinist. The mechanism finally reversed and they pulled him out, his arm crushed. Garth worked to stop the hemorrhage of blood in an effort to save his life.

Robert hung up the telephone at a desk in the corner of the room and turned to Garth. "I called for an ambulance, but the weather's too bad for them to come out."

"Then we'll just have to drive them ourselves. We both have cars, and although these tourniquets will do for now, we must leave immediately." For the second time that evening, he looked at Jess. "You ride with me and sit in the back, keeping Howard's leg elevated. Frank can sit up front. Robert, you and Charlie take John and Patrick. Visibility is probably bad, so we'll stay together." Turning he addressed the machinist working on the mechanism. "Walt! Can you free it? We have to get these men to hospital."

"No worries," waved the man named Walt. "Whatever happened when John got caught has broken it loose. We'll keep workin' to ensure it stays runnin'."

"Then we'll pack up and head out." After settling everyone into the cars with blankets tucked around them, Garth led the way with Robert following.

The heavily falling snow made driving difficult. All Jess could see was a glare from the snow in the headlights; she couldn't see the road at all. With Howard's head in her lap, she closed her eyes in prayer.

She'd never known such an agonizing ride. Inches of snow covered the road while Garth strained to see ahead. Not only were his own passengers' at risk, but with only his taillights to guide them, those in the car behind depended on him staying on the road as well.

Silently Garth concentrated on driving. Jess watched out her window, trying to determine where they were. Occasionally a faint glow from a house could be seen. In Pateley Bridge, they had difficulty climbing the hill on High Street. As the quickest way to Harrogate, there was no choice but to take it. Robert waited at the bottom while Garth slowly ascended, slipping as he went. He dared not stop until he reached level ground for fear he'd slide back down. At the top, he stopped and inhaled deeply. His shoulders and neck ached from the strain while his fingers hurt from gripping the steering wheel. He turned to Jess.

"Are you alright?" He barely saw her nod in the faint glow from the streetlights.

"I'm fine. Are you?"

"I'll be fine when we get there," Garth said, a smile in his voice. He checked his patients. "Stay here. I'll check on Robert's progress."

Pulling his coat collar higher and his hat lower, he got out to watch as Robert steered his vehicle slowly up the hill until he stopped by Garth's car.

Robert rolled down his window. "Everyone alright?"

"So far, so good. Just wanted to check on everyone before we leave Pateley. This hill's the worst part of the journey, but we've still a long way to go. Let's move on."

They drove slowly through the Dales, passing homes and farms closed up against the raging storm. The snow never let up, and the wind constantly battered them. Occasionally slipping, they never met another car until they reached Harrogate. It seemed like hours before they parked in front of the hospital on the far side of town. As Garth stopped the engine Jess sighed deeply, laying her head against the seat. *Thank you, Lord!*

~

Garth hurried inside, returning with several nurses and orderlies pushing gurneys. His patients were taken into the casualty ward as Garth explained the situation to the hospital doctors.

As Jess, Robert and Charlie sat in the waiting room Jess was amazed that it was after twelve-thirty. She'd left with Robert at five forty-five. Suddenly feeling very tired, she rested her head against the wall and closed her eyes, her body beginning to relax.

"Jess," someone touched her arm gently. Having dozed off, Jess opened her eyes and found a pair of smiling gray ones. Garth knelt by her chair holding a steaming cup.

"I hope tea will do." He grinned. "I tried for your coffee, but they didn't have any made."

Jess sat up, pushing her hair from her eyes. "Thank you. Tea is fine." She reached for the hot cup. "I need to call Grandmother. She'll be worried sick."

"I hope you don't mind, but I already called her. I wasn't sure if the phone lines would be intact and if they were, for how long. It's a good thing I did," he added grimly. "I tried to call Dad and the line was dead."

"Will he be worried?"

"He knew where I was going, so I doubt it. He'd have been

there too if he hadn't been on a call."

Charlie spoke up. "You don' think your Grandmother will have any problems without me and you bein' there, do ya? It's just her and the children."

Jess patted his worn hand. "They'll be fine, Charlie. If the power goes out, there's plenty of wood for the fires, and she has the older children to help."

"She's right, Charlie. They'll be fine," agreed Garth. "I spoke to the head nurse about a place for us to stay the night. There are some vacant beds in the private ward. She's having something sent up from the kitchen for us to eat before we turn in."

Jess teased, "I guess it pays to travel with a doctor, huh? First class service all the way."

"We aim to please," Garth replied with a crooked grin, a gleam in his eye.

Jess felt her cheeks warm. She could tell Garth was pleased at the effect his words had on her.

After eating cold ham, cheese and rolls, the nurse led them to two rooms where they'd sleep the remainder of the night. Jess took one while the three men shared the other. After washing her face and hands in the wash room down the hall, Jess came out to find Garth leaning against the wall outside the bathroom door.

"Oh," she exclaimed, startled. "I didn't know any one was waiting. I'm finished; it's all yours."

"Actually I wanted to speak to you, Jess. I know it's late, but I want to apologize for how I spoke to you at the mill. I was surprised to see you and couldn't stop to speak when I was up to my elbows in injured workers, but I realize you only came to help. It was a dangerous, cold and unpleasant place for you to be, but . . . your help was invaluable."

Jess lowered her gaze to her toes. "Thank you. And I'm sorry I responded in anger. I should've realized the strain you were under."

Lifting her chin with a gentle finger, he smiled into her dark eyes. "Thanks for the coffee. Even though I didn't have time to drink it, I noticed you brought it over. You've been a good sport about everything." He studied her face as if he wanted to say more but didn't. "Good night, Jess."

"Good night." Jess closed the door of her room and leaned against it, willing her heart to stop its trip-hammer beat, the result of Garth's gentle touch and the light in his eyes. Without undressing, she removed her shoes and climbed into bed, pulling the blankets up. Within minutes she was sound asleep.

Chapter Twelve

Jess awoke to a knock at her door. Opening her eyes, she looked around, trying to remember where she was.

"Jess," called Garth softly. "Are you awake?"

She sat up, rubbing the sleep from her eyes. "Yes. Just a minute.' Throwing back the covers, she got up and walked to the window, amazed at the view, nothing but white as far as she could see. Huge snowdrifts piled everywhere. She turned to the mirror above the dresser where she'd placed her hat and scarf the night before. Not even a comb to straighten her hair or a toothbrush to clean her teeth. Oh, well. Running her fingers through her disheveled hair, she opened the door where Garth waited. For a moment she wondered if he'd been there all night. He stood right where she'd left him the night before.

Garth caught his breath as Jess opened the door. Obvious she'd just woken, her cheeks were flushed and her hair had been hastily smoothed, but the disorder was endearing. Her eyes were still trying to focus and widened when she saw him. He'd love waking up to this vision every morning.

Jess's flushed cheeks reddened further. She knew she looked a mess, but did he have to stare so openly? "Good morning." She held her head high, hanging onto her dignity.

"Good morning." Garth smiled at her attempt to appear unembarrassed. Pulling his hand from his pocket, he held a small black comb. "I picked up a couple of these from the dispensary. Care for one?"

Jess smiled sheepishly, accepting it. "Thank you, Garth."

She stepped back into the room leaving the door open. Garth dug his hands into his pockets, watching as Jess combed and braided her hair into a single braid down her back. He'd been tempted before to reach out and touch that honey-colored hair, but never as strongly as now.

Turning to Garth, Jess shut the door behind her. "Much better." She smiled. "I don't suppose you have a toothbrush in your pocket as well?"

"Sorry. I'm afraid the comb was all I could find."

"I appreciate that much."

"You must be starved. I know I am." He led her down the hallway. "Robert and Charlie are waiting for us in the canteen. We'll eat breakfast before we head out."

Entering the canteen, they spotted Robert and Charlie standing near the door.

"Thought we'd wait on you before getting our food," said Robert. "Did you sleep well, Miss Montgomery?"

"Yes, I did. A bomb could've exploded in my room, and I wouldn't have heard it."

"Me as well," agreed Charlie as they got in line. Garth and Robert exchanged rueful looks. Jess guessed they hadn't slept much. Perhaps Charlie had snored all night?

After sitting down, Garth picked up his fork to begin eating but noticed the others waiting. He lowered his fork as he saw them bow their heads. He'd forgotten they prayed before eating. Robert prayed aloud, petitioning for their daily needs, particularly for a safe drive home. Bowing his head Garth listened to Robert's words. He realized Robert believed his request would be answered.

They discussed the drive home, planning to take their time

since it was still snowing, though lighter. Hopefully, the roads had been cleared, but closer to home they knew the roads would still be covered. No one had the equipment to clear roads. Most farmers owned horse-drawn sleds to use when it snowed.

"I'd like to check on my patients before we leave." Garth spread marmalade on his toast. "I hate leaving them, but they're in good hands here. Their families need to be told what happened last night."

"I'm sure Walt did what he could to inform them," said Robert. "When we get back, I'll visit the families to reassure them."

Jess, Robert and Charlie waited while Garth checked on his patients. Shortly, Jess saw him at the nurse's desk. As he spoke to the head nurse, a tall policeman approached him, clapping him on the shoulder. Garth turned, smiling broadly and shook his outstretched hand. As they talked Jess saw Garth's smile vanish. Two attendants pushed a gurney, bearing a sheet-covered body, past the desk. The uniformed officer pointed to it, and Garth shook his head sadly. Then Garth brought him over to their little group.

Garth affectionately punched the man's shoulder, smiling. "This chap's an old army buddy of mine. This is Inspector Paul Kendall. Paul, this is Jessica Montgomery, Robert Kilpatrick and Charlie Bernard. They helped bring the injured here last night when we couldn't get an ambulance."

"It's a pleasure to meet you all." Looking at Jess Paul added pleasantly, "You're Morag McDonald's granddaughter from America."

"Yes, I am. How did you know?"

"Oh, word gets around," was the evasive reply. "Well, I must go. I've reports to write up. I hope your stay is pleasant, Miss Montgomery." He nodded to Robert and Charlie. "Nice meeting you. Hope to see you again. Call me, Garth, and we'll get together." With a slight bow he walked away.

"Nice chap," said Charlie. "Does he work here in Harrogate?"

"Yes, but he directs most of the investigations throughout

North Yorkshire. By the way, our men went through the night quietly. They send their gratitude to you all. They couldn't save Howard's leg. Too badly damaged. But he's taking it quite well. The surgeons think they can save John's arm, though, it'll be a few days before they know for sure. The others are doing well and will go home soon, provided they can get home. Which reminds me, we need to get home ourselves."

~

Garth's eyes were glued to the road as Robert again followed him. Visibility was better, but Jess wasn't sure if she'd disturb Garth's concentration by talking, so she remained quiet.

"You can talk if you like, you know. My eyes are busy, not my ears."

Had he read her mind? She turned a surprised gaze on him. "How did you know what I was thinking?"

He flashed a smile but remained silent.

"Alright, you want me to talk, I'll talk. I noticed when you spoke to the Inspector how serious you were. Did it have anything to do with the body on the gurney?"

Garth glanced at her then turned his gaze back to the road. "You don't waste time on pleasantries, do you? Yes, it did. It was a body found last night in the snow."

"That's all? Just a body found in the snow? Was it another victim of the serial killer? Do they know who the victim is? Was it a man or a woman?"

Garth glanced at her again with an unreadable expression. "Can't we talk about the weather, or you, or anything else?"

"We know about the weather, and I know about me."

"Ah," Garth hoped to change the subject, "but I don't know as much as I'd like to. Tell me about your home in the States?"

"Garth, please. I'm a big girl. I can handle it."

He sighed heavily. "Alright. It was a woman, and the police think she's another victim. Dressed rather shabbily, there was no identification on her. They think she was killed just before the snow began. A farmer found her and called the police. Because of the way she was killed, the police assume she's another victim of the elusive murderer."

"Could there really be a cult in the area sacrificing homeless people?"

"Paul thinks it's possible. The m.o. is consistent with previous cult murders and with what is known about their historical ceremonies. Paul has studied the druids quite extensively and feels there's possibly a druid cult in the area. Occasionally you'll hear about one surfacing somewhere in the British Isles, but generally they meet and worship their deities and perform ceremonies without human sacrifice."

"Druids? So they're not just the fictitious group found in folk tales and legends?"

"Apparently not. Ritual sites have been found throughout Europe pre-dating Roman times. Archeologists have learned a lot about the ancient druids, but much less is known about the modern ones. They're very elusive, which begs the question, why? What are they trying to hide?"

"Do they perform human sacrifices?"

"Robert says most don't, but apparently there's a group out there that does. I guess the rub is in catching them. They cover their tracks well."

Jess leaned her head against the seat, a headache starting to pound behind her eyes.

Garth glanced to see if she was okay. Perhaps he should've avoided her question. Hopefully he hadn't frightened her, but he wanted her to be extra cautious. The fact that the children were orphans concerned him. He'd speak to Robert about dropping by a little more often to check on them.

They plowed their way through the snow, following some sled tracks and arrived at the orphanage just after lunch.

At the front door, Grandmother hugged Jess, relief in her shaky voice. "I'm so glad you're safe, luv. Thank the dear Lord above! And thank you for taking good care of her, Garth."

"It was my pleasure." His eyes were on Jess. As Grandmother held her at arm's length, Garth saw concern replace the relief.

"Jess, your face is flushed. Are you alright?"

"I'm fine. It's been a long, stressful night. I'm just tired." In truth, Jess wasn't feeling well, but she chalked it up to fatigue and her pounding headache. After greeting the children she turned to Grandmother. "Where's Michael?"

"He's sleeping." Grandmother turned as Charlie and Robert entered. "Charlie, Robert. I'm glad you're home. Won't you all come in to eat? You can warm up and rest a bit."

"Thank you, Mrs. McDonald." Robert flashed a tired smile. "I should get on. I've things to attend to. May I have a rain check?"

"Of course. Anytime." She turned to Garth. "I know it's been stressful for you. How about some lunch?"

"Thanks, but I must push on as well. I have to locate Dad and see what's happened in my absence. I'll take a rain check, too, if I may." Turning to Jess, he smiled tenderly, "You should rest. Doctor's orders. And take your Grandmother up on that tea."

"Absolutely," agreed Charlie eagerly. "I know I'm goin' to."

"Thank you, Doctor," said Jess wearily. "I just might obey those orders."

After Garth and Robert left, Jess removed her coat and turned to hang it on the coat rack but didn't get that far. Her head suddenly pounding horribly, everything spun around her. Putting her hand to her head, she felt herself falling. Then everything went black.

Chapter Thirteen

"*R*obert." Garth closed the door behind them. "Could I make an appointment to talk with you soon?"

"Certainly. With your schedule so uncertain, you tell me when."

"Thursday? I've plans for the day, but we could meet for supper and talk."

"The Kings Arms in Lofthouse has excellent veal cutlets."

"Sounds good."

Suddenly, Charlie ran out the front door. "Garth!" he called excitedly. "It's Miss Jess. She's done gone an' fainted. She's layin' on the floor all still like."

Garth's heart plummeted as he grabbed his bag from the car and followed Charlie back inside. Jess lay unconscious where she'd fallen. Kneeling, he grasped her wrist, finding a week pulse. Touching her forehead, his fingers were seared with a feverish heat.

"She's burning up." He glanced at Morag kneeling beside Jess. "Let's get her into bed and cool her down."

Lifting her into his arms and cradling her against his shoulder, Garth carried Jess upstairs. She hadn't indicated a fever in the car, but now he felt the heat radiating from her body.

Garth laid her gently on her bed, carefully checking her vital signs. Turning, he found Morag, eyes closed in prayer.

"We must act quickly. Her fever's sudden and high and her lungs are filling."

"What can I do?"

"Those heavy clothes are holding in the heat. Dress her in something light while I fetch some cool water. We'll start with a sponge bath."

Opening Jess's chest-of-drawers Grandmother found a cotton nightgown.

With another glance at Jess's still features, Garth went for the water. Robert, who'd followed Garth and Charlie inside, was praying with the children. The sight touched Garth's heart reminding him that Bible scripture said something about the faith of a child. These children prayed in faith believing God would answer their prayers. As they finished, Katie and Billy ran over, grabbing his hands.

"Will our Jess be alright?" Katie asked sadly.

Kneeling, Garth put his arms around them. "I'm doing all I can to see that she is, but you keep praying. I think that'll do more good than anything else." He realized he meant it.

Back upstairs, Garth set the bowl of water on the bedside table and rolled up his sleeves. Grandmother gathered cloths to bath Jess, who'd started coughing hoarsely. Dipping a cloth in the cool water, Garth wrung it out, placing it on Jess's forehead. She recoiled from the coolness, but he held it there until she settled down. Grandmother wiped down her arms and legs.

"Did she say anything before she collapsed?" Garth asked quietly.

"No, but she put her hands to her head before she fell. Perhaps her head was hurting."

"With a fever this high, I'm sure it was." He dipped and wrung out his cloth again. "Why don't you fetch some tea? I'll keep working here."

Garth lifted a finger to Jess's hot face. Tracing a line from her brow to her chin, he thrilled at the softness of her skin. He smoothed back tendrils of hair that had escaped her braid, her hair silky against his fingers. *I'll take care of you, Sweetheart. You've become precious to me!! So very precious!*

~

With the phones out Garth sent word to his father by Charlie, explaining what had happened and that he'd be at the orphanage for a while. Grandmother offered to send for Connie but Garth quickly said he wanted to ensure Jess's fever lowered before he left.

Her cough worsened as her lungs filled, her fever refusing to drop. She called out for her mother as Garth worked over her.

Claire brought him supper and a cold glass of milk. As he ate, Jess started shivering. Pulling the duvet up, he tucked it beneath her chin. When Claire returned to see if he wanted more to eat, he asked for more blankets. After tucking them around Jess, Garth sat back, rubbing his face with his hands. After the accident at the flax mill, the stressful ride to the hospital, little or no sleep last night, and now Jess, he was exhausted. But he couldn't go home.

Grandmother grew concerned. "Garth, go home and rest or you'll be sick, too. I'll sit with Jess through the night."

Garth looked up, dark circles beneath his eyes. "I want to ensure her fever breaks. Hopefully it'll be soon, but if not, perhaps I'll crash on your sofa while you sit with her. Will that do?" He smiled wearily.

Grandmother smiled back, a knowing look in her eyes. "Yes, luv. If that's as close as I can get to you resting, it'll do." She saw Garth's tender gaze on Jess. *So that's how it is. I'll have to pray about this. Jess needs a Christian man in her life, and I'm going to pray she gets one.*

"By the way. Gwen called this morning from Scotland. With the bad weather she can't get home yet so we'll just have to continue to muddle through. Hopefully the weather will allow Connie to make it in tomorrow."

~

When two hours later Jess still coughed heavily and her fever hadn't dropped, Garth kept his word. Grandmother sat with Jess while he rested on the sofa by the fire. He pulled up a blanket, planning to rest a while and then relieve Grandmother so she could go to bed.

Oddly, he was too tired to sleep and lay recalling the events of the past twenty-four hours. He was glad Jess had come to help at the mill. Then he recalled as they'd said goodnight at the hospital. As tired as he'd been, he couldn't sleep. Charlie's snoring was partly responsible, but he couldn't banish Jess from his thoughts. He always enjoyed her company. She was enchanting and maddening all in one. It was hard to watch her this afternoon and evening and never see her smile or even scowl at him. Seeing her lovely features contorted from the coughs that racked her body hurt him deeply. He wanted to take it from her and make her well again. He thought about praying, but doubted God would listen. Why should He when others like Jess, Morag and Robert shared a real relationship with Him?

Sooner than he expected the warmth from the fire and the fatigue both worked their magic, sending him to a dreamless sleep.

~

"Morning, Garth!" Morag set a cup of coffee on the table by the sofa. "I see you slept. Wonderful! Here's coffee for you."

Garth opened his eyes to see the morning sunlight streaming through the window. Sitting up, he ran his fingers through his disheveled hair.

"What time is it?" He tried driving the fog of sleep from his brain.

"Why, nearly a quarter past eight."

Suddenly wide-awake, he remembered why he was here. "Jess! How is she?"

"Her fever broke about four a.m. I came to tell you, but you slept so soundly, I hadn't the heart to wake you. I just checked on her, and she's still coughing, but she's resting. Wash up and have breakfast and perhaps afterward she'll be awake. I've put a washcloth and towel in the bathroom for you. When you're ready, come down, and I'll serve you breakfast."

Garth's stomach rumbled. He'd eaten supper last night but couldn't remember what or when. After washing up and combing his hair he felt much better. Breakfast should get him up to par.

He enjoyed the golden hotcakes with homemade raspberry syrup and sausages then wasted no time in checking on his favorite patient.

Knocking softly on her door, he was happy to hear a faint "Come in". Her face was pale, and she was weak from the fever, but Jess smiled, sending his heart leaping in his chest.

He placed a gentle hand on her forehead. "Good morning. How do you feel?"

"Like I've been hit by a freight train," was the hoarse reply.

"I'm sure. Has your grandmother told you anything?"

"Only that I had a high fever, that I was delirious and that you stayed with me most of the time." She paused, coughing hoarsely. "Thank you. I'm sorry I caused so much trouble. You were exhausted before, and this didn't help. Did you sleep at all?"

"Like the proverbial log. Your grandmother didn't wake me when your fever broke, so I slept on, oblivious."

"Good, then I don't feel so bad about taking up your time looking after me."

"No problem." Garth spoke casually while thinking *I wouldn't have wanted to be anywhere else.* "Since your fever's down, I'll head home, get a proper washing up and check in with Dad. I've left everything with him for a while and need to see what's happened in my absence." He added in a very doctor-like voice, "You stay in bed and rest. I'll leave some cough medicine with your grandmother. Take it as prescribed. I'll check on you soon."

"Yes, Doctor," croaked Jess meekly.

~

Later that morning Connie came to visit Jess.

"Well, you've had quite a time the last few days, haven't you?" Sitting on the edge of the bed she waited while Jess coughed then handed her a glass of water from the bedside table. "That's a nasty cough. Do you have anything for it?"

"Yes. Garth left a bottle with Grandmother. I've already had a dose this morning." She reached for a handkerchief on the bedside table, blowing her nose.

"Tell me about your adventures. I've only heard Charlie's sketchy review at breakfast this morning."

"You were here for breakfast?" Jess croaked.

"Actually I came to help your grandmother with the children. School's called off because of the weather."

"What's it like now?"

Walking to the window, Connie opened the curtains allowing bright morning sunshine into the room. "It's extremely cold, but it's beautiful. The frozen branches and twigs glitter with snow and ice like a magical wonderland."

"Did you drive yourself?"

"No. The chauffer brought me. Mother was livid. She was still protesting as we drove away." She grimaced then smiled. "But I'm here."

"I'm glad you are," sniffed Jess.

"Now, for those adventures I'm eagerly waiting for?" Returning to the edge of the bed, Connie listened as Jess recounted the events of the past two days.

When she'd finished, Connie shook her head slowly. "No wonder you're sick. I'm glad Garth could care for you."

Jess's cheeks warmed as she spoke casually. "Yes, he's a fine doctor."

"That he is." Connie looked smug. "But perhaps he had personal reasons for taking such good care of you."

Jess looked aghast. "What are you saying? He didn't care for me any more than he would've for any other patient."

"Um hum."

Jess ignored Connie's sarcasm. Coughing again, she thankfully accepted more water, both as a relief for her cough and also as a diversion.

~

At lunchtime, Claire brought a tray of clear chicken broth, toast and tea, setting it on the bedside table.

"Thank you," Jess said hoarsely. "I'm not hungry, but I'll see what I can get down."

"Grandmother thought as much but wanted you to at least try." Claire seemed distracted.

"If I don't she might come up and feed me herself." The attempted joke barely registered with Claire and instead of leaving promptly as usual, she hung around.

Jess reached for the tea. "Something on your mind you want to talk about?"

Blushing, Claire dropped her gaze. "Well..., sort of, but I don't know how to begin."

Jess guessed what it was but waited for Claire. "Something personal you have a question about?"

"Actually, yes," Claire twisted her long blond hair nervously, "but Grandmother's always busy, and I don't want to bother her. I thought perhaps you..., um..., have time since you're laid up."

"I'd be happy to help if I can. What is it?"

"Well, there's a boy at school. We talk a lot." She paused, unsure how to continue.

Jess was right. "What's his name?"

"Joshua. He's a year older than me. He graduates this year, and he's very smart. I just don't know what to do."

"Well, you're sixteen. It's natural for boys and girls to notice each other at that age."

"Yes, but I don't know him that well. He's only recently started noticing me."

"Why do you like him? Are you willing to get to know him better to find out if you really do or not? Tell me about him."

"Oh yes, I am. He's not extraordinarily handsome, but he's very nice looking. Polite and mannerly, too. His father sheep farms up near the old lead mines on Greenhow Hill."

Jess was relieved that Claire cared more for Joshua's personality than his looks. "Does he attend church?"

"He goes to our church. I see him there often."

"He sounds like a fine young man, but no matter how good he sounds, if he hasn't given his life to Christ, you need to rethink things. Pray for him, Claire, and ask God's guidance to do the right thing. He'll give it, you know"

Claire nodded in agreement. "He always has, but I've never asked about a boy before."

"Whatever we ask is important to God no matter how big or small it seems to us." Jess smiled. "This is definitely big, don't you think?"

Claire gave Jess a big hug. "Thanks for listening."

"Anytime. I hope something I said will help."

"It already has." Claire smiled as she left the room.

Jess looked at the cup of tea and bowl of soup. Cold and definitely unappetizing. No matter. She didn't want it anyway. She poured water from the pitcher by the bed, sipping it. Closing her eyes she prayed for Claire.

"Are you asleep?" asked a quiet, familiar male voice.

Her eyes flew open as Garth entered the room.

"I met Claire downstairs, and she said you were awake. Were you dozing?"

"Actually I was praying." Jess reached for the water again. "Claire asked me something, and I was praying for guidance for her."

"Nothing serious, I hope."

"To her it is, but nothing to worry about," Jess evaded. Claire wouldn't appreciate her discussing their conversation with others.

"How are you feeling?" Garth pulled out his thermometer and stethoscope.

"Tired and weak. I have no energy whatsoever."

"After the fever you had that's to be expected." Listening to her chest, he heard the rattle of congestion and frowned. Placing the thermometer in her mouth, he held her wrist between his fingers. Jess grew uncomfortable under his scrutiny. Surely he could tell by her heartbeat. With difficulty she willed herself to relax.

Releasing her wrist he checked her blood pressure then pulled the thermometer from her mouth.

"Well, Doctor, go ahead. Break it to me. I can take it," she said casually despite his nearness.

He looked at her with a lopsided grin. "I'm glad to say you'll survive. However, your recovery won't be immediate. Your lungs are filled and rattling. You're warm, but not like last night. Stay in bed a few more days. Lay back and relax. Read a good book or work a crossword puzzle. But stay in bed. At least until Saturday."

"So we're canceling our ride tomorrow?" She didn't feel like going, but was still disappointed.

Garth sighed. "As much as I was looking forward to it, you need to recover first. It's bitterly cold out, even though it's clear. There'll be another time. Count on it." An assured gleam filled his eyes as he closed his bag. "I'd like to stay and visit but I have to go. Dad and I have been running all day. Fortunately, most of the roads are pretty clear now. Take care of yourself and get well." Reaching for her hand, he gave it a quick squeeze before he left.

Chapter Fourteen

*F*or the next three days Jess stayed in bed, growing more and more bored. *You can only sleep so much,* she thought to herself. The children all visited with her. She listened as they read from their primers or told her about their day. Grandmother and Connie visited often, bringing magazines or books to read. Charlie even brought her the crossword puzzle from the newspaper. Her appetite returned as well.

On her second day of recovery, a box of beautiful hothouse flowers arrived for Jess. Grandmother put them in a vase and brought them up to her.

"These just arrived for you, luv." She set the mass of blooms on the dresser.

"Wow! They're beautiful! What an array of colors!"

"They certainly are. Here's the card that came with them." Grandmother handed Jess a small white envelope.

Tearing it open she extracted the card. In a flamboyant script the note read, "Jessica, my Darling. Sorry you've been ill. Get well soon and we'll paint the town red! Yours, Ian."

Grandmother arranged and re-arranged the kaleidoscope of flowers as she pretended disinterest.

Glancing at her, Jess knew she'd be unhappy about who'd sent them. Well, she hadn't asked him to send them. She hadn't even thought of him since their evening out.

"They're from Ian."

"How very thoughtful of him, luv. They look expensive."

"I'm sure they were, Grandmother. Ian doesn't do anything cheaply." Jess lay against the pillow, closing her eyes. "Have the children come in and take some of them. There are plenty here. You can even put some around the house if you like."

"But, luv, they're for you."

"And I want to share them. Send some out to Charlie's bungalow for his enjoyment as well."

"Certainly, luv. It's nearly time for your medicine. Want some tea to help you sleep?"

"No, thank you. I'll just close my eyes and rest a while."

Grandmother closed the door pausing to again pray for Jess to make the right choices.

~

"Jess, since you've been resting your body for a few days, I hope your mind's rested as well. I need ideas for the Christmas Fair." Connie breezed into Jess's room, sitting in the chair near the bed. She opened a note pad, ready to write.

"Let's just dispense with greetings and jump right to brainstorming." Jess chuckled, starting a coughing spasm. When she'd quieted down, she added, "Between the two of us we can dream up anything."

"I hope so," sighed Connie. "I thought it'd be easier than this. I haven't come up with much."

"Let's see your list." Jess accepted the notebook, briefly scanning the page. "Hmmm. Looks good so far, but you do need more. Has Robert been able to help?"

"Not yet. He's been ever so busy. We're meeting tomorrow to discuss plans, but I wanted to have more to share with him." She shook her head dejectedly. "He'll think I'm a dolt if I've nothing to show him."

"You don't have to worry about that, my dear," Jess smiled

knowingly. "But we'll work on it just in case I'm wrong. Now, the fair will be in George Higgins's barn, right? Is it big?"

"It's huge. There's a large open area in the middle perfect for folk dances. Game booths will line the sides. At one end will be the buffet and dining tables. The musicians will be at the other end."

"Have you found your musicians yet?"

"No. The only ones I know charge a mint to play. I don't know the Dale folk well enough to know who plays and if they'd donate their talents to the cause."

"Grandmother knows everyone in the Dales. So does Garth. Between them they could give you names of people to talk to."

"Excellent idea." Connie jotted it down.

"What will your game booths be?"

"The Ring Toss, Weight Guessing, Balloons and Darts, and the Duck Pond. I'd like to have at least eight booths."

"We'll think of more then ask for donations for the items needed for the games."

They brainstormed through the afternoon. When Grandmother checked on Jess, she found them deep in discussion surrounded by pages of notes, sketches for decorations and supply lists.

"What's all this?" Grandmother indicated the chaos on the bed. "You're not tiring yourself, are you, luv?"

Jess leaned her head back on the pillow, smiling wryly. "Now that you mention it, I am a bit tired. We've been at this all afternoon."

Connie glanced at her watch. "I didn't realize we'd worked so long. I shouldn't have kept you when you've been so ill. How thoughtless of me!"

Reaching over, Jess patted Connie's hand. "I'm glad you did. It can be boring up here with nothing to do, so don't apologize. We made real progress, don't you think?"

"Yes, I do. Thanks for all your help." Connie leaned over, giving Jess a quick hug.

"Before you go, ask Grandmother about the musicians?"

"What musicians?" Grandmother asked, puzzled.

"Connie needs musicians for the Christmas Fair. There'll be folk dancing and background music."

"I don't know anyone who plays," added Connie.

Grandmother smiled broadly. "That shouldn't be difficult. There are plenty of musicians about. I even know someone who can call out the dances. I'll handle that problem for you."

"Thanks," sighed Connie with relief.

"When is the Fair?"

"The first Saturday in December. We've three weeks to pull it all together, then three weeks after that to purchase and wrap the gifts for a Christmas Eve delivery."

"How exciting!" Grandmother was getting into the spirit. "You should have a baking contest and auction the bakery at the Fair as part of the fund raiser."

"That's a wonderful idea!" Connie jotted it down.

"We can auction off donated handcrafted items, too," added Jess. "We'll hang posters around, and soon, so that anyone who wants to donate items can start on them."

"I'll mention all of this to Robert when we meet tomorrow," said Connie. "Perhaps we can make some posters in the next few days, and the children can help place them in shop windows around the villages."

"Seeing as how I'm not particularly busy right now," Jess said, "I might have time to work up some posters for you. My calendar's empty for the next few days. Your timing's just right, you know."

~

Garth found himself working at his office on his day off. He'd looked forward to driving Jess to Aysgarth Falls, but they'd go another day. He'd make sure of it as he'd told her he would. In the mean time, he'd catch up on some paperwork and records needing his attention. With things so hectic lately, his deskwork had fallen behind. He hadn't realized how engrossed he was until he noticed the sun setting and evening approaching. Grabbing his coat and hat from the coat tree, he extinguished the lights and left to meet Robert at the King's Arms in Lofthouse. The food was good, and he ate there often. Malcolm, the proprietor, was Dad's distant cousin and forever trying to match Garth with his daughter, Kate. Smiling, he remembered all the times Malcolm had pushed Kate at him, only to see her roll her eyes in exasperation. He'd heard through the grapevine that she had a beau from Knaresborough. She should tell Malcolm so he'd leave him alone.

Passing the lane to Hope Orphanage, he longed to stop and check on Jess. He hadn't seen her since the day before yesterday, but Dad had examined her, assuring him that she was coming along fine. He'd stop by tomorrow. He tried to force his thoughts to his meeting with Robert but couldn't purge her from his mind. Not that he'd tried very hard. While working all day he managed to stay focused, but sometimes she was right there, brown eyes, gorgeous smile and all. He knew in his heart that he loved her.

Lofthouse was a small village made up of a few gritstone houses and shops. The King's Arms pub was the focal point of the village where locals came nightly to pass the time, throw a few darts and hear the latest news. Garth noticed a few vehicles and several horse-drawn wagons parked outside.

Inside the pub a lively game of darts was underway in the corner near the fire. Several customers sat watching the match. Removing his overcoat and hat Garth hung them on a peg-rack by the door. The fire's warmth felt good.

"Garth, me boy!" called Malcolm from behind the bar. Wiping his hands on the white apron around his waist, he came around to shake Garth's hand. "Good to see ya, lad. Haven't been by in a while. Been stayin' busy, no doubt."

"Hello, Malcolm. It's good to see you. Yes, we've been very busy."

"Yeah, heard about the problem at the flax mill." Malcolm shook his head. "Real nasty business, so I heard."

"Yeah, it was pretty bad." Garth didn't want to talk with Malcolm long. He'd bring up Kate soon. He looked around the room then back to the proprietor. "Malcolm, I'm meeting someone. He's the new minister in Pateley Bridge. Got a table where we can talk privately while we eat a good hot meal?"

"Course we do, me boy. Take a table in the dinin' room away from the lads in here. There's only a few folk in there. Nice an' quiet, it is. Maybe your party's there already."

"Thanks, Malcolm." Garth clapped the older man on the shoulder and walked into the dining room. A fire burned brightly in the fireplace, its warmth and glow filling the room. Garth spotted Robert at a table near the fire. He stood up, shaking Garth's hand.

"Evening, Robert. Good to see you. Hope you haven't been waiting long."

"I just arrived a few minutes ago." Robert sat back down. "I hope the rest of the week went better for you."

Garth nodded appreciatively. "We've been busy, but nothing major since Jess got sick."

"How is she?"

Garth answered as professionally as possible. "Dad went by yesterday and said she's improving. I haven't seen her in a few days."

Robert nodded. "Glad she's improving. She had Mrs. McDonald quite concerned."

No more than me, Garth thought.

Kate, Malcolm's daughter, approached the table, a tray tucked beneath her arm. She smiled brightly at Garth. "Well, now, we haven't seen you around for a bit. What've you been up to lately?"

"Oh, you know; the usual." Garth grinned. "But you can't keep me away for long. How have you been?"

"Smashing!" She held out her left hand displaying the small diamond on her finger. "Getting married, I am. So don't worry about Pops trying to match us up anymore. I told him about Peter. He was rather surprised. Had his heart set on you for a son-in-law, but he accepted it right enough. Don't be surprised if he says you've made a big mistake by not marrying me before. He'll say you've missed your chance."

"Thanks. I consider myself warned." Garth indicated Robert across the table. "This is Robert Kilpatrick, the new minister in Pateley. Robert, this is Kate, the proprietor's daughter."

Standing, Robert shook her outstretched hand. "A pleasure to meet you, Kate."

"Welcome to the Dales. You're not from around here, are you?"

"No, I'm from near Cambridge."

"Well, I'm glad to meet you. Now, what would you lads like to eat?"

"What's your special?" asked Garth. "I didn't notice the board when I came in."

"Shepherd's Pie with brussels sprouts, veal cutlets with mixed vegetables and rhubarb pie for dessert."

"Both are excellent choices, but I'll go with the veal with a pot of tea, please. Robert?"

"I'll have the same. I've had a taste for veal ever since we planned this meeting. And make it two teas."

Before Kate could respond, Malcolm stepped up, placing a hand on Garth's shoulder and an arm around Kate. "Well, me boy, ya waited too long to marry me daughter, here. She done went an' got herself spoken for, she did. Ya missed your chance." He shook his head sadly.

Kate rolled her eyes and sighed. The look she gave Garth said, *what did I tell you?* She shook her head. "Come on, Pops. Lay off, will you. Give the lad a break. You've gone on about this for years now."

"Just don't want him feeling bad for ya jiltin' him like ya did."

Garth saw Kate's glare and quickly said, "Don't feel bad for me, Malcolm. I've got my sights on someone, and I'm very happy for Kate. I've known all along she was meant for Peter, so don't fret. I won't pine away." As soon as Garth spoke he wished he hadn't. Robert looked at him, surprised, but didn't comment. Garth avoided his gaze.

Kate smiled her thanks as Malcolm clapped Garth on the shoulder. "Well, that's good news, me boy. Who's the lucky lady?

She must be pretty special to grab the attention of a lad like you."

Garth didn't like where this conversation was headed and started back peddling. "Well, I haven't talked to her yet."

"Well, what are ya waitin' on, lad? Tell her."

Kate elbowed her father. "Pop, leave him be. He'll talk to her when he's ready. Or when she's ready. Besides, it's his business, not yours." She spoke to Garth and Robert. "Pay him no mind. I'll bring your food shortly." Turning, she glared at Malcolm then taking his arm walked him out of the room.

Garth chuckled and turned to find Robert watching him thoughtfully.

"It's Jess, isn't it," Robert said quietly.

With gaze downward, Garth fingered the silverware. "What's Jess?" he asked evasively.

Chapter Fifteen

Robert smiled knowingly. "Garth, Jess is 'the someone' you 'have your eye on', isn't she?"

Garth looked at Robert thoughtfully. He didn't know him very well but somehow knew he was trustworthy. "Is it that obvious?"

"Honestly, I hadn't thought about it until your statement. Looking back, I recall times when you said or did things that showed you care." He paused. "Does it bother you that I know?"

Garth thought about his question. "No. It's the first time I've said it aloud, but it's true. I do love her."

Robert smiled broadly. "Then why haven't you told her how you feel?"

Garth shook his head wearily. "Because, like you and her grandmother, she has a deep faith in God that I don't have. Which is why I wanted to talk with you. I know Jess loves God very much, but I don't understand why? What draws people to Him? What am I missing?"

Robert's heart leapt at this opportunity to share the gospel. Garth had been on his mind for weeks, so he'd prayed for God to open his mind and heart to Jesus Christ.

"Garth, do you believe in God?"

"Yes. Mother taught me about Him when I was young, but as I grew older, other things took precedence, and I didn't bother with religion anymore."

"Well, not knowing what you were taught, I'll start at the beginning." Robert pulled out a pocket Bible and shared scripture with Garth explaining how sin had entered the world and what God did for mankind to make an escape from the consequences of sin

"John 3:16 says 'For God so loved the world that He gave His only begotten son, that whosoever believeth in Him should not perish, but have ever lasting life.' Death is the consequence of sin and the only way to escape it is through Jesus Christ. He came to teach, preach and heal, but most importantly to die on Calvary's cross. He loved us so much He took on Himself the sins of the whole world. If we trust in Him, He gives us eternal life, and we don't have to fear an eternal death. It's His free gift to us."

Kate brought their plates, and as they ate, Garth mulled over Robert's words. "How does this affect me personally?"

"Have you ever done anything wrong?"

"I've done my share, but nothing terrible."

"Sin is sin in God's eyes. That's why He sent Christ to die for us. Nothing we could ever do would be good enough to wipe out our sins. But the blood that He shed on the cross for us will cover them completely."

"Why is Jess always so at peace about problems and difficult situations? Not just her, but her grandmother, and you, too?"

"When we make Him Lord of our life, he sends the Holy Spirit and He gives us that peace. We're human, however, and we often exert our will over His. When we do, we're not at peace. That's why it's important to give ourselves to Him daily."

"What does that mean, to give our will over to Him?"

"When God made us, He gave us a free will to choose whether to accept Him or to reject Him. When we accept Him as Lord, we're changed, but we're still human, weak and susceptible to sin. He wants us to let Him lead us. After all, He made us. He knows what's best for us. He's given so many promises in His

Word that He'll take care of us in every aspect of our lives, but He won't force us to. He wants us to serve Him willingly. And when we do, we'll have the most precious relationship with Him possible, and more."

Garth thought about Robert's words. Yes, he believed in God, but he'd always assumed He was a distant figure that created the universe but had little interest in mankind. But according to Robert, He really cared. He wanted a close relationship with man. With him.

"And if we reject Him?"

"God said that sin must be punished by death. Christ died in our place on the cross, but if we reject Him, we must pay our own penalty. There's a place prepared for Satan and his demons that God will one day send them to. But we'll go there, too, if we reject Christ, and remain there for eternity. The Bible describes it as a terrible place."

At that moment Kate returned. "Well, lads, how about some of my rhubarb pie? It's quite good, you know."

Robert smiled. "I'd love some, and coffee, please."

"And you, luv?" she asked Garth.

Garth stared at his plate, thinking.

"Garth, luv," said Kate, concerned. "Are you alright?"

He suddenly realized Kate was speaking to him. "Sorry, Kate. My mind was elsewhere. You were saying?"

"It certainly was. Thought we were going to have to call the doctor. But you are the doctor," she teased. "I asked if you'd like a big slice of my rhubarb pie."

Garth smiled. "Actually, I'd like a slice of your apple pie, if you have any. With a dollop of whipped cream."

Kate chuckled. "Just for you, luv."

Retrieving their plates, she hurried away.

Robert turned back to Garth. "Can I answer anything else?"

Garth leaned forward on his elbows. "I understand the difference between Jess and me. She has a relationship with Christ and I don't. We could never truly be close until we're of the same mind about this. Yet, even if I'd never met her, I'd still need to know Him, wouldn't I?"

"Yes. We all must settle the age old question of where we'll spend eternity. One day we'll all face it. Who we knew or what we did in life won't help us. We'll each stand before God and answer for ourselves, and we must prepare now because we're not promised tomorrow. When we stand before Him, it'll be too late to change things."

Garth stared into the flames burning brightly in the fireplace. He'd known about hell but thought it was only for bad people. Now he knew he was headed there, too, if he didn't accept Christ. No, he wasn't a murderer or a criminal, but he was guilty of not allowing Christ into his life. He wanted the peace that Jess had. He wanted to turn things over to God and say, "Here, You take control and work it all out for me." He'd made a mess of things long enough.

After Kate brought their dessert and coffee, Garth gazed at Robert, yearning in his eyes. "How do I begin this relationship with Christ?"

Robert smiled. "He made it easy for us because He did it all. Tell Him you realize you're a sinner and ask Him to forgive you and to be Lord of your life. Just give yourself to Him."

"That's all?"

"That's all, Garth. If someone gives you a gift, all you have to do is reach out and take it. It's yours. That's what He's done. He paid the price of the 'gift' by dying on the cross. Just believe and trust in Him."

"May I accept His gift now?"

"He'd love for you to, my friend. Simply bow your head and talk to Him. He's waiting for you."

Garth felt awkward at first but was soon pouring out his heart to God. "Oh, Father, I realize I'm a sinner, but I want to know you. Please forgive my sins and take my life. Help me live for you."

Garth felt peace and joy fill his heart like he'd never known before. He didn't have to face difficulties alone anymore. He had Someone to help him face them. "Thanks for helping me understand. I can't wait to tell Jess."

"I'll be praying for you, my friend. Call anytime you want to talk."

~

Saturday morning Jess decided enough was enough. She was getting up. However, as she threw back the covers and swung her legs over the edge of the bed, she found it wasn't so easy. She hadn't realized how weak she'd become. Reaching for her robe and warm clothes, she slowly headed to the bathroom. A half-hour later, bathed and dressed, she attempted the stairs.

On the way down she was greeted by some of the children heading upstairs to make beds. Since Jess's illness, everyone pitched in, taking on more chores than usual.

They gave Jess hugs then helped her down the rest of the way. Very vocal and solicitous in their help, they had her laughing as they reached the bottom.

"What's this?" Grandmother came to investigate the noise. Seeing Jess, she exclaimed. "What are you doing out of bed?"

"I couldn't stand it another minute. I had to get up." She coughed, bringing a doubtful expression to Grandmother's face.

"I don't like that cough. You shouldn't be up."

"I'll be fine. Besides, the cough is improving. It'll just take a while to get over it, that's all."

"Well then, come have breakfast. Children, let's get to your jobs. We've a lot to do today."

As the children moaned, mostly for effect, Jess followed Grandmother into the kitchen where Claire washed dishes while Jason dried them.

"Good morning." Jess sat down wearily at the table.

The teens turned in surprise. "What are you doing up?" exclaimed Jason.

"Shouldn't you be in bed?" Claire scolded.

"Out of the mouths of babes." Grandmother commented smugly, pouring coffee for Jess.

"Thanks for your concern, but I'm feeling much better," croaked Jess. "Besides, I needed a change of scenery."

Grandmother served her food. "Well, don't push it, luv."

"I promise to take it easy," Jess responded meekly.

"Um-hum," Grandmother nodded, unconvinced.

Charlie entered carrying a load of firewood. Jess shivered as cold air whipped in behind him.

Walking through the kitchen and the dining room, Charlie carried the wood to the living room hearth. Suddenly popping back through the kitchen door, he stared at Jess.

"Miss Jess, what are you doin' out o' bed? You'll be catchin' your death down here," he scolded.

"I'm pleased everyone's so happy to see me." Jess laughed hoarsely. "Anyone else want to scold me?" She threw her hands in the air, exasperated.

"Now that you mention it," said Garth from the kitchen doorway.

Turning, Jess saw him standing, hands on his hips, one eyebrow cocked and a half smile on his lips. *Well, he'll say whether I should be out of bed or not,* she thought sarcastically. *And from the look on his face, maybe I should've stayed in bed.*

"Well, everyone else has fussed at me. What do you say, Doctor?" She tried unsuccessfully to stifle a cough.

Setting his bag on the table, Garth placed a practiced hand on her forehead and probed her neck glands before checking her pulse.

"How long has your fever been down?"

"For two days." Jess tried unsuccessfully to ignore how his touch affected her heartbeat. He couldn't have missed it as he checked her pulse. Her cheeks warmed.

"I suppose you can stay up a while as long as you do nothing but sit by the fire with a book. Nothing more. Understand? Your cough's improved but not enough. Above all, stay warm."

"Thank you, Garth. I couldn't stay in that bed any longer." She laughed. "I sound like a broken record."

Garth smiled. "That's understandable. A change of scenery should do you good as long as it's inside."

"Garth," said Grandmother, "have you eaten?"

"Actually, no. I had an early call, and I'm just returning from it. Thought I'd stop by to check on Jess."

"Have a seat and I'll fetch you a plate. Claire, please pour him some coffee."

Charlie left to tend to the fire and Jason headed for the barn. Garth sat opposite Jess, eating his breakfast.

"So what or who had you out so early?" Jess asked.

Garth sipped his coffee. "Margaret Sipes delivered around six o'clock this morning. Twins! The first was easy, but the second wouldn't cooperate. Happy where she was, it took some coaxing before she gave in. Margaret's husband Sam called about eleven last night, saying she was in labor. At eleven-thirty I stopped to check her. She wasn't ready so Elizabeth Miller sat with her and called me at three forty-five when things were moving along."

"When you said an early call, that's exactly what you meant."

Grandmother placed a gentle hand on Garth's shoulder. "You're a good doctor, luv. A very good doctor."

"Don't I know it," agreed Jess. "Any doctor who personally sits with a patient all night to lower a fever is the best."

Garth looked into her eyes, seeing her sincerity. *I'd do anything for you.* Jess felt her cheeks warm at the look in his eyes. Lowering hers, she took a bite of toast.

"Thanks for the kind words, but that's what doctors do, you know."

As Jess carried her plate to the sink, she swayed, feeling lightheaded. Grasping her chair, she closed her eyes. Before she knew what was happening, she was lifted off her feet. Her eyes flew open and looked right into Garth's gaze, only inches from her own. Instinctively she wrapped her arms around his neck and instantly wished she hadn't. Pulling back slightly, she heard Garth's deep chuckle.

"Please put me down. I'm fine. I just stood up too quickly."

Ignoring her, Garth headed for the living room. Grandmother started to follow, but changing her mind, returned to the sink. Jess was in good hands.

Although she wanted him to put her down, Jess felt secure where she was. Still shaky, she relaxed and laid her head against his shoulder, causing his heartbeat to race.

Garth savored the feel of Jess in his arms, wanting her there for always. In the living room, he reluctantly but gently laid her against the pillows on the couch, pulling an afghan over her.

"I'm fine, you know." Jess whispered.

"I know you are. It's to be expected when you're weak and first start getting up. Just promise you'll take it easy."

"I promise. You need to get some rest yourself after your morning."

"In time, but first I've something to tell you." Pulling up a footstool, he sat by the couch.

Jess straightened against the pillows. "What is it?"

Garth was eager to tell her about what had happened the night before but didn't know how to begin. "Well, I'm a bit new at this, so I may not explain very well, but I hope you'll understand. Last night I met with Robert Kilpatrick. I've had a lot of questions lately. I wanted to know why you, he and your grandmother trust in God. He explained it to me and I realized what was missing from my life. I'd never trusted in Christ. Last night, I did." Jess saw joy shining in his eyes. He was different. He had a peace that wasn't there before.

"Oh, Garth! That's wonderful! Can I tell Grandmother?"

"Of course. I intend to do some telling myself. It's wonderful having peace and knowing He's in control." He reached out, taking her hand. "I have you to thank for showing me as well."

"Me?" Jess was puzzled.

"Yes, you. Telling me about your faith and living it is what got me thinking. As well as inviting me to church to hear Robert preach."

"I invited you to church?" Jess didn't remember asking him exactly.

"Well, perhaps not directly, but you got me interested in hearing more." He originally came because of his interest in her, but he couldn't tell her that. Not yet.

"Well, for whatever reason, I'm happy for you. Christ makes all the difference," Jess smiled. "But now you should get some rest."

"Right. I'll be off then. And you remember the doctor's orders."

Chapter Sixteen

*R*elaxing by the warm fire, Jess thrilled again at Garth's news. The angels in heaven rejoice when a soul is saved and so did she. It had nothing to do with personal feelings. She tried to convince herself she didn't have any, except for friendship, of course. He was a respected doctor and had become a trusted friend since she'd arrived; nothing more. She'd return home eventually, and it wouldn't do to fall for him. She would just keep things status quo.

She tried to read, but the children came through dusting the furniture and straightening the room. Grandmother checked on her and inspected the clean-up in progress. She set a tray of tea, soup and sandwiches by the couch.

"You're not tiring yourself, are you, luv?" Sitting on the footstool by the couch, Grandmother handed Jess the tea.

"Thank you. No, just following the doctor's orders, but I think I'll nap after lunch."

"Good idea."

Jess sipped the hot amber liquid. "When Garth was here, he told me he and Robert talked last night and that Robert led him to the Lord. Isn't that wonderful?"

Grandmother's eyes lit up as she clapped her hands together.

"Praise God! I've prayed for Garth for years, and now God's answered my prayers."

"How long have you known Garth?"

"Oh, a very long time. I attended school with his grandmother when we were girls, and I knew his mother, Sarah, very well. She grew up and married Neville Samuels, a young medical student from York. After graduation, he started a practice in the Dales. She came from a Christian home, but I'm not sure about Neville. When Garth came along, they attended St. Cuthbert's, but with Neville busy with patients so much, it wasn't often. Sarah tried to teach Garth about God, but after her death, there was no further encouragement. Neville was too busy with his practice. He was a good father and did his best alone, but God wasn't a priority."

"I'm glad God doesn't give up on us even when the odds are against us." Jess reached for the soup.

"Me, too." Grandmother stood up. "I'd better get back to work. Those children are a cleaning miracle today. Jason and the older boys are helping Charlie drop hay in the pasture for the sheep. Now, when you're finished, leave the tray and take that nap. If you need help getting upstairs, just call."

~

Note pad in hand, Connie entered the church at the time she and Robert had agreed to meet. Hopefully he had some ideas to add to the ones she and Jess had discussed. Between them, they would devise an awesome Christmas fundraiser!

Glancing around the sanctuary, Connie wondered if Robert was here. As she checked her watch, he entered from the rear of the building.

"Good morning," he greeted cheerily.

"Good morning."

"Do you mind sitting in the office? It's chilly in here, but I have the heater on there."

"Not at all."

Shelves filled with books lined the office walls while a large wooden desk sat in the middle of the room, a leather-upholstered chair behind it. Robert pulled a chair forward, holding it for

Connie.

"Have you thought of any new ideas since we last spoke?" He took his seat behind the desk.

Opening her note pad, Connie updated him on the newest ideas. They still needed musicians. She'd been unable to reach the people Morag had suggested.

"Our church pianist is very good, and a man in the congregation plays the violin. Perhaps you could ask them." Connie jotted down the names Robert gave her.

His gaze rested on her features as she wrote, enjoying the faint color in her cheeks and her long dark lashes. He longed to reach out and touch the wispy curl on her temple. She was blessed with a lovely face, but what about her soul? Did she know Christ? He wanted to know more about her. She came from a wealthy family, but that didn't affect her desire to help others. She didn't seem at all selfish; just the opposite and it was more than just charity to her. God could use her willingness to give of herself to others.

Connie raised her eyes and met his, glimpsing something in his gaze that sent warmth into her cheeks. Robert looked down at his hands, his mind racing to remember what they'd been talking about.

"I'll call on them this afternoon to ask if they'll play at the fair."

Ah, yes. The musicians! "That would be fine," he agreed lamely. *Yeah, really fine, you dolt.* A pretty face and he couldn't keep his mind on the matter at hand. "Before you leave, I'll give you directions. May I see the list?"

Connie handed him the note pad. Looking it over, he tried to get a handle on the conversation.

"This looks good so far. I'll help place the posters and fliers. The teens from the church can team up with the adults to post them in the villages, and I'll make some calls and visits. We'll spread the news quickly enough." He looked at the list again. "The craft and baked goods auction is a splendid idea."

"Would you approach some of the merchants to donate

items for game prizes? Since you're a minister, perhaps they'd be more willing to give."

"Certainly. Let's list the merchants to ask and what we need." They spent the next hour and a half making more lists and plans.

Robert glanced at the wall clock, surprised at how quickly the time had flown while they pored over the papers spread across the desktop.

"I'm sorry. I've kept you here much too long, causing you to miss lunch."

Connie chortled. "Honestly, I hadn't noticed. I was so engrossed in all this," she gestured toward the desk, "I lost track of time."

"But I feel responsible, and the least I can do is take you to lunch, belated as it is."

"That's not necessary. Besides, I have several people to contact this afternoon." She reached for the scattered papers, stuffing them into her notebook.

"It would be my pleasure," Robert said seriously.

Connie saw the sincerity on his face. Well, why not? He was very nice, and it had been a while since she'd lunched with a very nice young man. And she *was* hungry. Her visits could wait. "Then it would be my pleasure, too."

~

The old Miner's Arms pub sat at the top of Greenhow Hill for nearly two centuries, withstanding high winds and storms that swept across the moors. Connie heard the wind whipping around the old building as she sat across from Robert. She'd never been allowed to mingle with the "common folk" as her Mother labeled the locals, but glancing around the room, she knew these folk were hardworking and proud. Several glanced her way, indicating she was the topic of discussion at several tables around the room.

Looking at Robert she found his gaze resting on her. "They know who you are, you know."

"What does it matter to them who I am?" she asked curiously, without malice.

"It isn't every day the daughter of the richest man in the

Dales comes in. They're probably just surprised you did."

"But why? I'm no different from them, not really."

"In their eyes you're very different. You come from a world they're unfamiliar with. Most struggle daily just to exist. They'll never know what it's like to have every want or need met without exception."

Connie shook her head sadly. "Not every need."

"Do you need something?"

"Oh, yes! That's why I'm working at the orphanage and pursuing this Christmas fundraiser. I need to be a part of the real world, to make a difference in the Dales. My mother's idea of making a difference is keeping her hairstyle and wardrobe one step ahead of the ladies in her bridge club. When she discovered I'd volunteered at the orphanage, she was livid."

"I'm sorry. I wasn't aware you don't have family support. That makes it especially difficult to accomplish something."

"My father isn't against it. He feels it's a passing whim that I'll eventually grow bored with and move on to something else. When I don't, he'll still support me, but to my mother it's an embarrassment. They support charities financially, but she'd never become personally involved. I love her, but she's a first class snob."

The bitterness in her voice saddened Robert. "Perhaps she loves you so much, she's just being over-protective."

Connie sighed heavily. "No, she just can't let go of control over my life. I'm old enough to make my own decisions, but she still thinks she can do a better job than I can. I know I'll make mistakes, but how will I ever know what I'm supposed to do in life if I don't try. I refuse to sit and be waited on or think life involves just moving from one social event to another."

Robert nodded in agreement. "I understand. My dad was against my entering the ministry. He's an architect as was his father before him. It's a fine profession, and he's good at it, but it wasn't what God wanted me to do. I tried it. I attended school intending to become an architect because Dad wanted me to. But the more I studied and planned, the more I knew it wasn't what

God planned for me. I knew He wanted me in the ministry. I struggled because of my father's disapproval, but I had to follow God's plan for me."

"What is your relationship with your father now?"

"He still doesn't understand, but he doesn't have a personal relationship with Christ. We get along, considering. I tell him at every opportunity that I love him and that God does as well." He prayed Connie would realize that God loved her.

Connie ate, considering his words. She didn't have a relationship with God. Only attending church occasionally, she never thought much about it.

"When did you begin a relationship with God?" she asked curiously.

"As a Christian, my mother taught me, but I was fifteen when I trusted in Him."

"How did you know you needed to?"

Robert smiled tenderly then shared God's Word with Connie, as he had with Garth, praying she'd understand and accept Christ, too. They talked on, Connie asking questions and Robert answering them. The waitress had long since cleared their table, but they still sat discussing the most important decision anyone could ever make.

Glancing at the wall clock, Connie decided it was well past time to go. "I'd like to talk again sometime, if you don't mind. You've given me food for thought, and I want to know more. I appreciate your time."

Robert was disappointed and encouraged at the same time. At least she hadn't rejected Christ. She wanted to hear more. He'd continue praying and talk with her when the opportunity arose, and he'd see that it did.

"Any time, and I'll be praying for you. Not only concerning your decision about God, but also about your mother."

"Thank you. Although I don't know anything about prayer, I'm sure God hears and answers your prayers. And I need all the prayers I can get."

Chapter Seventeen

"*I* like the red and green," commented Grandmother. "They're Christmas colors after all."

"I agree," Connie nodded. "They're more cheerful looking than plain black letters."

Sitting at the dining room table surrounded by poster board, paint pots and brushes, Jess designed posters for the Christmas Fair.

"Then red and green it shall be. They'll definitely draw attention then we'll have people knocking down the barn door to get into this gala affair. What do you think?"

"It'll be a night to remember," Grandmother agreed. "We haven't had a big to do in the Dales in a long time. The war put an end to such doings."

"Well, the war's just ended! We can celebrate!" cheered Jess.

Connie laughed. "I hate to dampen your enthusiasm, but there's a lot to do before we can celebrate."

"Ho-hum! Details, details! The slave driver has spoken. What's next on your list, Sergeant?"

"When you've finished those posters, Robert, the children and the teenagers from church will post them. Charlie, George Higgins and some parents will drive them around. Robert contacted several merchants in Harrogate, Knaresborough and Pateley Bridge about donating items for the auction and for the game prizes. We're going tomorrow morning to start collecting them."

"Where are you going to keep everything?" asked Grandmother.

"We thought of the church, but there's not much room there. We may have to store everything in different locations."

"That's not necessary." Grandmother waved a dismissive hand. "There's a room in the barn that should do quite nicely. It's just sitting there, perfectly sturdy and dry. Slip on your coat and we'll go see if you think it'll do."

As they left for the barn, Jess dipped her paintbrush, returning to the posters. Claire walked in and sat across from her.

Jess glanced up. "Hello, Claire. What's up?"

Claire smiled sheepishly. "I wanted to tell you that Joshua asked me to the Christmas Fair. And he's going to help hang posters this afternoon."

Jess smiled. "That's wonderful, Claire. Did you pray about it?"

"Oh, yes! I even asked if he knows Christ, and he does."

"I'm glad! Once again you see how God hears and answers our prayers."

"Yes, I do. He doesn't always answer what we want or when we want it, but He answers with what's best for us. Grandmother taught me that." She paused before continuing shyly. "I wondered if you'd help me the night of the Fair, to dress up a bit, you know?"

"I'd love to! We'll fix up your hair and find something pretty for you to wear."

Claire came around, giving Jess a hug. "Thank you."

As Claire hurried from the room, Jess returned to her task, recalling her first date. At sixteen, just like Claire, she'd attended a church function with the pastor's son. Nothing ever came of it, but she remembered her crush on him and the excitement of her first date. She'd look through some of her dresses and see if anything could be altered to fit Claire. Every girl should have a "new" dress to wear on her first date.

~

Jess had avoided Michael while she was sick, but since she was better and coughing less, she couldn't stay away any longer. While busy upstairs, she heard him cooing in his crib. He'd stayed in Grandmother's room when Jess was sick and his crib was still there. Peeking around the doorway, Jess watched Michael waving his arms and kicking his legs. Unaware of his audience, he kicked and waved and cooed. He was a good baby, with a happy temperament. She often wondered about his mother. Who was she? Where was she? And most of all why had she given up such a precious baby?

Jess quietly approached the crib. Seeing her, Michael gave her a bright eyed, toothless grin. "Hello, my little heart stealer. Did you sleep well?"

Cooing, Michael raised his arms toward Jess. Lifting him into her arms, she cradled him against her shoulder, kissing his downy soft cheek. "You've been busy in other ways, haven't you?" Reaching for a clean folded diaper, she gently laid him on Grandmother's bed.

Katie and Billy tiptoed into the room and leaned against the bed, watching as Jess changed the baby's diaper.

"Hello, you two. What are you up to?"

Katie shrugged and sighed heavily. "Ohhhh, I don't know."

Billy gently stroked the top of Michael's head. When the baby saw him and waved his hand, Billy let him grab a finger and hold on. A smile formed on the usually somber face. Jess had rarely seen that smile.

"He likes you, Billy. He knows that's a strong hand he's holding onto."

Watching Michael, Billy nodded and continued stroking the downy head.

"Would you two like to help me get his bottle ready and feed him?"

Katie jumped up. "Oh, yes! We would!"

Billy nodded emphatically.

"Alright, then follow me. We'll go to the kitchen and get to work." Picking up Michael, Jess headed downstairs, the youngsters at her heels.

She helped them prepare the bottle, ensuring each had something to do then they all went to the living room where they sat side by side on the couch. "Billy, you hold Michael while Katie holds the bottle. You must sit very still, and Katie, you must hold the bottle up so he drinks the milk and not air. Both jobs are very important. Alright?"

"A'right!" Katie answered while Billy nodded. They were feeding the baby after all, and that was an important job. Jess told them so.

Sitting on the footstool in front of them, she watched closely. Grandmother returned from fetching the mail.

"What's this?" She hung up her coat. "Do you have new helpers?"

"I certainly do. And they're doing a great job." Jess winked at Grandmother.

The children gave their full attention to the job at hand, concentrating on sitting still, something alien to them both.

Grandmother handed Jess an envelope. "Here's something for you, luv. I'll take over here while you open it."

Taking the letter, Jess gave Grandmother her seat and moved to the armchair. The letter was postmarked in the States, but she didn't recognize the address. Opening it, she quickly read the short note then returned it to the envelope.

"What is it, luv? Not bad news, I hope."

"No, it's from Mother's lawyer. He didn't write sooner because he felt it was too soon after her death, but now he says I must make some decisions. He wants to know if I'm keeping the house or selling it."

"Have you thought about it?"

"Not really. After Mother died, I just wanted to come see you. I suppose I knew I'd have to return sometime to deal with the property and return to teaching, but it wasn't pressing at the time. I suppose I should think about it."

"We'll pray about it, but remember you're more than welcome to stay here as long as you like."

"Thanks, Grandmother. I'll pray and think about it. He wants a decision in the next few weeks if possible."

Michael finished his bottle and Katie gently pulled it from his mouth, holding it up proudly. "We did it." Looking at Grandmother, she said importantly, "Jess said it's very important to feed a baby."

"She's right, luv. You and Billy did an excellent job. Now, let's give him back to Jess to burp him."

She handed Michael to Jess. "Now I have another important job for you. Come with me." Taking each by the hand, Grandmother led them from the room.

Draping a cloth diaper across her shoulder, Jess held Michael close as she gently patted his back. Burping loudly, he snuggled close, sucking his fist happily.

Father, what should I do? Not just about the house, but with my life. What do You have planned for me? Do I return to America and continue where I left off before Mother got sick, or do I sell the house and stay here? Give me wisdom, Father. Please.

~

Connie and Robert borrowed Charlie's old truck, driving into Harrogate to collect donations from various businesses. Robert had exchanged his suit and tie for casual pants and shirt, topped by a warm coat. Connie liked him dressed up but decided she liked this casual side of him, too. While driving from place to place, they enjoyed getting to know each other. Connie felt at ease with Robert and liked being with him.

By late afternoon, they'd collected the last donation and returned to Hope Orphanage. After Robert backed the pickup to the barn, Connie went to the house in search of help to unload it.

Jess grabbed a coat and hat, calling the older children to give a hand. Within an hour everything was unloaded and organized. On one side of the room were small tables, lamps, kitchenware, and household items for the auction. Across the room were boxes of game prizes. In a couple, Jess discovered a variety of hatpins, costume jewelry, gloves, scarves, picture frames, and porcelain dolls.

"Robert, you're a miracle worker. How did you get people to donate such wonderful things?"

Robert shook his head. "It wasn't me. All I did was make some phone calls, asking for donations. The merchants had their boxes packed and ready when we got there. I had no idea what was in them. I just prayed beforehand that the Lord would prepare their hearts to meet the need."

"Well, He certainly did that. This is going to be fun! Since these things are so nice, whatever's left from the Fair, if anything, can become Christmas gifts for the Dale folk. Look at this box." Jess opened another. "It's full of tin toys, teddy bears and china tea sets."

Robert and Connie exchanged smiles at Jess's excitement. This really was fun!

~

As they left the barn and the children left to do chores or homework, Jess invited Robert to supper.

"Thanks, but I've some things to attend to."

Turning to Connie, she hooked her arm within her friend's. "You won't turn me down, will you?"

"Of course not," Connie said in mock seriousness. "After all this work, I'm famished."

Robert bade them goodbye as Connie and Jess went inside to help with supper.

The phone rang as they worked, and Grandmother answered it. She returned a moment later, displeasure on her face. "Jess, it's for you." She returned to the stove.

Jess sent Connie a puzzled look before leaving the room.

"Hello?"

"Hello, my sweet Jessica. Haven't forgotten me, have you?"

Jess suddenly understood Grandmother's displeasure. "Hello, Ian. How are you?"

"Fantastic, but I've missed you terribly. I'd like to see you again. We'll do dinner and a movie tomorrow night."

To Jess it sounded very much like he wasn't giving her a choice, but she knew she still had one. She suddenly knew she clearly had no business going out with Ian. She hadn't thought of him since he'd sent flowers during her illness. But above all, he didn't know Christ, and she couldn't have a relationship with someone who didn't believe as she did.

"I'm sorry Ian, but I don't think so. I appreciate the invitation, but it just won't work out."

After a pause he asked almost harshly, "And why not?"

This wouldn't be easy. "Ian, we come from two different worlds with different beliefs. How could we hope to make a relationship work? Besides," she added gently, "I like you as a friend, and I'd like us to stay that way. As friends."

The long silence that followed her words brought a physical chill that Jess felt through the phone line. She started to ask if he was still there when he finally spoke. "I won't give up," was the low, harsh reply before the line went dead. Jess hung up the receiver, leaning her head against the wall.

When she'd first met Ian, she thought there might be a cold and ruthless side to him. He was spoiled and used to getting his way. How had Connie escaped such a personality? Returning to the kitchen, she continued what she'd been doing. Connie tried to catch her eye, but she didn't look up. Grandmother never even turned around. Jess knew she'd talk to them both about it later. But not now.

~

After supper the children sat listening to their favorite radio serial while Jess prepared Michael's bottle. As it warmed, she sat in the kitchen with him while Connie filled a kettle with water.

"Your Grandmother wants some tea, and I thought I'd have some as well. How about you?" She reached for cups and saucers.

"Yes, please." Jess tested the bottle before feeding the hungry infant. "You'd think this child never ate."

Connie laughed. "That's what he wants you to think."

"I think you're right."

"Be right back." Connie carried a cup to the living room.

Jess listened to the silence, broken only by Michael's suckling noise as he ate hungrily. She remembered the silence on the phone when Ian called. He'd said he wouldn't give up. He wasn't going to make it easy for her, and she just didn't know what to expect.

Returning to the kitchen, Connie brought their tea to the table and sat down. "Here you go."

"Thanks. I'll wait until his highness finishes. I don't want to accidentally spill any on him."

Connie sipped her own tea then leaned forward, cradling the cup between her hands.

"Ready to tell me what happened before supper with the phone call? From your behavior and your Grandmother's silence, I knew something wasn't right."

"You don't miss much, do you? Ian called. Without trying to offend you, Grandmother doesn't approve of him. She's concerned about his reputation and his life style."

"And she should be. I know Ian very well, and although I love him dearly, I don't want my best friend involved with him."

"Well, that's what he wants," Jess sighed. "He wanted to go out tomorrow night, and it sounded like he expected me to. I told him I didn't want to see him anymore except as friends. He asked why, so I told him we were from different worlds, with different beliefs." She glanced up for Connie's response. She was from the same world as Ian even if she didn't seem like it.

Connie smiled. "It's alright, Jess. I understand. I'm from that world, but I left because I wanted to. Ian's still there, because he wants to be. And concerning the different beliefs, I'm starting to understand what that means. He believes in himself and what he can do for himself. I suppose he took after Mother in that way. Then what did he say?"

"There was a long, chilly silence. I thought he'd hung up then in a cold voice he said, 'I won't give up'. He hung up after that."

"Ian wants his way no matter what. Avoid him, Jess. He's not dangerous, but I've seen him ruthless."

"Well, I don't want hard feelings between us, but that may

not be possible."

They heard voices in the dining room just before Grandmother came in followed by Garth.

He smiled broadly at Jess and Connie then placed a brown paper bag on the table between them. "Good evening, ladies. I come bearing gifts of unspeakable value."

Jess looked at Grandmother. "What's this all about?"

"I've no idea, luv. He wanted to show us all at once." She took a seat at the table.

"Now that I have your attention, feast your eyes on these." Opening the bag he pulled out a bundle of cloth items, displaying them one by one. There were hand-embroidered aprons, guest towels, pillowcases and daintily crocheted baby bonnets and booties.

"Garth!" Jess exclaimed. "These are beautiful! Where on earth did you get them?"

"Mrs. Sixsmith is donating them for the Fair." He loved the flush of excitement on her cheeks and thrilled at the picture she made holding the sleeping Michael in her arms. She'd make a wonderful mother.

"Did she make all these herself?" Connie fingered the fine linen pieces.

"She certainly did."

Grandmother held up an apron. "She's been working on these for a long time. The posters asking for donations were only put up yesterday."

"She's always making things and keeps them on hand. When she needs a gift, she has one ready. She wanted to be the first to donate handmade items."

"I'll call in the morning and thank her," said Connie. "They're simply beautiful. I can't wait to see what other handmade items will be donated."

Grandmother noticed Michael asleep in Jess's arms. "Luv, I'll put Michael to bed. You drink your tea before it's too cold."

"Thanks! My arm's fallen asleep." Handing her the infant, Jess reached for her cup. "Garth, can I fix you some tea?"

"No thanks. I must be going," he said regretfully. "I'm on a call but wanted to drop these by. They'll be good sellers at the Fair."

"They'll be snapped up quickly. I may even purchase an apron myself," said Grandmother as she left the room.

Connie took her cup to the sink. "I have to go, Jess. Mother won't be happy with me for not coming home sooner, but I'm glad I stayed. I'll see you in the morning. Goodnight, Garth."

"Goodnight."

"See you tomorrow and thanks for your help," Jess said

Connie looked at her questioningly before understanding her meaning. "Anytime. Goodnight."

After she'd left Jess folded the items back into the bag.

"Is there a problem, Jess D---?" Garth almost called her Dear. *Watch it.*

"No, nothing to worry about."

"Would you tell me if there were?"

"Maybe," she evaded. "If I thought it was something you could help with, but since it's nothing, we don't have to worry about it now, do we?"

Garth gently caught her hand and her full attention at the same time. Surprised, she looked up. Her cheeks burned, but she couldn't look away from the sincerity in his eyes. "Jess, please come to me if there's ever a problem. If nothing else, I can listen. I've a strong shoulder to lean on or cry on. I mightn't have an answer, but now I know where to find them. And I can help you pray. I'm not very good at it yet, but I'm learning."

Jess smiled, placing her hand over his. "Thank you. That means a lot." She dropped her gaze. "I have some decisions to make, and I'd appreciate your prayers."

"You have them." He didn't push further. Something was bothering her, but he'd bide his time. "Well, I've a patient waiting. See you soon." And he was gone.

~

As Jess climbed into bed, she remembered Ian's call, disturbed more than she'd let on to Connie. He was a worldly man and she'd never be close to him. Handsome and charming, he used those traits to his advantage. She might've fallen for him, but she thanked God she'd seen the real Ian before becoming involved with him.

Her thoughts turned to Garth. What time she'd spent with him showed her how shallow Ian really was. So unlike him Garth was selfless and caring and now loved God. She looked forward to his visits and enjoyed being with him. Tonight she'd thought he almost called her Dear or Darling, but decided that couldn't be. He was just a very good friend.

But as she closed her eyes and drifted off, she knew she was falling in love with him.

Chapter Eighteen

Over the next few days, folks from all over the Dales dropped by with handmade items. Jess and Connie kept a donation inventory: baby clothes, dolls, stuffed animals, crocheted doilies, and knitted sweaters of all sizes, to name a few. A Knaresborough stationary store donated Christmas party decorations. Charlie collected them and after he returned, there was something else to fetch. The list seemed endless. With two weeks until the Fair, there was much to do. The whole community got involved. When people met on the street or in a shop, the conversation invariably turned to the Fair.

One morning after the children left for school, Garth breezed in, a blast of cold air following him. Jess, washing breakfast dishes, turned as he entered.

"Good morning, Sunshine!"

Her breath caught at the light in his eye. "Good morning to you, too. What brings you breezing in so happily?"

"It's a beautiful, sunny day out, if a bit cold. I have the day off and thought perhaps we'd take that ride we missed a few weeks ago. How about it?" He held up a checkered cloth covered basket. "Mrs. Sixsmith packs an amazing lunch basket."

Everything Jess planned to accomplish today flew out the window. They'd been busy with Fair preparations, and a day out was very appealing. "I'll have to tell Grandmother and change into something warmer. Can you wait?"

Coming to stand beside her, Garth stroked a gentle finger down her cheek. She felt herself drowning in his warm gray eyes. "I'd wait forever, if necessary," he whispered.

"Wait forever for what?" Grandmother walked into the kitchen just then, not indicating that she'd noticed their closeness but smiling inwardly.

Garth and Jess each stepped back self-consciously, her cheeks flaming as she returned to the sink.

"I was just saying I'd wait, uh... forever... for her to, um... get ready to go riding with me," Garth stammered lamely.

"I see." Grandmother saw more than they realized. "Where are you riding to?"

"Before I was sick Garth invited me to ride into the Dales but never said where. When I got sick, we had to cancel." Jess cheeks were finally cool enough to turn and face her.

Grandmother looked expectantly at Garth.

"I thought we'd drive to Aysgarth Falls. It's a beautiful ride and the falls are spectacular."

"Oh, yes!" exclaimed Grandmother. "I haven't been there in a long time. We should all take a ride in the spring when it's warmer and the flowers are blooming."

Jess abruptly left the room.

Grandmother realized too late what she'd said. Jess might not be here in the spring. She followed her upstairs, leaving Garth wondering what had happened.

Grandmother knocked on Jess's door.

"Come in."

Jess had changed into a navy wool skirt and a yellow blouse, topping it with a navy cardigan.

"Jess, I'm sorry. I'm so used to you being here that I feel like you'll always be here. It's hard to imagine you leaving because I don't want you to. But I won't pressure you into staying if you want to go back. That's why I haven't mentioned it. It's your decision."

Jess turned from brushing her hair. "I know, Grandmother. It's just that I don't know what I'm supposed to do. I may not be here in the spring." She braided her hair into a single long braid. "I've written the school where I taught to see if they have any positions available. When I hear from them, I'll go from there."

Grandmother hugged Jess. "I love you, Jess. You've very special to me, and as much as I want you to stay, I'll support your decision."

Jess returned her hug. "Thank you. I need to go. Garth's waiting."

"Put everything aside for now and have a wonderful time."

"I will." Jess blew her a kiss and ran downstairs.

~

Garth was right. The day was beautiful! Apparently days like this were rare in wintertime. The temperature was near freezing, but Jess was bundled up and didn't notice. It was exhilarating to be out on such a day. They talked about the Fair and the events of the last week. As Garth drove, Jess enjoyed the countryside. The snow was melting slowly, but the sun was bright on the remaining snow, patches of faded grass poking up here and there. Jess loved the Dales even with its temperamental weather.

Perched on a hillside, Aysgarth village consisted of an old church, a few shops and a gristmill standing on the river bank. Crossing the bridge by the mill they parked on the other side.

Jess was thankful for her warm boots as Garth guided her up the path into a wide-open area, the falls on the left and trees far to the right. Straight ahead the path led to the river above the falls. Here the snow was deeper, and the falls were ice crusted, sparkling brightly in the sun. The water ran steadily beneath the ice and over the rocks.

Standing quietly they listened to the gentle rush of water, the falls dropping gradually from one tier to the next.

"It's so quiet and peaceful here," Jess almost whispered.

"This time of year, but in the spring it's louder with the force of the melted snows. But it's beautiful with the blooming flowers and trees." He remembered Grandmother mentioning that earlier, sending Jess quickly from the room.

"Jess, why did you leave the room when your Grandmother suggested coming here in the spring?"

Sitting on a nearby boulder, Jess looked up at him openly. "Last week I received a letter from Mother's lawyer, asking what I intended to do with my parents' house. He suggested I sell it unless I'm returning to live there. I need to give him an answer in a few weeks. I may not be here in the spring."

Garth felt like he'd been punched in the gut. *No, you can't leave!* He jammed his hands deep inside his pockets and walked to the river bank. He didn't know what he'd expected but this wasn't it. He wanted to pull Jess into his arms, never letting her go.

"Have you made a decision yet?" His voice was surprisingly steady.

"Not yet." Garth gained hope. "I've written to the school where I used to teach to see if any positions are available. Depending on their reply, I'll decide then."

"You know your Grandmother would miss you terribly if you left." *Not to mention me!*

"I know, but she's managed all these years without me and she can again. She said she'd support my decision."

"Have you thought there might be others who'd be affected by your leaving?" he asked gruffly. He coughed to clear his throat.

Jess stood up, walking upstream. He wasn't making this easy.

Garth caught up with her. "I'm sorry, Jess. This can't be an easy decision to make, and I don't want to make it harder than it already is. I'll help pray about it."

"That's the best thing anyone can do for me," she said with a cheerfulness she didn't feel. "God has a purpose. He'll show me when He's ready."

They walked downstream to where more waterfalls fell in tiers, each fall as beautiful as the last. They talked about Grandmother, the children, and the Dale folk Jess had come to know during her stay.

"You know, folks here have accepted me and considered me one of them since I've been here." Jess gazed at the scenery around them. "They pay no mind that I'm not English."

"But you're half English, and they know that."

"I think they'd treat me the same if I weren't."

"They're simply good folk, Jess, and they know a good person when they see one. They've also noticed how you help not only your grandmother, but the whole community." He chuckled. "Do you know what they call you? The Yorkshire Lass."

Jess stopped on the path, raising sad eyes toward the sky. "If I leave, it'll be very hard."

Garth stepped in front of her, taking her chilled face between his gloved hands, his gaze burrowing into hers. "Then don't go," he spoke gruffly, lowering his face to hers.

Jess closed her eyes and thrilled as his lips touched hers, wanting him to wrap her tightly in his arms. She could face anything held securely by him.

The kiss, brief but tender, left Jess wanting more, her heart racing with the feelings welling inside her.

Garth longed to pull her close and kiss her until she promised to stay, but he'd already made things difficult with his first kiss. He stepped back, grasping her hands gently.

"I'm sorry, Jess. I shouldn't complicate things for you. You've already a lot to think about." Dropping her hands he draped a friendly arm across her shoulders. "Come on, we've lunch waiting in the car, and I don't know about you, but all this fresh air has made me hungry."

Jess wouldn't admit that her confused feelings had chased away her appetite. As they headed toward the car, she determined she wouldn't let him see how much his kiss had affected her.

~

Connie entered the back door quietly, hoping Mother wasn't around but was surprised to find Ian in the kitchen. Slouched in a chair in the breakfast nook, his feet were propped on another chair. If Mother saw his shoes on the chair, she'd be angry, but Connie realized he didn't care at this point. A half-empty bottle of liquor stood beside an empty tumbler on the table.

Without looking up as she quietly closed the door, he spoke with slurred words. "Shneakin' in, Sis? Now, now, Mudder dear would never approof. Those do-gooders at that orph'nage of yours are too high and mighty for their own good. I'd hate to shee you become like 'em," he sneered.

Connie approached her brother. "You're drunk, Ian, and you don't know what you're saying."

"Don't I?" Dropping his feet to the floor loudly, he sat forward, leaning on the table. "Your 'ittle friend turned me down cold. I don't like that. She'll be shorry." Falling silent, he dropped his head onto his folded arms, then stirred and repeated, "Yessiree, she'll be real shorry." He snored as he dozed off.

Connie wasn't sure if he knew what he was saying or if the liquor was talking. Picking up the bottle, she poured the golden liquid down the sink drain. Ashamed of her brother, she'd never seen him this drunk. Going to the parlor she brought back an afghan, covered him with it and turned the lights low.

In her room she sat wearily on her bed. Ian's words disturbed her, but tomorrow he probably wouldn't even remember what he'd said. Perhaps she should call Robert. No, she wouldn't bother him with it.

He'd told her how he turned to God for guidance with his problems, but she didn't have a relationship with God. In her heart she knew she needed Him. Dropping to her knees by the bed, she felt hot tears on her cheeks.

"Oh, dear God," she cried softly. "I need you in my life. Seeing Ian, I'm ashamed. But I'm just as sinful and ashamed of my own sins. I've followed my own way without caring about You. But Robert says You're real, and he loves You so much. Please forgive me. Help me live my life for You. And please help Jess. I love her like a sister, and please help Ian to leave her alone. Thank you, Father."

She knew God had heard her prayer and felt a peace like

she'd never felt before. After climbing into bed, she fell asleep, resting in her new-found Father's love.

~

Garth placed a practiced hand on the carotid artery, already certain the man was dead and had been for hours, but as a physician he had to check.

Pulling the sheet over the man's head, he stood, sighing heavily. "May I use your phone to call the police, George?"

"Course you can," replied George Higgins.

"They'll want to question you about finding the body. Don't allow Mrs. Higgins out here."

"No, I won't. She'd likely faint dead away, she would."

Thirty minutes later a police car stopped in front of the farmhouse. Inspector Paul Kendall climbed out, followed by two uniformed officers

"Hello, Paul." Garth approached his friend.

"You know, the last time we spoke I told you to call and we'd get together. This wasn't what I had in mind," Paul said grimly.

"I know." Garth led Paul behind an old wagon by the sheep pasture wall where the body lay. Kneeling down, he pulled back the sheet. Paul held up a lantern, examining the body.

"So, we've another one. No identification and his clothes suggest hard times. Whoever's doing this is a real lunatic." He shook his head, disgusted. "The coroner's on his way. I wouldn't get my hopes up that he'll find much. This psychopath doesn't leave many clues."

He stood up. "Who found him?"

Garth led him inside to meet the Higgins's while the two uniformed officers guarded the body.

"George, this is Inspector Paul Kendall of the North Yorkshire Police. He has some questions."

"Nice to meet ya, sir." George nodded politely. "Ask away."

Paul asked when George had found the body and how. Had he seen the man anytime before he'd been killed?

"I found him 'bout an hour ago. I went out to check me sheep. The gate's near there, ya know. Soon as I found him, I called Garth. I knowed he was dead so I didn' touch him. Ain't never seen him before. Dead or alive."

"And you, Mrs. Higgins? Have you noticed anyone unusual around recently?"

"No, sir." She poured coffee for the men. "Just like me man here, I never seen nothin'. And I'm sure I'd remember if I did."

After further questioning, Paul thanked Mrs. Higgins for the coffee, and he and Garth went outside to find the coroner had arrived and begun a preliminary examination.

"Well, Morgan, what can you tell us?" asked Paul.

"Not much, I'm afraid, until I perform a thorough autopsy." Returning his instruments to his bag, he stood. "However, I can tell you he wasn't murdered here. He was killed elsewhere and brought here. He bled out, but there's none around the body. Like all the rest, he wasn't killed in these clothes, although they're probably his. He was then redressed and dumped here. He died in the same manner as all the rest: repeated stab wounds to the heart. Quick, powerful thrusts right up to the hilt, suggesting the murderer is a man. Unless she was very strong, a woman couldn't inflict this much damage, but we won't rule it out. An ambulance will arrive to take him to the hospital. I'll jump on it and give you a detailed report in the morning."

"Another late night, eh, Morgan?" sighed Paul.

"Another late night." An ambulance pulled into the barnyard. "Here's the wagon, lads. I'll see you later." Tipping his hat, he approached the ambulance driver.

Paul turned to Garth. "Will the Higgins's keep quiet about this?'

Garth chuckled. "I wouldn't be surprised if half the Dales know about it already. If one didn't grab the phone when we walked out, then the other one did."

"It's always hard to keep something like this quiet. It'll surely be in the morning paper. Well, next time you want to get together, let's choose something a little more mundane, shall we?"

"Agreed!"

Paul walked away, suddenly turning back. "By the way, the young American woman you introduced me to at the hospital. Are you seeing her?"

"I'm working on it. Why?"

"You'd be a fool if you weren't. Cheerio."

Chapter Nineteen

*"J*ess, I have something to tell you." Connie folded a towel and dropped it into the clothesbasket on a chair by the kitchen table.

Jess knew from her voice that Connie was excited about something. "What is it?"

"You know how I've been asking you and Robert about God? Well, the night before last I gave my life to Him."

Jess gave her a hug. "Praise the Lord! First Garth, now you! God's answering prayers!"

"I appreciate those prayers." Connie paused, looking at Jess uncertainly. "That night when I got home, I found Ian drunk. I was ashamed for him then realized I was just as bad. I know I can't answer to God for Ian, but I have to for myself, so I asked for His forgiveness." Picking up another towel, she continued hesitantly. "There's something else you should know."

"What?"

"Ian said you'd be sorry for turning him down. Perhaps he didn't know what he was saying, or perhaps it was the liquor talking. He fell asleep, so he may not even remember it."

Jess picked up another towel, folding it. "What can he do? We only went out once. It must've been the drink."

"I hope so." Connie effectively changed the subject. "Are you going to bake something for the Christmas Fair baking contest?"

"I thought I might. How about you? What are you baking?"

Connie laughed. "Me? I can't cook. The judges would be ill then I'd lose for sure. No, I don't think so. You'll have to do the baking for this contest."

Jess propped her hands on her hips. "Now just a minute. You've cooked breakfast for the children several times. You mean you really don't cook?"

"No, I don't. I've learned from watching you and your grandmother. I was always shooed from the kitchen by Mother or the cook. Anything more than brewing tea, I learned here."

Jess shook her head in disbelief. "You're a fast learner. If you can learn to cook breakfast from watching someone else, why can't you bake something for the contest? We'll find a simple recipe and experiment. Would you at least try?"

"I don't know," Connie said doubtfully. "I wouldn't know where to begin."

"With a recipe book." Jess reached for the shelf above the stove and pulled down a worn cookbook, flipping through the pages. "Here's a simple recipe. First, check the oven temperature and set it. See? It tells you here. Then collect all your ingredients, bowls and utensils, and then follow the directions. It's easier than you think."

"I suppose I could try. Do you really think I could?"

"Of course! And I'll help if you need me to."

"Well, I'd have to bake here. Mother would become apoplectic if I baked at home."

Jess handed Connie the recipe book. "Here, find something you'd like to try. I'll finish folding clothes and put them away then we'll begin Beginners Baking Class."

Later, when Connie opened the oven door, removing the cake she'd so painstakingly baked under Jess's watchful eye, Jess exclaimed, "Wow! I thought you'd never baked before. That looks delicious!"

"Looks can be deceiving. The real test will be the taste."

"Then let's taste it!" Jess gathered plates and forks as Charlie entered the back door, a box of wood in his arms. "Charlie, would you taste something for us?"

Setting down the box, Charlie closed the back door. "What might that be, lass?"

"Connie baked a cake and we want your opinion of how it turned out."

"With pleasure! I love cake." Removing his coat, he accepted the plate Jess handed him.

"Jess, perhaps you should explain that this is the first time I've ever baked anything," Connie said apprehensively.

Charlie shook his head. "No matter, Miss Constance. I don't mind tryin' it. Looks tasty, it does." He took a bite, his brows furrowing thoughtfully. Then his eyes lit up. "Miss Constance! This *is* delicious. You say you never baked before?"

Connie's cheeks flushed with pleasure. "Thank you, Charlie. This is the first."

Jess ate some, readily agreeing. "Connie, you must make one for the fair. It's wonderful! I bet you'll be trying out that cookbook some more, too."

"It was fun, but don't tell Mother. She'd faint if she knew her daughter was actually cooking." She shuddered in disgust then laughed happily.

"What's so funny?" Garth entered the kitchen.

Jess placed another slice of cake on a plate, handing it to him. "Here, try this."

Taking the plate, he ate it as instructed, all eyes on his face eagerly awaiting his opinion. After another bite he looked from one to another. "Why are you all staring? What's wrong?"

"Nothing," Jess replied happily. "How's the cake?"

"Delicious. Why shouldn't it be?"

Connie smiled apologetically at Garth. "I'm sorry you weren't told beforehand," she quirked an eyebrow at Jess, "but, with Jess's help, this is my first attempt at baking. Charlie and Jess were tasting it when you came in and you were recruited for the taste test, too. As for what's so funny, I said if my mother knew I was cooking she'd probably faint."

"Then we won't tell her, will we, fellows? And when Grandmother returns from Bertha's she'll try it and agree."

"You got that right." Charlie cut another slice.

"Mums the word," agreed Garth. "But why are you baking?"

"There will be a baking contest at the Christmas Fair," explained Jess. "Afterwards the food will be sold, the proceeds going toward the Christmas gifts. Connie was trying out a recipe."

Garth eyed Jess questioningly. "And are you entering the contest?"

"Of course!" She wrinkled her nose at him. "But I'm not telling what."

She caught her breath at the light in his eyes. "Is that a challenge for me to find out?"

Jess turned to wash up the plates. "I don't know what you're talking about."

Charlie cleared his throat self-consciously. "Well, Miss Constance, I don't think you have anythin' to worry about. Your cake'll be real tasty, it will. Now I need to get to the fire, before it goes out."

"Thanks, Charlie," said Connie, turning to Jess. "I'll do those dishes. I used them, so I'll wash them."

Garth put down his empty plate and, leaning against the counter, crossed his arms, waiting for Jess to turn and face him.

Reluctantly she gave up the dishrag and turned from the sink. "So what brings you here today?"

"Actually, I've a donation for the Fair." Reaching into his pocket he pulled out a fifty-pound note. "It was donated anonymously, and the donor wants it used wherever it's needed, either in preparation for the Fair or toward the gifts."

Jess held out her hand and he laid the note in it. Her cheeks warmed as his fingers brushed her palm. Her gaze flew to his, and what she saw tripped up her heartbeat. Attempting a casual tone, she heard the breathlessness in her voice. "Please tell whoever donated this thank you. It'll go a long way in helping out. I just wish we could tell them somehow."

"I'll make sure they know," Garth spoke softly. He wouldn't tell her he was the donor. This seemed the best way for him to contribute. With not much time to help, he knew they needed money.

"I can't wait to shop for the gifts," said Connie, her attention on the dishes. "It'll be fun buying things for the folks that they wouldn't buy for themselves."

"Which reminds me, Garth," said Jess. "Since you're always in and out of the homes in the Dales, could you help us compile a list of individuals and families who need help this Christmas?"

"Certainly! I'll work on it the next few days and get back to you. When do you need it?"

"Not until the Fair."

"I'll have it to you before then." He walked toward the back door.

"Thank you." Jess followed him. "I hope you know how much we appreciate all your help."

One hand on the door knob, he asked offhandedly, "Who me? I haven't done anything."

"Yes, you have." Jess smiled, crinkling the bill in her hand.

Looking into her eyes Garth knew he hadn't fooled her. He reached up, gently cupping her cheek. "I wish I could help more. Depending on my schedule, perhaps I can help with decorating the barn,"

Jess found it hard to breath. "I hope so." Surely he knew how his touch affected her breathing. Surely the whole world could hear her heartbeat.

"I'll see what I can do." He let his hand drop from her silky cheek. He couldn't stand like this all day, as much as he might want to. Dared he hope she loved him as much as he loved her? The look in her eyes told him she felt something. Was it love?

"See you soon," Garth promised and was gone.

Jess stood by the door, not realizing the minutes ticking away. Connie came over, draping an arm across her shoulders. "You care for him, don't you?" It was more a statement of understanding than a question.

Jess turned to deny the words, but seeing the understanding in Connie's eyes, she couldn't. "Yes, I do."

Chapter Twenty

When Jess answered the knock at the door, it took a moment to recognize the gentleman. "Why, Mr. Cameron. Please come in."

"Thank you, Miss Montgomery." He removed his hat and gloves. "Is my daughter here?"

"Yes, she is." Jess wondered what brought this wealthy man to the orphanage. "Please have a seat, and I'll get her."

"Thank you." Sitting near the fire, he stretched out chilly hands to its warmth.

In the kitchen Jess whispered excitedly, "Connie! Your father's here."

Connie whirled in surprise. "What? Father? Here?"

Jess nodded, reaching for the teakettle.

Connie removed her apron and hurried to the living room. Mr. Cameron stood as she entered and gave him a quick kiss. "Father, what are you doing here?"

"Well, my dear, don't tell your mother or I'll never hear the end of it. I've a donation for your Christmas Fair."

"A donation?"

"Have a seat and I'll explain." He waited until she sat down then seated himself.

"Constance, I understand what you're doing here is important to you as well as to these people, but your mother doesn't understand. Her idea of charity is giving a ball to raise money for the needy, but that's as close to charity as she'll ever get. Don't feel harshly toward her for what she says. She loves you very much and only wants what's best for you, but she's never known what it means to be needy. Her family gave her everything. However, I do understand. I often reflect on where I started and how far I've come. I understand the needs of the Dale Folk are real."

"Yes, Father, they are. Since working here, I've realized that money isn't everything. It doesn't bring happiness. People bring happiness. The close loving relationships they share are what get them through hard times."

Her father nodded sadly. "Yes, but sometimes we forget that, don't we." He paused before continuing. "Anyway, the reason I'm here is to tell you I want to help with the Christmas Fair."

Jess brought in the tea tray and, pouring a cup, handed it to Mr. Cameron.

Connie looked at her father questioningly. "You mentioned a donation. What kind?"

"I've purchased several farm animals and am donating them for the auction. There are three cows, five sheep, and three large pigs, all show quality."

"Mr. Cameron!" Jess exclaimed, dropping into a chair. "Why, that's wonderful!"

"I don't know what to say! It's fantastic!" Jumping up, Connie flung her arms around her father's neck. "Thank you! This will be a fair everyone will remember."

Mr. Cameron's face reddened as he cleared his throat. "Yes, well, ah-hum. The animals will be delivered to George Higgins' farm two days before the fair along with enough feed to keep them until after they're auctioned. Please check with George to ensure that day is satisfactory with him." He stood, turning his hat between his hands. "Well, I must be going. I have another appointment shortly."

Connie smiled at her father's embarrassment. Every now and then he descended from his pedestal to be the father she loved, and when he grew uncomfortable, he climbed back up, pulling on the façade of social correctness. Loving him dearly, she enjoyed the times when he was more relaxed. Unfortunately, it was usually when her mother was absent.

"Mr. Cameron," Jess was saying. "Auctioning farm animals will be a real draw for the Dale folk, and prize-winning show animals at that. How can we thank you enough?"

Waving her words away, he returned his bowler hat to his head and bowed slightly. "Think nothing of it, but remember, if Mrs. Cameron finds out, I'll deny everything. Good day." He returned to the big shiny black car awaiting him. The chauffeur opened the door and he climbed in.

Jess closed the door, leaning against it. "What a blessing! Is God good, or what?"

Connie nodded solemnly. "I'm finding out just how good He really is. I'd never dreamed this could happen."

Jess linked her arm through Connie's. "Come on. Let's see if Grandmother's returned from Bertha's. I can't wait to tell her the news."

~

As the Fair date drew closer, Connie, Jess and Robert doubted they'd be ready in time. Grandmother, the children and folks from the church pitched in to get things done. Jess altered Claire's dress. Connie baked another cake...just for practice. Lists were checked off and prizes wrapped. Jess and Grandmother decided what they'd bake for the contest.

On Friday, the day before the Fair, Jess, Connie and Robert met to decorate George's barn. Inside, at the far end of the barn, several animals were stalled.

Setting down the box of decorations she carried, Jess approached them. Sure enough, there were three cows, five sheep and three pigs. Removing her gloves, she stroked the course hair of one cow that turned her head sideways trying to get closer to Jess. Her slippery gray tongue whipped out, swiping across Jess's cheek. Surprised, Jess stepped back.

"Thanks, but no cow kisses, please!" Laughing, she pulled out a handkerchief, wiping her cheek.

Bringing in more boxes, Connie and Robert laughed. "She's an affectionate cow, Jess," said Robert. "I think she likes you."

"You could bid on her," teased Connie. "You might even get her at a good price."

Retrieving her box, Jess shook her head. "Again, thanks, but no thanks."

Before long everything was unloaded and they began decorating. The day before, Robert, Charlie and some of the children had filled boxes with running cedar and pine boughs they'd found. Jess decided to hang a large beribboned pine wreath above the inside of the main barn door. George had left a tall ladder for their use. Propping the ladder in front of the door, Jess slung the wreath over her shoulder, climbing carefully. As she reached to hang it on a nail, someone opened the door, bumping the ladder and knocking it backwards. Before she knew what was happening, Jess felt herself falling. It felt like slow motion as she braced to hit the floor.

She never made it that far. Caught between strong arms and a hard chest, she lay momentarily, eyes closed tight, unsure what had happened. It registered that Robert couldn't have caught her. He was clear across the barn when she'd climbed up.

Her eyes flew open, meeting Garth's horrified gaze only inches from hers. "Garth," she whispered softly.

His look of horror stilled her rapid heartbeat. His face drained of color and his breathing rapid, he held her tightly as he spoke in a ragged voice. "Oh, my... Jess! I'm sorry! I'd no idea you were there. If I hadn't caught you...." Leaving the sentence unfinished, he slowly set her on her feet. "Can you stand?"

Jess averted her gaze. "Yes, I'm fine." Her heartbeat picked up where it had left off. She looked back at him, seeing his concern. "I really am, Garth, but thank you for catching me. It would've been a nasty fall if you hadn't."

He still held gently onto her arms. "Yes, it would've been," his voice gruff.

"Jess!" Connie and Robert approached them. "Are you alright? I saw you falling but couldn't move fast enough to help. Thank God Garth caught you."

"I thank Him and Garth!" Jess looked sincerely at Garth.

Retrieving the wreath from the floor, Garth steadied the ladder, climbed up and hung the wreath on the nail. "How's that?"

Jess eyed it thoughtfully, thankful she had something to concentrate on besides the look in Garth's eyes and the feel of his strong arms around her. She still felt their pressure. And the look in his eyes.... *No, concentrate on the wreath.*

"It...it needs to go left a bit. Yes, that's better."

Climbing down, Garth moved the ladder to the wall beside the door. Turning around, he eyed her closely. "Are you sure you're alright? Perhaps you should sit for a bit." He glanced at Connie for support.

"You're the doctor." Connie returned to what she was doing.

"Garth, I'm fine." Jess approached a stack of boxes. "Besides, there's too much to do right now."

He looked at Robert who shrugged his shoulders and returned to work.

"You're stubborn, you know that?" Garth said gruffly, running an exasperated hand through his hair.

She laughed happily. "So I've been told. Have you come to help or to tell me I'm stubborn?"

He sighed heavily. "I came to help. I'd no idea I would almost cause an accident that could've injured you."

Jess laid a gentle hand on his arm. "But I wasn't, Garth. Now please, let's forget it. There's a lot to do, and we can enjoy doing it."

She suddenly wished she hadn't phrased it quite that way. The light in his eyes burned her cheeks. Again. Looking into his eyes was dangerous for her heart.

At lunchtime, Mrs. Higgins brought a basket of food and a huge thermos of hot tea for them. Hungry from the morning's labor, they ate heartily. Jess glanced around the cheerfully decorated barn. From the loft Robert and Garth had hung a huge welcome banner. Then they'd climbed up and carefully hung green, red and gold streamers from the oak beam rafters, making Jess nervous as they'd worked. Trying not to watch, she couldn't help glancing up often until they were back safely on the ground.

Several folks stopped by with tables and chairs. Jess and Connie covered the tables with borrowed tablecloths and simple holiday centerpieces then hung red crepe paper bows on the support posts and over the animal stalls. Robert and Garth set up a tall Christmas tree that George had cut that morning then they'd enjoyed decorating it. After building game booths from donated wood, they decorated them while George cleaned out the old potbelly stove and brought in a good supply of wood. Robert and Garth returned to the orphanage for the auction items which Jess and Connie displayed next to the newly built bandstand.

It was getting late when they finally stopped to consider their handiwork. George's barn was very festive indeed.

Jess rubbed the back of her neck. "I never realized how many muscles I don't normally use. A nice long soak in hot water is in order."

"Sounds delightful." Connie slumped onto a nearby chair. "I'm bushed."

"And rightly so," Robert laughed. "You've both gone non-stop all day."

"And you two haven't?" Jess pointed at Robert and Garth. "You've not exactly been twiddling your thumbs. We couldn't have done it without you, you know."

Garth propped a foot on a nearby hay bale, leaning his elbow on his knee. "I'm glad I could help. Dad handled the practice so I could."

"Please thank him for us," Robert said. "You were a tremendous help."

"If it had been too hectic he'd have called." Garth pulled out his pocket watch. "I'll call and see how things went."

"You can call from the orphanage." Jess offered. "We've

missed supper. Why don't you all come over and eat?"

They agreed it was a good idea. Having enjoyed the camaraderie, they weren't ready for it to end yet. Connie climbed into Charlie's pickup with Robert while Garth led Jess to his car.

Leaning her head against the seat cushion, Jess relaxed. Garth glanced at her as he started the car. "It's been quite a day."

"Yes, it has. I don't know if I'm more tired or hungry. I'm glad George lives close to Grandmother. If we had to drive any further, I'd fall asleep."

"I have a very comfortable shoulder," he offered, a teasing note in his voice.

Jess sat up straight in her seat. "Thanks, but I can stay awake."

The low rumble of Garth's chuckle sent warmth flooding Jess's cheeks. She was thankful the interior of the car was dark.

Chapter Twenty-One

*J*ess slipped into the forest green velvet dress, surveying her reflection in the Cheval mirror. She and Grandmother had found it in a little dress shop in Harrogate. Ankle length and with a rounded neckline, its skirt draped softly from the empire waist. Long full sleeves gathered at the wrists with green satin cuffs. Grandmother said the dark green highlighted Jess's honey-colored hair. Jess loved the soft fabric that should keep her warm in the old stone barn.

Hearing a light tap at her door, Jess opened it to find Claire in her "new" dress. "Claire! You look beautiful! When is Joshua picking you up?"

"Soon. I'm a bit nervous." She twisted her fingers together.

"I'm sure you are." Jess put her arm around Claire's slender shoulders. "You'll have a wonderful time."

"Claire," Grandmother called from downstairs. "Joshua's here, luv."

Claire looked at Jess, crossing her fingers on both hands. "Wish me luck."

Jess took the girl's hands, uncrossing the tense fingers. "You don't need luck. God's with you and you'll do fine."

Claire nodded and turned to run downstairs. Then taking a deep breath, forced herself to descend slowly.

Pulling back the window curtain Jess watched as the teenagers left the house. As Joshua helped Claire into his father's horse-drawn sleigh, Claire looked up and waved at Jess.

Downstairs Jess helped load the children into the truck bed, then holding Michael, climbed into the cab with Charlie and Grandmother. Their baked contest entries were secured within a crate in the back with Jason holding tightly.

When they arrived, Jess found the musicians on the bandstand setting up. Connie reviewed her last minute list while Robert waited by the door to greet the first arrivals. Jess and Grandmother placed their desserts on the contest entry table.

"Yum!" Connie stopped at the table.

"Well, I plan to give the other contestants a run for the prize." Grandmother winked. "Knowing how the local ladies cook, I'd hate to be a judge. It'll be a tough decision."

As the game volunteers arrived Jess and Connie helped them set up. The children played tag while they waited for their friends to arrive.

George Higgins entered with Martha who set her cake on the table. "Evenin', ladies." He tipped his tweed cap. "This here's real fancy lookin'. Ya did a bang up job, ya did. Don't look like me barn no more. A regular party house, it is. The last time we had a party here, was long afore the war. And it didn't look half as good."

"Now, George, don't get started on that. We've heard it all afore. Come now." Martha smiled at the ladies and grabbed George's arm, pulling him away.

"Thank you, Martha," Grandmother whispered. "Get George started reminiscing and we'll be here a while."

The musicians played Christmas tunes as folks arrived. Ladies added their desserts to the contest table as food donations filled the crates by the front door. Robert greeted everyone as they entered.

Grandmother was in charge of serving the supper that would begin shortly. She and several ladies had prepared huge pots of soups and stews. Baked bread, donated by a Harrogate bakery, was delivered fresh and hot.

Garth entered and shook Robert's hand, speaking with him while his eyes scanned the room for someone else.

Robert chuckled. "If you're looking for Jess, I saw her near the makeshift kitchen. She's helping the ladies prepare supper."

"Am I that obvious?"

"To me you are, but I know how you feel about her. Perhaps it's time you told her." He turned to greet more people as they entered.

Garth slowly drifted around the room, stopping to speak with folks as he went. He spotted Jess slicing bread into baskets to be set on the tables.

His heart kicked into high gear as he watched her work. She was gorgeous! Her green dress set off her slenderness, highlighting her hair. She'd twisted it into a loose chignon, but wisps had slipped out, framing her flushed cheeks. He recalled the feel of her in his arms as he'd caught her yesterday. Oh, to hold her close again! She laughed at something one of the ladies said, the sweet sound reaching his ears. If she could only love him back. If she'd only stay in England, he'd teach her to love him. He shook himself mentally. *Get hold of yourself, lad. You're acting like a lovesick schoolboy. Well, I've got the lovesick part right. Help me, dear God,* he prayed. *I love her so much.*

"Good evening, ladies." He approached the table.

Jess looked up as Garth spoke, catching her breath at the sight of him in a tan corduroy jacket and brown wool sweater, a white shirt collar peering from the top. He'd run his fingers through his dark hair before approaching the table, but already the endearing stubborn forelock had fallen forward. She busied her fingers, ensuring they wouldn't reach up and smooth it back into place.

"Good evening, Garth." She spoke casually while reaching for another loaf of warm bread.

"Why, Garth!" exclaimed Bertha Myers, beside Jess. "I haven't seen you in a while. But then Frank and I have been very fortunate so far this winter. We've not been sick once. But the winter's young, you know."

"I'm glad to hear it, Mrs. Myers." He smiled at the elderly lady. "I wish you continued good health. Perhaps I'll see you on the street in Lofthouse sometime. I'd prefer that over a visit due to illness."

"As would I, lad. If you'll excuse me, Jess, I'll see what else Morag has for me to do. You've got this in hand."

As she left, Garth stepped closer to the table, ramming his hands into his trouser pockets. "You look lovely this evening, Jess." Trying to keep his voice casual, he couldn't help as huskiness slipped in.

She looked up, smiling. "Thank you. Grandmother and I found this dress in Harrogate. I hadn't been shopping since I've been here, so I splurged."

"I'm glad you did. It's breathtaking," he breathed softly.

Jess caught the look in his eyes and the tone of his voice. As the telltale warmth crept into her cheeks, she was unaware that it enhanced the picture she made. For once she couldn't drag her eyes from his and was relieved when Robert spoke from the musician's platform. Dropping her gaze, she filled the last basket with bread.

"Ladies, gentlemen, and children," Robert spoke loudly. "Welcome to the Christmas Fair! Let's give a hand to all those who've worked hard in preparing for this event."

As everyone applauded, Garth turned to look, and when he turned back around, he spotted the back of Jess's dress disappearing behind a group of people. Furrowing his brow, he started to follow, but was suddenly caught by the arm. An elder of the church was speaking to him, and he forced himself to concentrate on his words.

Jess slipped behind a stack of crates. Putting her hands to her warm cheeks, she closed her eyes, trying to still her breathing. She must stop reacting this way whenever Garth appeared!

"Jess, are you alright?" Connie whispered, suddenly at her side.

Jess opened her eyes, nodding slowly.

"I saw Garth speaking to you. Did he upset you?"

"No, Garth's always the perfect gentleman and would never offend me. It's just… I feel…, well…, a little confused."

"About what?"

Jess shook her head. "I don't know how I should feel right now. I may return home soon, but the thought of leaving hurts so much." She looked at Connie helplessly.

"I'm not really experienced myself, but I've heard that love can hurt." Connie placed a hand on Jess's arm. "Do you think he loves you?"

Jess shook her head again. "I don't know. He's never said anything, but sometimes there's something in his voice or in his eyes that makes my heart race." She laughed lightly. "Pretty silly, huh? Wishful thinking, maybe? Besides, he's friendly and kind to everyone, and there's a fair to run so this will have to wait. Come on." They stepped from behind the crates to see the dinner line forming.

Jess ladled chicken soup from a cast iron pot into bowls, handing them to people in the line. She was unaware of Garth's presence until she held out a bowl and he reached for it, his fingers lightly touching hers. Her gaze instantly flew to his face. Jerking slightly, she spilled soup on the table.

"I'm sorry, Garth." She reached for a towel. "Did it burn you?"

Garth grinned in delight at her confusion. "Not at all. It's all on the table. Here, I'll do that." He reached for the towel, intentionally touching her hand again. Jerking back, she banged her elbow on the cast iron pot.

"I don't know what's wrong with me." She rubbed her elbow gingerly. "Just clumsy tonight, I suppose."

Garth wiped up the soup and laid down the towel. "Are you alright? You hit that pot pretty hard."

Jess picked up another bowl, filled it, and handed it to the man waiting behind Garth. "I'm fine." She busied herself filling more bowls.

The line had backed up behind Garth, so he moved on;

thrilled that she was so aware of him. It gave him hope.

After everyone was served, Jess filled a bowl, took some bread, and joined Grandmother, who sat chatting with some ladies.

Grandmother observed her closely. "Jess, luv. Are you alright? I saw what happened at the serving table. Your cheeks are flushed. You're not taking ill again, are you?"

Jess avoided Grandmother's gaze as she broke off a bite of bread. "No, I'm fine. Just a bit clumsy."

Grandmother spotted Garth approaching their table. "Garth, luv," she called as he approached. Jess accidently dropped her spoon into her soup, splashing some onto the tablecloth. Grandmother looked at her curiously then back to Garth as he sat opposite Jess.

Jess retrieved her spoon, casually glancing at him then back at her bowl.

"Garth, I'm glad to see you here," Grandmother was saying. "I wasn't sure you'd make it."

His eyes rested on Jess's downcast face. "I wouldn't have missed it for anything. Besides, Dad and I both came. If anyone needs us they know where to find us. Most everyone's here tonight anyway."

"Neville's here as well?" Grandmother asked in surprise, her eyes scanning the room.

Garth looked around. "He's here somewhere."

Jess was thankful for Grandmother's presence when she suddenly slid her chair back from the table. "Excuse me, my luvs, but I need to speak to someone."

Jess groaned inwardly. Maybe Garth would see someone he needed to speak with and would go away. His presence was making her uncomfortable.

He sat quietly as she finished her supper. She glanced up and found him watching her. If she wasn't self-conscious before, she certainly was now.

He leaned forward on his elbows. "The musicians are really good together, aren't they?"

"Yes, they are." *Ah, a safe subject.* "They practiced a lot to prepare for tonight."

One musician stepped forward and began playing bagpipes, the other instruments joining in. An older gentleman stepped forward, calling everyone to the floor. Jess, prepared to sit and watch, was suddenly pulled to her feet and into the line of people forming a huge circle in the center of the barn.

"It's a Scottish Reel," Garth explained. "Just follow my lead."

The music began slowly as Jess imitated what Garth and the others did. She missed several steps but noticed she wasn't the only one. Soon she caught on, and as the tempo grew and the circle moved faster, she realized this was fun. She laughed as Garth missed a step then tried to catch up, making her laugh even more. Suddenly her shoe came off, and as she reached for it, it skittered between feet as someone unknowingly kicked it. Unsure what to do, she saw it flung through the air, landing in the middle of the circle.

Garth chuckled. "Keep going. We'll fetch it later."

Shrugging her shoulders, Jess concentrated on the quick steps of the reel.

Just when she thought she had the hang of it, the music ended. Everyone applauded as they dispersed from the floor. Jess tried to catch her breath when, without warning, Garth swung her up into his arms and carried her to a chair by the wall. "Don't move. I'll be right back."

He soon returned with two cups of punch and her shoe tucked beneath his arm. "Here, this should help." He handed her a cup and set the second one on another chair then taking the shoe from under his arm, he knelt down, tenderly lifting her foot. Jess's breath caught as his gentle fingers removed bits of straw from the bottom of her stocking clad foot then replaced the shoe.

"Did you enjoy the reel?" He took the seat beside her.

"Yes! I haven't moved that fast in a while. Half shoeless, no less. I assume the Scottish are in good health if they do this often."

Garth chuckled. "I haven't danced a reel in ages. I'm out of practice."

"You looked perfect to me. I couldn't have done it without your lead. You made it seem easy."

"I'm glad you enjoyed it." Noting her flushed face and tousled hair, he longed to reach out and touch her cheek. Shifting in his seat, he ran a finger under his collar. "It's quite warm in here, don't you think?"

Jess noticed he'd discarded his jacket earlier. "A little. Why don't you remove your sweater? With this crowd, I don't think George has stoked the stove much."

Before Garth could comment, Connie approached. "Garth, we need another judge for the baking contest. Would you help us out?"

He looked at Jess who smiled brightly, nodding her head in agreement. "Alright." He handed his punch cup to her and winked. "At least I get dessert first."

Setting down the cups, Jess followed them to the judging table where the crowd was gathering. Garth took his place behind the table beside four other men. There were at least forty-five desserts spread across the tables waiting to be tasted. A lady handed each of them a plate and so the judging began.

Jess and Connie watched as the judges tasted the desserts one by one. Occasionally their brows rose and their eyes lit up. With the not so tasty samples, they quietly sat the plates on the table, moving on to the next. All the ladies stood with rapt attention, awaiting the final decision. Once during the judging, Garth glanced at Jess then taking a bite of the dessert on his plate, he winked at her. She simply smiled back.

Finally the judges laid down their forks and huddled together, comparing notes. Their final decision written on a piece of paper, they handed it to Robert. Glancing at it briefly, he spoke to the crowd.

"Ladies and gentlemen, the judges have made their decision. However, before I announce the winners, I'd like to thank everyone who entered the contest to help raise money for those in need. Now, we'll begin with the third place winner." Clearing his throat, he looked across the crowd. "Third place goes to Mrs. George Higgins." Applause followed the excited lady as she split the crowd, making her way to the front. Robert handed her a bundle of wooden spoons and shiny new utensils wrapped in a red bow. Nodding toward the crowd she thanked the judges.

"Second place goes to Mrs. Mildred Simms." Mildred approached, hands on her flushed cheeks. She received a shiny new stainless steel pot and lid. Thanking the judges graciously she returned to her husband's side.

"First place goes to..." and he paused for effect, "Miss Jessica Montgomery."

Jess didn't think she'd heard him right, until Connie squeezed her arm, pushing her toward the platform.

Feeling awkward, she stepped up beside Robert. Grandmother was waving happily. Applause and cheers rang out as Robert handed her a brand new box of stainless steel cookware.

"Congratulations to the 'Yorkshire Lass'." Robert joined in the applause.

Jess thanked the judges, each stopping to shake her hand. Garth took her hand, smiling mischievously. "I told you I'd find out which was yours," he whispered for her ears alone.

He winked again and she suddenly knew that the dessert he'd been eating when he winked the first time was hers.

Robert addressed the crowd. "Folks, all these desserts are for sale. You can purchase them anytime. We want to thank Perkins Department Store for donating the prizes. Now we'll begin the auction. Bill, come on up and start the bidding for us."

The auction drew lots of bids. The farm animals were the biggest draw, each going at a great price. Connie was pleased as she and Jess watched the bidding.

"Your father will be happy to know his donation is bringing such a good price."

"I'll tell him. You know, this whole evening has been great, and it seems everyone's enjoying themselves. By the way," she draped an arm over Jess's shoulders, "I knew I'd picked the right person to teach me how to cook. Congratulations!"

"Thanks. I didn't think I'd place, much less win first prize. Did you see the cookware I won? It just might come in handy someday."

"I'm sure it will," Garth said from behind her. "You can cook for me anytime. That cake was spectacular."

"I'm glad you liked it."

"Liked it? It was so good I bought the rest of it." He held up a brown box tied with string.

Connie covered her mouth with her hand, chuckling behind it.

Jess eyed the box doubtfully. "How could you even want more dessert after all you've eaten?"

"There's always tomorrow." Then before he lost his courage he asked, "Would you take a walk outside with me?"

Jess considered for a moment. Why not? It was warm in here, and she could use some fresh air.

Leaving Connie watching the auction, and, after placing his brown box with her box of cookware, they grabbed their coats and headed outside. The pale moon shone softly on the snow as they strolled across the barnyard. The wagon near the pasture wall reminded Garth what George had recently found there, so he guided Jess in another direction. But she'd heard the stories circulating the Dales.

"George told Charlie what happened here the other night." She shuddered at the thought.

"Are you cold?" Garth pulled her scarf beneath her chin then reached for her gloved hand. "We'll return inside if you are."

"No, I was just thinking about the poor man they found, another victim of the maniac who's committing these awful murders."

"Jess, I'd rather not talk about that right now," Garth began slowly. "There's something else I want to talk to you about."

"Oh? What is it?"

He stopped walking and took her gloved hands in his. Looking straight into her eyes, he spoke fervently. "Jess, I'm probably going to bungle this up good, but I can't wait any longer. I've got to tell you how I feel. I love you more than life itself and have since the first day I saw you." He stroked her cheek tenderly. "I feel like I'll go out of my mind if I don't tell you. Could you possibly learn to love me as well?"

Jess couldn't believe her ears! Tears spilled down her cold cheeks unheeded. "Oh, Garth!" she whispered.

Seeing her tears, Garth touched one with his finger. "Jess, Darling! Why are you crying? Are you disappointed? Please tell me what's wrong."

"No, there's absolutely nothing wrong! Now that you've told me that, everything is so right."

Groaning in relief, Garth pulled her into his arms, gently covering her lips with his. As she eagerly responded, his kiss grew deeper.

"Garth, I do love you," Jess breathed, as she drew back slightly. "You had me so confused tonight, I didn't know if I was coming or going."

"I suppose I did put the pressure on a bit, but I had to know how you felt about me. I was so unsure. But when you spilt the soup and banged your elbow," he rubbed it gently through her sleeve, "I knew I at least had your attention."

"I just don't understand how you could love me. Me, Jessica Montgomery."

He cupped her face tenderly between his gloved hands. "Jess, I've loved you since I saw you sitting in your grandmother's living room the day you arrived, but I was attracted to you before that." He smiled at the question in her eyes. "For years I've seen your picture on your Grandmother's mantle. Whenever I went to the orphanage I saw it and longed to meet that girl. I wanted to know the color of her hair and of her eyes. I wanted to know what she was like. Then when your grandmother said you were coming to visit, I was ecstatic. Without realizing it, I'd built up an ideal of what you'd be like, but I wasn't prepared when I walked in and saw you sitting amongst the children. You took my breath away. Afterward I tried to tell myself I wasn't really in love with you. How could I be? I didn't know you. But the more I got to know you, the more I knew I was."

Jess lowered her eyes self-consciously, her cheeks flaming at his words.

He lifted her chin, bringing her gaze back to his. "Lift up those gorgeous lashes, sweetheart. No more self-consciousness. I love you, and you love me. There's nothing we can't share. We have the most important things in life in common. Our love for God and our love for each other." He grinned before adding, "But keep the blush. I love it."

This time she didn't look away. "You know, the first time we met, you made me blush. I hadn't done that much before, but since I've known you, I've made up for it."

He chuckled before sobering. "What did I do or say that day that turned you cool toward me."

Jess smiled. "You made me blush like a schoolgirl."

Garth lowered his head, his gaze on her parted lips. "Good." Catching her close, he kissed her again.

Chapter Twenty-Two

"I want it done, and I want it done right," the man spoke menacingly into the phone. "This is important."

"Course it is, Gov'ner. We know the deal." The second man responded with a malevolent laugh. "Have we ever failed ya afore?"

"No, and I don't want this to be the first time. This will be the last, do you understand?"

"It will be. Jus' relax, Gov."

"There can be no slip ups, no mistakes."

"Course not. Everybody'll meet as usual and plan it all out. You'll be there?"

"Of course! There's too much at stake for me not to direct the plans."

"Right, Gov," the weasel shuddered inwardly. There'd always been a cold detachment before, but this was personal. The Boss was angry. "Well, I gotta go. When do we meet?"

"Saturday night, the usual place. Notify everyone."

"Will do." The weasel hung up before his boss could say more.

~

Jess and Garth returned to the barn, wanting to share their news with Grandmother but instead found something wrong. Everyone was gathered around the bandstand, the previous merriment now gone. The stillness of the crowd sent apprehension into the pit of Jess's stomach. She and Garth made their way through the crowd until they reached the front where Grandmother sat, a crying Katie held tenderly in her arms.

Jess knelt beside Grandmother. "What's happened?"

Grandmother stroked the little girl's hair. "Billy's disappeared. Katie said they were playing before she went off with another child. When she looked for Billy, she couldn't find him."

"We're starting a search for him," Robert said. "We'll break into teams and search in different directions."

"Oh, he's probably just hidin' somewhere," an older man said. "You know wee boys an' their games. He's just waitin' for someone to find him's all."

"But we can't wait to see if that's the case," Garth spoke up. "He's small and it's freezing outside." A murmur of agreement surged through the crowd. "I suggest we listen to Robert and search for him. The ladies can thoroughly check in and around the barn, while the men search the fields and around the house."

Splitting into groups, Robert, Garth, George Higgins and two other men led them outside while the women searched inside the barn. Before Garth joined the other men, Jess pulled him aside.

"Garth, do you think... I mean could the murderer have taken Billy? He's always killed those without family. Billy's an orphan and thus a target. If he wondered off...."

Stilling her lips with a gentle finger, Garth looked into her troubled eyes, smiling reassuringly. "Don't worry, darling, we'll find him. If we haven't found him after searching the area thoroughly, I'll call Paul Kendall. Don't give up on him, Jess. Like Hank said, he may be hiding somewhere." He wouldn't let himself think that her fears could be reality. "Just pray. Our heavenly Father knows exactly where he is."

Jess nodded hopefully. "Right and we'll trust Him to help us find Billy."

Young Geoffrey stopped beside Grandmother, awkwardly patting the sobbing Katie's back. "Grandmother, a while ago I heard one o' the big boys making fun o' Billy. He's a bully, and he called Billy names like dolt, dunce and imbecile. He said Billy was too stupid to learn anything."

"Did you see where Billy went?" Grandmother asked.

"He didn't go anywhere. He just took it and walked over and sat in a chair. I asked if he was okay, and he just nodded. I went back to playing and that's the last I saw of him."

"Who's the bully?" asked Garth.

"Frankie Potts," Geoffrey replied importantly. Maybe he'd get what was coming to him.

Garth glanced around until he saw several fourteen and fifteen-year old boys huddled together. He approached them, hands casually thrust into his pockets.

"Boys, have any of you seen little Billy from the orphanage?"

The boys shook their heads, murmuring that they hadn't. Garth looked directly at Frankie who was trying to blend into the barn wall.

"And you, Frankie? Have you seen Billy this evening?"

"Yeah, I seen him around. Why?" he asked belligerently.

"He's disappeared, and you were overheard telling him he was stupid and calling him names."

Frankie refused to meet Garth's gaze. "Yeah, what of it?"

Garth stepped closer, speaking in a quietly, threatening voice that left Frankie in no doubt to the sincerity of his words.

"Frankie, for your sake, I hope we find Billy soon. If you can tell us anything about his whereabouts, I advise you to tell us now."

Frankie shrank against the wall. "Yeah, I picked on him some. But I don't know where he went. Honest, I don't."

Garth shook his head contemptuously. "Aren't you too old to be picking on little kids? Or does that make you feel like a man? You've a lot of growing up to do before you reach manhood and choosing not to be a bully would be a good start."

Garth joined the search as everyone agreed to meet back

inside the barn after investigating the whole farm. Jess and Connie searched the loft while the other ladies searched stalls, in and behind crates and under tables. The tool room at the back of the barn was searched thoroughly. Outside, the men called Billy's name while searching the out-buildings and around the farmhouse. Martha Higgins searched her home in case he'd hidden there. With lanterns, the men searched the pastures and behind pasture walls.

An hour later everyone met to decide the next step and to grab hot coffee prepared by the ladies after their fruitless search.

"Could he have gone home?" Jess asked suddenly, a mug of coffee cupped between her chilled hands.

"Possibly," agreed Robert. "If he was that upset, he may have walked home."

Garth set down his mug, wrapping his scarf around his neck. "I'll head there, driving slowly and checking the road along the way."

"I'm coming with you," Jess set her mug next to his.

Garth started to protest then nodded in agreement. "George, I'll call when we arrive and let you know what we find."

Driving slowly, Garth and Jess searched the darkness by the road for Billy's small form. A few shadows made them stop the car and look, to no avail. They were relieved when each shadow turned out to be only a shadow.

At the orphanage, they searched every room, the barn and all the out buildings.

"We can't waste any more time with just the villagers searching." Garth reached for the phone. "I'm calling Paul."

While he placed the call, Jess sat on the couch, head leaned back. Jossie laid her soft, white and brown head in Jess's lap. She licked her hand, understanding something was wrong, but not knowing what. The dog tried to comfort her the only way she knew how. Without opening her eyes, Jess stroked the silky head as her heart petitioned her heavenly Father. *Please, Lord. Lead us to Billy and please keep him warm wherever he is. Help him not to be afraid, but to know You're with him.*

Garth hung up the receiver grimly. "Paul isn't in the office, but the officer will contact him. He suggested someone stay here and at George's in case Billy returns."

"George is still waiting to hear from you."

Reaching for the phone again, Garth told George what the police had said. After hanging up, he and Jess knelt beside the couch, held hands and prayed together. They didn't realize how long they'd knelt praying until they heard a loud knock on the door.

Jess's heart lodged hopefully in her throat as Garth answered it. Paul Kendall stood there in his uniform, hat in hand.

"Evening, Garth, Miss Montgomery." Stepping inside, he shut the door behind him. "I've been told one of the orphans is missing?"

"Yes, Billy. He's only three," Jess informed him.

"Three, eh?" Paul didn't like the sound of it. "How long's he been missing?"

Garth glanced at his watch. "About three hours, perhaps longer."

"Where have you searched?" Paul removed a note pad from his pocket, taking notes.

Garth told him everything, including about Frankie Potts teasing Billy.

"Was he wearing a coat?"

"I believe so," Jess replied. "When we searched Mr. Higgins barn, we didn't find it."

"Right." Paul looked grim. "I've called out officers from York and Harrogate. They'll arrive shortly. We'll set up base here since he'll likely come home if he shows up on his own. I'm heading to Mr. Higgins to question the folks there."

Garth turned to Jess. "I'll ride over with Paul. Will you be alright here?"

"Of course. I'll make coffee and sandwiches. It's probably going to be a long night."

Jess was in the kitchen when Connie came in.

"Any news?" Connie hung up her coat.

Jess explained everything as Connie helped her prepare food for the men who would be coming.

"How's Grandmother?" asked Jess

"She's a strong lady. I hope I can handle difficult situations as well as she does. She and Charlie are bringing the other children home. I have some leftover food in my car."

"How's Katie?"

"She was asleep in Claire's lap when I left. The poor thing cried herself to sleep."

"She and Billy are very close. Let's bring in the food and add it to what we have here. It's going to get hectic around here soon."

As they brought in the food, Charlie's pickup stopped in the backyard, the children spilling from the back.

"Children," Grandmother got out of the cab, Katie in her arms, "it's late. Please get ready for bed. Jess, will you take Michael from Claire? He's hungry and needs changing. I'll take Katie upstairs."

"I'll see to the other children." Connie followed them from the kitchen.

Michael fretted when Jess didn't move fast enough for his liking. While warming his bottle, she heard a knock at the front door. Several men in heavy clothing identified themselves as the York Police. Letting them in Jess hurried back to the kitchen to feed Michael as they set up their base of operations in the living room.

Grandmother came into the kitchen, surprise on her face. "Who are those men in the living room?"

"Police from York and Harrogate. Paul Kendall called them to help find Billy."

"Who's Paul Kendall?"

"A police inspector from Harrogate and a friend of Garth's."

Just then Garth walked in the back door followed by Paul.

"Here they are now." Jess searched Garth's face hopefully. She hadn't even told Grandmother about Garth's proposal yet.

"Mrs. McDonald?" Paul approached her. "I'm Inspector Paul Kendall, North Yorkshire Police."

She shook his outstretched hand. "Yes, I saw you at the Higgins' farm as we were leaving. There are policemen waiting for you in the living room."

"Yes, they called when they arrived. Please excuse me and I'll get them started."

Grandmother poured a cup of tea as Garth sat beside Jess. He gently stroked Michael's head, smiling tenderly at Jess. Grandmother joined them, absently spooning sugar into her tea.

Jess placed a hand on Grandmother's arm. "Don't worry. They'll find Billy."

"I keep telling myself that, luv," swiping a tear from the corner of her eye. "I know he's in God's hands, but I keep thinking of him out in the cold, all alone, or worse. He's so small; almost a baby."

"Let's not borrow trouble," said Garth gently. "Let's trust God to look after him."

Paul returned to the kitchen. "Garth, will you help with the search? We need all the able-bodied men we can find."

Garth stood up. "Certainly, I'll be right in." As Paul left, he tipped Jess's chin up to look into her eyes. "I'll return as soon as I can." Then he looked at Grandmother. "Keep praying and trusting."

The living room had been transformed into a search and rescue base station. Garth found Robert joining the search teams that consisted of local village men lead by policemen. Lanterns, ropes, and first-aid supplies were distributed as the teams left for the search areas as Paul directed them. A policeman stayed behind in case Billy returned on his own. With the children in bed, Jess, Connie and Grandmother settled into the kitchen to wait.

"Won't your parents be concerned about you, Connie?" Grandmother pulled out a ball of wool and a crochet hook.

"I should call, but they're probably already asleep."

"Then stay here tonight," Jess suggested. "You can call in the morning."

"I'll stay to help with whatever is needed here. The searchers can't stay out too long because of the cold. They'll return to warm up and eat before heading back out again."

"It'll be hard searching in the dark," commented Grandmother. "I pray safety for them all."

Chapter Twenty-Three

*P*aul's team consisted of Garth, Robert and five other men. Returning to the Higgins' farm they searched in the direction of Pateley Bridge. Each carried a lantern as they walked slowly through the pastures and fields, keeping their lantern light touching the light from the next man's lantern. They climbed over stone walls and continued across pastures, checking every shadow or hollow in the ground, dreading what they might find.

At Pateley Bridge, Paul directed their return to the orphanage. Barely feeling his toes and fingers, Garth was grateful for Paul's decision.

As the men entered the house, Jess, Connie and Grandmother served warm drinks and food. The policeman manning the base station had kept the fire stoked, and after shedding their coats, the men gathered around it to warm themselves.

Jess carried a tray of cups and a pot of coffee. Connie followed with sandwiches while Grandmother served slices of pie and cake. The men ate hungrily.

"I'm glad we had these ready," Jess whispered to Connie.

Paul addressed the men. "I know you're tired and cold, but

time is of the utmost importance. We must get back out there and continue searching." Using a thin stick from the kindling box by the fire, he drew an imaginary circle on a map laid over a chair. "We'll extend our search area out this far, which means we each must cover a larger area. We've searched up to Pateley Bridge. The local constabulary is searching the village. We'll continue on the other side. The other teams will return soon to warm up and rest before continuing their search. I'm leaving instructions with Sgt. Stevens for the other teams to extend their search areas, too."

The phone rang, and Paul nodded for Grandmother to answer it.

"Hello?" she answered quietly, the room silent.

"Morag, its Sam Phillips," came the voice of the grocer in Pateley Bridge.

"Yes, Sam. What can I do for you?"

"Well, after me an' the missus left the fair this evening, we stopped by the store before driving to me daughter's house. She and her husband were tellin' us one of the young ones from the orphanage was missin'. They left after us, when everyone was lookin' for him. When we was drivin' home, I seen a small child up near the Miner's Arms on Greenhow Hill. We stopped and looked about, but the child disappeared. Could be hidin' up there anywhere. Don't know if it was a boy or girl, but that was less than an hour ago. I had to drive back to the store to call you. I'm there now."

"Oh, my!" exclaimed Grandmother excitedly. "Here, speak to the policeman in charge of the search." She turned to Paul. "It's Sam Phillips, the grocer in Pateley Bridge. He saw a child up on Greenhow Hill but wasn't sure if it was a boy or a girl."

Paul took the phone. "This is Inspector Kendall, Mr. Phillips. Could you repeat everything, please?" He nodded as he listened. "We'll meet you at the Minor's Arms, and you can show us where you last saw the child. Thank you, Mr. Phillips." Hanging up he turned to the waiting group, filling them in.

"It's possible Billy's up there. We'll ride up and see what we find."

"Greenhow Hill?" asked one man skeptically. "How could a three year ol' make it up there? It's a long walk for an adult, but a three year ol'?And in the dark?"

"Billy's smart," Jess said. "Maybe he caught a ride with someone or stowed away in the back of a truck."

"Stranger things have happened," agreed Paul. "Alright men, let's go. No time to waste."

The phone rang again as they gathered coats and hats and swallowed the last of their coffee. Jess answered it.

"Garth, its Mrs. Sixsmith." She held out the receiver to him.

The women returned to the kitchen to prepare food for the next search group. Moments later, Garth came in coat in hand.

"Connie, Mrs. Sixsmith just received a call from your father. Your mother's taken ill. Dad's out with a patient so I'm on my way there now. Would you like to ride along?"

Shaken, Connie laid down her knife, wiping her hands on a towel. "Yes, thank you." Looking at Jess helplessly, she opened her lips to speak, but Jess stopped her.

"Connie, go with Garth. Don't worry. We'll take care of things here." She hugged her friend. "We'll be praying for her, too, okay? Remember you're God's child now. He'll be with you no matter what."

Connie smiled weakly. "I know. Thank you." She turned to Garth. "I'll get my coat."

Garth took Jess's chilled hands in his warm ones then kissed her tenderly. "I love you," he whispered. "Whatever problems may arise in our lives, that will never change. Remember that. I'll let you know something as soon as I can. Perhaps you'll even have good news for me. Alright?" He stroked her cheek tenderly.

She nodded, smiling through misty eyes. "Alright. Take care of Connie. I'll let Robert know."

When they were gone, Grandmother hugged Jess. "It's been quite a night, hasn't it, luv?"

"And it isn't over yet."

Returning to the living room she found the search team gone.

201

She'd tell Robert about Connie's mother later. Hopefully they'd find Billy soon then one of their problems would be over.

~

When he'd nodded to Geoffrey that he was okay, Billy didn't feel okay. Frankie Potts made him feel bad. Looking to see if anyone was watching, Billy slipped out the back door of the barn and walked around to the front. As he rounded the corner, the front barn door opened. Hiding behind a rain barrel, he slowly moved his head around until he could see. Jess and Garth were walking across the barnyard.

Returning to the back of the barn, he tried to see in the dark. It reminded him of the night the lights went out at his home in London. He remembered how he'd crawled through the darkness to find Mother, Father and big brother, Bryan. And he had. But they weren't moving. No matter how hard he'd tried, they wouldn't answer his cries. He remembered distant screams and flashes of light as explosions damaged the city. He didn't realize he was crying until his cheeks suddenly felt cold. Reaching up, he wiped them with the back of this mitten.

He wouldn't think about that now. It always hurt inside when he did. Reaching the other side of the barn, he looked around the corner. Jess and Garth had stopped across the barnyard.

He sat on the cold ground in the darkness. Maybe he was a stupid. Frankie Potts said he was. He didn't want to embarrass Grandmother and the other children, so maybe he'd just go away.

Looking around the corner again, he saw lots of wagons and trucks parked in the barnyard. Standing, he ran to a pickup truck in the back, furthest from the barn. Climbing onto the back bumper, he looked over the tailgate where hay bales and empty gunnysacks lay in a pile. Tumbling over the tailgate, he pulled the sacks over himself. If he was going to run away, the best way was to hide here and go wherever the truck went.

Before long someone exited the barn and climbed into the truck cab. A man and woman talked in low tones as the truck started and drove away from the barn. Peeking from under the sack, Billy watched the dimly lit barn disappear into the distance.

They rode for a while before the truck stopped in front of a building. The people got out and went inside. Billy heard music and voices as the door of the building opened then the sound was cut off as the door closed. The silence was scary. Pushing the sacks away, he stood up, looking around. It was dark, and except for the building, he couldn't see any houses or lights nearby. With no idea where he was, he climbed down from the truck and started walking up the road.

Maybe this wasn't such a good idea after all. It was awfully dark and cold and he didn't know where to go. Sobbing quietly, he walked until he saw lights in the distance. Maybe a small village or a farm! If only it weren't so dark between the lights and where he stood. He wished he was back at the orphanage! The other children were probably already tucked into their warm beds.

Leaving the road, he started across what he thought was a field, walking slowly so he wouldn't run into any stone walls in the darkness. He'd run into one at the orphanage in the dark once. It hurt a lot. Stretching his arms out in front, he groped along with his feet, trying not to think about his warm bed and the lights at the orphanage. And about Grandmother's comforting lap.

A car passed on the road near him and stopped, two people getting out. Were they looking at him? Grandmother had always told him not to talk to strangers. Of course he never talked to anyone. He also knew not to have anything to do with strangers when Grandmother wasn't with him. He wished she were with him now. A man called to him. He dropped on all fours, his heart banging against his ribs. Hidden by tall grass and moor scrub, he lay quietly, hoping they couldn't hear his heart pounding.

After calling out and looking around a bit, the people returned to their car and drove away. After they were gone, Billy stood up, and, with tears streaming down his cold cheeks, started walking toward the lights again. Maybe someone there could take him home.

~

The lights weren't getting closer even though he must've walked a long way. Suddenly his hand touched a stone wall.

Running his hands over it, it wasn't like the stone fences at the orphanage. It was cracked and broken in places; large chunks lay on the ground. He stumbled and fell, tearing his mittens and scratching his palms. Whimpering quietly, he stood up, walking until his hands touched wood.

What was this? It wasn't very high, but with all the rubble on the ground, it could have been a building. He shuffled his feet along until his foot hit a raised board. He stepped over expecting another obstruction blocking his path. As he did, he pitched forward and down. As he fell, Billy screamed before the wind was knocked from his lungs. Stunned by the fall, he lay staring up through the darkness, unsure what had swallowed him.

~

Garth stopped his car beneath the portico at Connie's house. She was out and running up the massive stone steps before he could open his door.

Inside he followed her up the grand staircase to a hallway running the length of the house and into a large bedroom where a huge bed sat on a raised platform. Heavy drapes hung from the canopy and over the two tall windows on either side of the bed. It reminded Garth of a picture he'd once seen of a bedroom in one of the royal castles. Mrs. Cameron lay in the center of the bed, eyes closed and her face pale.

Mr. Cameron sat on the edge of the bed, tenderly holding her hand. He looked up as Connie and Garth hurried in. "Constance, dear." He laid his wife's hand gently on the duvet and stood. "I'm glad you've come. When I realized she was sick, I searched for you. I was worried when you weren't in your room." He hugged her to his broad chest then held her away.

Opening his bag, Garth began examining his patient.

"I'm sorry, Father." Tears filled Connie's eyes. "A child from the orphanage disappeared, and they're searching for him. I thought you and mother would be asleep so I didn't call. I was helping when Garth received the call about Mother." She looked at her mother lying on the bed. "What's wrong with her?"

Mr. Cameron shook his head wretchedly. "I don't know."

Garth draped his stethoscope around his neck and pulled out a thermometer. "Mr. Cameron, tell me everything that happened this evening. Were there any symptoms you know of?"

The older man thought momentarily. "Earlier this evening she complained of a headache, a stiff neck, and nausea. I told her she should turn in early, but she refused, saying she had charity paperwork to do. She wouldn't eat dinner."

"Does she have headaches often?" Garth noted the thermometer reading.

"Occasionally. She grew sleepy while reading her paperwork, but she resisted. She finally went to bed but was soon back up... um... you know, vomiting." He said it distastefully. "She returned to bed. When I checked on her, she was feverish and unresponsive. After checking her breathing, I called you."

"Mr. Cameron, your wife may be seriously ill," Garth replied. "She must go to the hospital for further evaluation, but she may have meningitis, an illness causing inflammation of the brain and spinal cord tissues. Has she had a cold recently?"

Connie sat by the bed, watching her mother lying motionless against the pillows. "Yes, last week. Instead of resting, she pushed herself. Too much to do before the holidays, she said."

"Where can I wash up?" asked Garth. "Afterward, I'll arrange her transportation to the hospital."

Connie apologetically explained that Mother was very particular about anyone using her bathroom. She led him to the one adjacent to Ian's room. He wasn't home, or he would've been at his mother's bedside.

Washing his hands in the marble basin, Garth glanced around the meticulously appointed bathroom for a hand towel. The towel rod was empty. The corner of a towel stuck out of the hamper across the room. Opening the warming cupboard, he grabbed the first towel he saw.

As he dried his hands he noticed a long white robe hanging inside the cupboard door. Unlike a bathrobe, it was unusual. Hanging up the towel, he removed the robe and examined it. The garment was a heavy cotton weave, with long, full sleeves and a draped cowl-neck. A matching sash hung on the hook.

Garth thought it odd, but it wasn't his business what Ian chose to wear. Returning it to the hook, he closed the cupboard and went to call the hospital.

Chapter Twenty-Four

After serving the search teams, Jess and Grandmother waited in the kitchen as they had all night. Jess glanced at the kitchen clock. The sun would be up shortly. She was exhausted, but Grandmother needed her right now.

"Jess," Grandmother held her teacup between her hands. "I noticed Garth was, shall we say, attentive this evening. Has something happened that I'm not aware of?"

Jess smiled. "Actually, yes. Tonight, rather last night, he proposed. We were coming to tell you when Billy disappeared. Our news had to wait."

Grandmother patted Jess's hand. "How splendid! Garth's a fine man, and he'll make a wonderful husband. I've known for some time that he loved you. I see it every time he looks at you." She chuckled. "I suppose this means you'll be staying?"

Jess smiled wearily. "I suppose so. I'll still have to go back and settle things."

"Well, the two of you'll discuss that later. I'm very happy for you, luv."

When Paul's team returned, unsuccessful, Jess asked Robert into the kitchen.

"When Garth left earlier, it was Connie's mother who was sick. She went with him." Jess watched sadness cross Robert's face.

"Have you heard from them since?"

"Garth called earlier. They were taking her to Harrogate hospital. He thinks she has meningitis, but they're running tests." She placed a hand on his arm. "Robert, I know you care for Connie. Am I right?"

"Yes." He paced the kitchen floor. "I can't help it. I've prayed about my feelings just as I've prayed for her salvation. I can't stop how I feel."

"But, Robert, didn't she tell you?"

At his look of uncertainty, she smiled brightly. "She's accepted Christ!"

Utter joy crossed his face. "She has? Praise God! My prayers are answered! I have to get to her." He suddenly stopped, remembering the search for Billy. "But it'll wait until we find Billy."

Jess understood his dilemma. He wanted to run to Connie, to share his love and to comfort her, but his sense of duty stopped him. Every able bodied man was needed in the search effort. Billy could even now be freezing somewhere.

Robert shook his head. "I'll finish this first. They need me here. After we find Billy, I'll go to Connie and declare my feelings.

~

Billy couldn't see anything but a few faint stars in the sky above the deep hole he'd fallen into. The surface he'd landed on felt like rough wood. Where was he? How was he going to get out? Tears flowed down his cold cheeks until his torn mittens were wet from wiping them away. What was he going to do?

He remembered a Bible story Grandmother had read to them recently. She said a man was put into a hole with some lions. What was his name? David? No, that wasn't it. He concentrated harder. Daniel! That was his name. Daniel was put into a deep hole with hungry lions. Billy searched the darkness for possible eyes peering at him. He was scared to think lions might be in this hole.

Grandmother read that an angel came and shut the lion's mouths so they wouldn't eat Daniel. He glanced around for an angel. There was a picture of one in his picture book. Grandmother said you couldn't see angels, unless God wanted you to. He'd just imagine them standing around him with big bright swords, keeping the lions away.

Before long he fell asleep, back to the dirt wall, his chin on his chest. There in the dark he slept, knowing with childlike faith that God's angels watched over him.

~

Traveling the winding road past stonewalled pastures as he returned to the orphanage, Garth noticed the sky begin to lighten. It would be sunup soon. What a night! Recalling the night before in George's barnyard, he knew his love for Jess couldn't be contained any longer. He'd told her, and she'd loved him back.

Thank you, Father. You've given me a precious gift. Help me care for her and love her with everything in me. Help me to be a good husband and to always put her needs before my own.

He thrilled again at the memory of her in his arms, the look in her eyes for him alone. By now Grandmother knew, and he hoped she'd be happy for them. Hopefully Billy had been found. Oh, for this long night to be over and for everything to return to normal. He sighed wearily. Until then, he'd trust the Lord through it all.

At the orphanage, he found most of the searchers were still searching. Jess hugged him, pulling his tired face down for a kiss. She told him how Robert longed to be with Connie.

Garth drank some coffee then donned the heavy coat and boots he'd used the night before. After accepting instructions from Sgt. Stevens, he turned to Jess. "I'm returning to the search. There are lots of old abandoned mines across the moors. I explored there as a youth and I still remember their locations. If Paul hasn't already checked them, then I will." With a kiss for Jess and a hug for Grandmother, he was gone again.

~

Garth found Paul and his team on the windswept moors near

the Miner's Arms. The sky had lightened but the sun hid behind dreary clouds. Paul said more snow was predicted by the end of the day.

"Have you searched the old lead mines?" asked Garth.

"We checked the ones I know about. Do you know of others?"

"I roamed all over these moors as a lad." Garth pointed to various areas on Paul's map. "You've mainly checked this area? There are mine entrances beyond that hill." He pointed to the map then to the area in the distance. "Robert and I will search over there."

"Sounds good." Paul clapped Garth's shoulder. "Yell if you find anything."

Pulling a coiled rope from the search supplies, Garth called to Robert, who searched a short distance away. Waving his arms, he motioned him over.

When Robert joined him, they grabbed two lanterns, and walked into the snowy heather and moor scrub. Spreading a short distance apart, they searched slowly, zigzagging across the moor. Cresting a hill, Garth spotted a mineshaft entrance. They searched as they walked toward it.

Garth stepped over chunks of wood and stone debris. "The mine entrance is behind that low wall."

At the opening in the side of the hill, they lit their lanterns, proceeding into a small chamber. The floor sloped steeply downward, through a passageway. Following the passage about two hundred feet, it opened into another chamber, empty except for scattered rubble.

Lifting his lantern high, Garth looked around. "I thought perhaps he'd slid down the passage and couldn't find his way out of the dark, but there's no sign anyone's been here in years."

"Could he be further back?" Robert indicated the passage leading further under the hill.

Garth shook his head doubtfully. "With no light that we know of, it's doubtful." He turned to leave the chamber. "Let's keep looking. Some of these mines had several openings. Most are considered extremely dangerous due to underwater rivers running through these hills. The mineshafts are unsafe because of rotted wood supports. If they give way, the dirt and rock may give way, too."

Robert extinguished his light as they stepped outside. "Then I certainly hope Billy isn't in one of them."

"So do I," Garth replied, dread slipping into his voice.

~

Opening his eyes, Billy looked up. No, he wasn't dreaming. He really was in a hole. Looking around, he saw he'd landed on a wooden platform only a few feet wide. Looking over the edge, it was too dark to see. Looking up again he saw it was getting lighter outside. Bracing against the dirt wall, he stood up, avoiding the platform edge. Reaching his little arms upward, he couldn't reach the top. He couldn't climb out.

Sitting down again, he propped his chin in his hands, elbows on his knees. Somebody would miss him and come looking for him. Poor Katie would be sad. He prayed God would send someone to find him.

He thought he heard his name called. Was it God? He'd never heard Him before. Listening carefully, he heard it again, only two voices were calling him, and they were closer and louder. He stood up, holding onto the wall. There they were again. His heart leapt happily. Was someone coming for him? He opened his mouth to yell, but all that escaped was a croak. Trying harder, a small cry lifted from the hole. He tried calling "Help!"

~

Robert and Garth continued calling Billy's name as they crossed the snowy moor. The sun was higher but still hidden behind heavy clouds. Cresting a small rise, they heard a faint sound. Both stopped, confirming that the other had heard it.

"Billy!" Garth called loudly.

"Billy!" echoed Robert.

Listening, they heard the sound again, trying to locate it.

"It's coming from over there!" Garth pointed to another hill. They broke into a run, calling Billy's name as they went. Cresting another hill, they spotted a jumble of wood and stone around an old building foundation. Running downhill, they searched until they found an opening in the ground surrounded by old rotten boards.

"Hold my feet!" Garth laid flat across the boards, looking over the edge. There, about eight feet below was Billy, tears streaming down his cheeks.

"He's here!" Garth called triumphantly.

"Thank you, God!" Robert closed his eyes.

Looking around the hole, Garth noted the boards where Billy stood were unsteady. Beyond, the hole dropped indefinitely. With little support, the dirt around the boards shifted with Billy's movements.

"Billy," Garth said quietly. "Don't move. We'll get you out, but you must be brave and do exactly as I tell you, alright?"

The little boy nodded, wiping tears with his already damp mittens.

Garth backed carefully from the edge of the hole and tied one end of the rope around his waist, then made a loop with a slipknot in the other end. With Robert holding his feet, he lay back across the boards, lowering the looped end into the hole.

"Billy, slide the loop over your head and under your arms. I'll pull you up, alright?"

Billy nodded and followed Garth's instructions.

"Okay, Billy. I'm going to pull you up. Hold onto the rope with your hands."

Hand over hand he pulled the rope upward. Just as Billy's feet lifted, some boards gave way, falling into the hole. Looking down, Billy gasped.

"Look at me, Billy. That's right. I've got you. Steady now." Looking him in the eye, Garth spoke quietly while pulling the rope steadily upward.

When Billy reached the top, Garth pulled him out. Sliding back across the boards, he sat up, hugging Billy tightly to his chest. Billy hugged Garth's neck, sobbing.

"It's alright," Garth soothed, rubbing Billy's head. "You're safe." He looked into the little boy's eyes, smiling. "Let's get you home where you belong, alright?" Pulling a handkerchief from his pocket, he wiped away the tears coursing down Billy's dirty cheeks. Billy nodded emphatically. "Go home!"

Robert and Garth exchanged surprised glances, but made no comment about him speaking.

"Let's go home." Garth hoisted Billy onto his shoulders.

"We'll have that hole sealed up," said Robert. "No telling how deep it is and we don't want anyone else falling in."

"No," said Billy softly. "We don't."

~

Jess and Grandmother were in the living room when Garth and Robert carried Billy in, Paul and the other searchers right on their heels. The reunion was a loud one, everyone talking at once. The children came from the dining room where they were eating breakfast. Everyone had to touch or hold Billy, reassuring themselves he was really home.

After several minutes of pandemonium, Paul called for silence. "The search is over, men. Thank you for searching for this lad." He patted Billy's head then turned to Grandmother. "And you, Mrs. McDonald, have been gracious to let us use your living room as a base for our search."

She shook her head. "No, Inspector Kendall. I'm the one who's grateful for what you've all done. You brought my wee one back to me." She held Billy closely. "Thank you all."

Robert spoke up. "Let's thank God for His guidance. He knew right where Billy was and kept him safe."

All heads bowed as Robert prayed, several wiping tears from their eyes. Garth reached down and grasped Jess's hand, gently squeezing her fingers.

Chapter Twenty-Five

As the searchers left for a much-deserved rest Garth clapped Paul on the shoulder. "I can't thank you enough for all you've done."

Paul waved aside his thanks. "It took teamwork and the next time I need help with a particularly difficult case, I'll know who to call." Shaking Garth's hand then Robert's, he tipped his hat to the ladies and left.

"He's a fine young man!" Grandmother gathered used dishes from around the room.

"The best," agreed Garth.

"Well," Robert sighed heavily, "I don't know if you remember or not, but its Sunday morning. I have to preach in a few hours."

"Robert, what are you going to do?" Jess asked. "You're so tired, and there's hardly time for you to rest."

"As they say in show business, 'the show must go on.'"

"But you're not in show business."

"True, but I'm in God's business, and He'll give me the strength I need." He added with a yawn, "However, the sermon may be shorter than usual."

Garth relieved Grandmother of the tray of dishes and headed for the kitchen. "If you can do it, so can we."

Breakfast was prepared for the two men. They ate then hurried home to wash up and change for church.

~

As predicted, Robert's sermon was shorter than usual. Afterward, he led the congregation in prayer, thanking God for the generosity of all who attended the Christmas Fair and for God's protection of Billy and those who searched for him.

After the closing hymn, many folks stopped to speak to Grandmother and Billy who, in spite of his cold experience, had suffered no ill effects.

Jess and Garth walked toward his car. "Please get some rest." She searched his tired eyes. "You can't go on much longer without it."

"And you?" He cupped her cool cheek in his warm hand. "You didn't sleep last night either. If I go home to rest then you must promise to do the same. At least for a while."

"Alright, I will."

"Good. May I pick you up about four-thirty? To take a drive?"

"A drive? To where?"

"I'm not telling, but we'll stop somewhere for supper."

"I'd love to. Now go home and get some rest."

"Alright, alright, I'm going. But don't forget your part of the bargain."

Jess saw the children and Grandmother climbing into the truck. "My ride's leaving. See you later." Reaching up, she gave him a quick kiss.

He caught her close as she started to step back. "Not so fast. This is what dreams are made of, and since I'm going to sleep...." He left the sentence hanging as he kissed her thoroughly. As he let her go, everyone in the truck and in the parking lot applauded with approval.

~

Robert approached Mrs. Cameron's hospital room, the door slightly open. Sitting beside her mother's bed, Connie's head was bowed, her eyes closed. He knocked softly causing her to look up. Seeing Robert, she tiptoed into the hallway, leaving the door ajar.

Connie smiled wearily. "Thank you for coming."

Robert gathered her hands in his. "I wanted to come sooner but felt I needed to continue searching for Billy."

"Of course, they needed you. Have they found him?"

"Garth and I found him this morning about sunup. He'd fallen into an abandoned mineshaft on Greenhow Hill. Garth pulled him out just as the floor gave way."

"Praise God!" Connie closed her eyes briefly. As she opened them, she found Robert's gaze on her, his heart in his eyes.

"How's your mother?"

"She's seriously ill. Garth was right. It's meningitis. There's been no change since he brought her in, but she's stable. Now we wait. Father was here most of the night, but I sent him home to rest." Robert saw sadness in her eyes. "Ian never came home last night so it's doubtful he knows about Mother. Robert, I'm concerned about him. I've a feeling he's into something he shouldn't be. I've seen him meeting mysterious men after dark. He doesn't know I saw them. And the other night he said something when he was drunk that made me uneasy."

Robert glanced down the corridor. "Can we get something hot to drink?"

They walked to the canteen, and after buying two cups of tea, they sat at a table in the corner.

"What do you think your brother's doing?"

"I don't know. I've thought about it but it's all so mysterious. It could be anything. Or nothing. Perhaps I'm reading more into it than I should."

Robert drank his tea. "You mentioned he said something that made you uneasy. What was it?"

"He was drunk," she said sadly. "Apparently he'd asked Jess out and she turned him down. He didn't like it and said 'she'd be sorry. Real sorry'."

"What do you think he meant?"

"I don't know." She shrugged her shoulders helplessly. "Ian can be ruthless sometimes, but Jess is so sweet, I don't know why he'd want to punish her."

"Is there anything else you've noticed about his behaviour?"

"I've overheard strange phone conversations. I'm sure what I heard was meant to be vague, so only the person on the other end would know what he's talking about. Robert, I've a bad feeling about Ian's behaviour, but what should I do?"

"Without anything definite to go on, what can you do? Don't approach him about it, because if he's into something dangerous, you could be in danger."

"Me? But I'm his sister. Surely he wouldn't harm me."

Robert doubted Ian's devotion to his family but kept it to himself. "Just continue watching him and his activities. Perhaps Inspector Kendall could better advise you." He placed his hand over hers. "You can always come to me when you need to talk."

She smiled. "I know I can. Thank you."

Robert swirled his cup distractedly. "Jess said you'd accepted Christ as your saviour. Is that true?" His eyes searched hers desperately.

"Yes, it's true."

Robert closed his eyes briefly, thanking God. "Praise God!" he whispered. He squeezed her hand gently. "You don't know how happy that makes me."

She looked a little surprised. "But why?"

"Two reasons really. One, you're now a child of God, and you're promised a home in heaven." He paused, pulling her hand closer as his gaze held hers. "Secondly, as well as selfishly, I knew I couldn't marry anyone who didn't know my Lord, and I desperately want to marry you. You see, I love you and have for some time. I fought it, all the while praying for your salvation. Could you possibly love me enough to marry me?"

Connie touched his cheek gently. "Of course I could. I love you, too."

Robert placed a kiss on her soft palm. "My dear, you've made me very happy." Pushing back his chair he stood up, pulling her into his arms. Oblivious to the people in the canteen, he kissed her tenderly. "Would you mind very much becoming the wife of a young minister with no definite future? I've no idea where I'll go after Pastor Wright returns. All I know is that I'll go wherever the Lord leads me."

"Then that's where I'll be going, too. It doesn't matter where as long as I'm with you, doing what God wants us to do."

"What about your family? They won't be happy that you're marrying a penniless preacher."

"I don't care." Connie shrugged. "I'm marrying you, not them"

Robert shook his head in wonder. "I don't deserve you, and yet here you are returning my love. I'll talk to your father when you think it's a good time."

"No, we'll talk to him together."

"Alright. We'll go together." Robert glanced at his watch. "Let's check on your mother then I need to get some rest. I'd love to stand here all day holding you, but I do need sleep."

Finding no change with Connie's mother, Robert offered to take Connie home.

"No, thank you. I'll wait until Father returns, in case she awakens. I don't want her waking up in a strange place alone." She looked at her mother's still form on the bed. "I know whatever happens I can trust God to help me through it. I just pray that she and the rest of my family come to know Christ, too."

~

After church Garth drove toward his boarding house. Yawning, he ran a hand over his tired eyes, hoping he'd make it home without driving into a ditch. The overcast sky promised snow. Hopefully it would wait until he and Jess returned from their drive. He wanted to spend some quiet time with her alone. Since declaring his love, they hadn't had much time to talk.

Passing through Pateley Bridge, he noticed two cars parked near the bridge at the end of town, no one in or around them. No other cars were parked on the street. Thinking it strange, he turned around and parked a distance from them, looking around for the occupants. The only shop open on Sunday afternoon was the teashop at the top of the town. Those customers wouldn't park down here.

Leaving his car, he walked up the street, all the while unsure why he was doing this. As tired as he was, why was he checking into something that likely meant nothing? He was probably still edgy from the search for Billy and dealing with Connie's mother. Glancing into shop windows, he berated himself for being suspicious. The more he thought about it the more ridiculous he felt. Deciding to return to his car, he stopped suddenly, ducking behind a shop window.

By the cars stood four men, three dressed in old coats with caps pulled low. The fourth wore a brown fedora and an expensive coat. Garth watched as they spoke, unable to hear them. If he could just glimpse their faces he'd know how ridiculous this was and could go home to sleep.

Suddenly, the fedora man turned, looking up the street. Garth ducked back, gasping as realization hit him. Ian Cameron! Peeking around the edge of the shop window, he saw one man pull a white cloth bundle from one of the cars. Ian took the cloth, throwing it into his car. After again speaking to the men, he climbed in and drove away, the remaining men leaving in the other car.

Garth waited for them to leave then ran to his car. He'd follow Ian. If it were anyone but Ian his behaviour might be innocent. He'd never trusted the man.

Disappointed when Ian drove to Cameron Hall and pulled into the long winding driveway, Garth turned around toward home.

There was something about the meeting that was familiar, but he couldn't place it. Perhaps after resting he'd think more clearly. But all the way home, he couldn't shake the feeling that something eluded his memory.

~

Grandmother gently shook Jess. "Luv, Garth's here. Says he's come to take you driving." She turned on the bedside lamp. "You didn't mention you'd be going out this evening."

Jess yawned, stretching her arms over her head. "Sorry. All I could think of was sleep. Did you rest well?"

"I did, until Michael woke demanding a bottle and a

changing."

Jess picked up her brush from the dresser and brushed her wavy hair. "I never heard him, or I would've taken care of him."

"Here, I'll do that for you." Grandmother took the brush.

"Thank you," Jess said absently. "He's such a sweet baby and I love caring for him."

"Yes, he is." Grandmother brushed Jess's hair and began braiding it, before adding, "Jess. I know you and Garth have just discovered your love for one another and haven't begun making plans, but when you do, perhaps you should discuss children and when you'd like to start a family."

Turning Jess looked at Grandmother, her cheeks reddening. "No, we haven't, but I'm sure in time we'll discuss those things. Why do you mention it?"

Grandmother sighed, finishing the braid. "Because you'd make a better mother for Michael than me." She put up a hand to still Jess's protest. "Please, hear me out. I meant that you're young and will soon have a husband. Michael needs a father and a mother. I'm not young anymore. I can handle the children that are here now, but I don't think I can meet Michael's needs. All I ask is that you and Garth think and pray about it. Should you decide you don't want to adopt him then we'll find another Christian home to place him with."

Jess hugged Grandmother's neck. "I'd love to be Michael's mother. I disagree about your lack of ability, but you know best. I'll talk to Garth. We'll pray and see where the Lord leads us."

Grandmother returned her hug. "You're fiancée is waiting, luv."

"Right. I love you!" She kissed Grandmother's cheek and hurried downstairs.

Garth's breath halted as Jess descended the stairs, her cheeks flushed and her eyes hazy from sleep. He thrilled knowing that once they were married, he'd wake up next to this woman every morning. Helping her into her coat, he kissed her before they headed out to his car and drove away.

~

The group dispersed, leaving the two standing by the still form.

"Where do I dump it this time?" The smaller of the two shuddered, tired of being left with the grizzly tasks.

"I don't care," he snapped, walking away. "There's no evidence pointing to us, so it really doesn't matter. Just get rid of it."

Chapter Twenty-Six

"Have I mentioned recently that I love you?" Garth drew Jess's hand to his lips.

"Not in the last few hours." She laughed happily before sobering. "I'll never tire of hearing that. Please, never stop saying it."

Garth looked into her eyes, saying softly, "I can promise I'll always love you, and I'll never tire of saying so."

Dusk fell as they drove through the Dales to Grassington. Parking on the edge of the small village, Garth helped Jess from the car. Although the village was small, crowds meandered everywhere. Evergreen wreaths with red ribbons decorated shop doors and houses alike while white candles lit shop windows and gas street lamps burned brightly. Christmas music filled the air as carollers and musicians sang and played.

Jess looked at Garth curiously, "What is this place?"

He smiled, pulling her gloved hand into his coat pocket, giving it a squeeze. "This is Grassington, a quiet little village, at least until December when it's transformed into a very festive place. People come from all over to see the Morris dancers and hear the music." As they strolled, he pointed to a puppet booth on the street. "See that? They always have a Punch and Judy puppet show."

"How delightful!" Jess stared as a couple walked by dressed in Dickens era clothing.

Garth laughed heartily. "You've never been to anything like this before?"

"No, I haven't."

"Well then, follow me." He gently pulled her along.

They joined a group gathered around the puppet booth. Jess laughed delightedly as the hook-nosed Punch clobbered Judy on the head with his club. The girl puppet screeched and ran offstage, returning shortly, a constable puppet in tow.

Garth led Jess to a street vendor roasting chestnuts over a cast iron brazier with hot coals. "Want some roasted chestnuts?"

"I'd love some! I haven't had any since I was a child."

Paying the vendor, Garth took a bag from the large basket sitting near the brazier. "Here you go." Handing her the bag, they nibbled the warm nuts as they strolled.

"What's that?" Jess pointed to a group of strangely-dressed dancers.

They wore black clothing decorated with colourful ribbon rosettes and streamers, black stovepipe hats with bright ribbons and flowers, and clog shoes, their faces smudged black with coal dust. Pads with little bells were strapped to their shins. A one-man band played a fife and tabor as eight men dancers clacked wooden sticks together in rhythm with the music while stamping their feet with vitality. The merry jingling of the bells mixed with the rhythmic clacking and stamping made a delightful sound.

"They're Morris dancers," Garth explained. "Centuries ago, folk dance was forbidden by the church, but the common folk refused to stop, so smudging their faces with coal dust, they dressed like this to keep from being recognized. The costumes vary from village to village. The dancers were very elusive and very few were caught. Notice, they never speak so they can't be recognized by their voices. Even after the folk dance was again permitted, it was already a tradition."

"Amazing!" Jess tapped her toe to the music of the drum and

fife. "What does it mean? Why do they do it?"

"Well, nowadays, it's more for entertainment during holidays, but," Garth paused, taking on a sly expression, "it once had a more useful purpose."

"Really? What was it?"

"Fertility rites."

"What? Oh!" Jess's cheeks warmed.

Garth chuckled at her discomfort. "Originally it was a pagan ritual thought to affect young women to bear children more easily. They also believed crops would produce better, too."

"I'm glad we don't rely on those methods nowadays," Jess said emphatically as the dancers clapped their sticks, stamped their feet and swung around and around. Before long the dancers pulled individuals from the crowd, leading them in the dance.

A particularly tall dancer pulled Jess into the group. She looked at Garth helplessly. He shrugged his shoulders, chuckling until another dancer pulled him in, too. Jess watched carefully, trying to imitate the dancer's steps. Clapping when he clapped, stamping when he stamped. When the music stopped, her partner bowed grandly and strode off, never speaking. The whole group moved on, dancing in other areas of the village.

"You did quite well for your first street dance," Garth teased. "Promise me you'll never smudge that beautiful face of yours."

"I promise," Jess laughed.

They found a warm inn where they ordered steaming bowls of beef stew and fresh rolls with butter. While waiting for their meal, Jess broached the subject of Michael.

"Garth, I'd like you to pray about something."

He covered her hand with his. "What is it, darling?"

Jess warmed at the endearment. "I love the sound of that."

"So do I." His gruff voice and the look in his eyes made her heart race. "What did you want to ask me?"

"About children." Jess didn't know how to begin.

"That's a good thing to pray about." His eyes lit gleefully. "Any particular children to pray about?"

"Ours!"

"Even better. Every time you look at the children at the orphanage I see how much you love them, and you look so natural holding Michael. I look forward to having our own."

"Well, how would you feel about adopting Michael? Because of her age, Grandmother doesn't think she can give him the personal care she gives to the older children. His needs are different from theirs, more demanding." She smiled slightly. "I've been told the first year of marriage is the hardest because of adjustments and learning to live with someone else. Added care of a child could make it even harder. And perhaps you only want your own children and not an adopted child."

Garth watched Jess tenderly. Oh, how he loved her! He was so blessed to have her return his love!

"Jess, that prayer's already been answered. I'd love to raise Michael as our son and love him just like any future children the Lord may bless us with." He kissed her hand. "I remember the night you found him. I'll never forget walking in and seeing you by the fire with Michael in your arms. I could hardly breathe. I already knew I loved you, but then I knew I wanted you to share my life."

The waitress arrived with their supper and they ate quietly until Garth asked, "When will you return to the States?"

"I don't know. I have to return soon to settle things with the house."

"Will you sell it? If you want to keep it, I'm sure something can be arranged, but finding a buyer would mean less hassle later."

"If I'm going to be living here…." Jess paused, looking at him expectantly.

"Which, of course you are!" Garth replied vehemently.

"Of course," smiled Jess. "So, I'll sell the house."

"Can you wait until after we're married? Then we'll go together. What do you say? Will you marry me soon?" He held her gaze ardently.

Jess smiled happily. "Yes, I'll marry you soon. And I'd love for you to go with me."

"You know, now that the war is over, ocean travel is safer. It might make a nice honeymoon." He smiled mischievously.

"Well, we can certainly find out, can't we?" Jess flashed her own impish smile.

After supper, they strolled back through the cold, narrow streets where the crowds had diminished to a few scattered people.

After settling Jess in the car, Garth drove back through the Dales. Soft lights shone from houses they passed, a welcome vision in the cold dark night.

Climbing Greenhow Hill, the car's headlights illuminated a dark shape on the left side of the road. Jess, sitting on that side of the car, saw it first.

"Garth, we just passed something on the roadside. I'm not sure what it was, but it shouldn't be there."

Garth braked the car then reversed beyond it, headlights illuminating the roadside. Most of the object lay in the high weeds and snow beyond the roadbed.

Jess reached for the door handle, but Garth put a hand on her arm.

"Wait, Jess. I'll look first. It might be nothing, but I'd rather you wait here."

Jess watched as Garth walked in front of the headlights and examined the object before returning to sit in the car, saying nothing at first.

"Garth, what is it? What's the matter?" She saw the grim expression on his face. "Garth?"

"It's a young woman. And she's dead."

Jess looked toward the dark shape by the road. "Oh, no. Not again."

~

Garth and a uniformed officer observed Paul examining the body. Standing, Paul handed the officer a small bag, indicating for Garth to follow him. They approached the car where Jess sat watching, but stopped a short distance away.

"What can you tell from the body?" Garth asked quietly.

"Not much out here. She's young, possibly sixteen or seventeen. She's been stabbed repeatedly like all the others. We'll get more information from the coroner."

"Who could be doing this?" Garth asked harshly. "For what purpose?"

Paul clapped him gently on the shoulder. "Garth, my friend, the world is full of lunatics. We just finished fighting a war against several. Whoever's doing this just hasn't taken on the whole world yet."

"No. Just the Dales."

"Well, we'll have to catch him or her or them before they get ambitious and start on the rest of England."

Garth suddenly remembered Ian's strange meeting in Pateley Bridge earlier that day and shared it with Paul.

"Ian Cameron, eh? Yes, I know who he is. A big shot. Lots of money."

"That's right. I was stationed in France with him. He was just as unpleasant then."

"Even if the meeting was unusual, with nothing to go on, we can't do anything. But we'll keep an eye on him."

"That's a good idea. I don't trust him." He still couldn't remember what Ian's strange meeting should remind him of.

"If you're done with me, I should get Jess home. It's been a long two days."

"That it has, my friend." Paul sighed heavily. "Until the murderer or murderers are found, I'm afraid we'll have more long days. I'll let you know what we find out about this one." He pointed a thumb over his shoulder toward the body.

At the orphanage, Garth followed Jess inside. Grandmother held Michael who cooed happily. Jess removed her coat, reaching for the baby.

"How was your ride?" Grandmother handed Michael to Jess.

"Wonderful. We drove to Grassington to see the Christmas festivities."

"I used to go when I was younger," said Grandmother. "They celebrate every weekend in December until after Christmas. Its lots of fun, isn't it? Garth, take off your coat and stay a while? Have some tea?"

Garth had unbuttoned his coat but left it on. "Thanks, but no. I can't stay." His voice was tired. "I have sleep to catch up on." He took Jess and baby Michael into his arms, giving each a kiss. Looking into Jess's eyes, he smiled. "Don't worry. Everything will work out. You just take care of this little one, and yourself, too. I'll call tomorrow and let you know what's happening, alright?"

Jess nodded. Giving her another kiss, he bid the ladies goodnight.

"Jess, what's happened? You look upset." Grandmother turned as the door closed behind Garth.

Jess sat in the big chair by the fire, hugging Michael closely. "Garth and I found another body by the road just this side of Hebdon. It was a teenage girl. She wasn't there when we drove to Grassington, but we found her on the way back. Paul thinks she was killed elsewhere and dropped there."

Grandmother pressed a hand over her mouth, closing her eyes. "Oh, dear Lord, what is happening in our Dales?"

~

"You had a phone call earlier this evening," Mrs. Sixsmith greeted Garth at the back door. "Pastor Kilpatrick left a message for you to call when you returned. Said it was important but not urgent."

Garth hung his coat by the door. "Thank you. Did he say he'd be in this evening?"

"Yes. Call even if it's late, he said."

Garth glanced at his watch. "Well, it's not late. I'll call him now."

"Did you have a pleasant evening with Miss Montgomery?" asked the kind landlady.

"A very pleasant evening," Garth smiled. "If you haven't heard yet, Miss Montgomery has agreed to marry me."

"Oh, that's wonderful news! She's such a lovely girl. I'm happy for you both." She patted his arm. "Is there anything you need before I retire?"

"No, thank you. It's kind of you to ask, but after I call Pastor Kilpatrick, I'm going to retire as well. I'm still rather tired from last night."

"Of course you are," she crooned sympathetically. "Rest well. If you need anything, just call. Goodnight."

"Goodnight." In the living room, Garth dialled Robert's number.

"Hello?"

"Robert, its Garth. You called earlier about something important?"

"There's something you should know, but I'd rather not discuss it over the phone. Can we meet somewhere?"

"I can be at your place in five minutes." Hanging up the receiver, he hurried out the back door, pulling on his coat as he went.

He parked by the church parsonage where Robert was staying in Pastor Wright's absence. Robert met him at the door.

Removing his coat, Garth followed Robert into the study, where they sat in armchairs by a brightly burning fire.

"Alright, shoot." Garth settled into the armchair. *This is a mistake. This chair, the warm fire and my fatigue are a bad combination.*

"I visited Connie and her mother at the hospital after this morning's service. Connie was uptight, mostly because of her mother's condition, but something else has upset her. Recently she found Ian after he'd been drinking heavily. He'd asked Jess to go out with him, and she turned him down."

Garth leaned forward, his fatigue forgotten. "Go on."

"I don't know Ian, but Connie's concerned about his behaviour. In his drunken state, he commented that Jess would be sorry for turning him down."

Garth gazed into the fire, his mind racing. "What does Connie think he's capable of?"

Robert shook his head. "She doesn't know. She's hoping it was just the liquor talking."

Garth stood, leaning an arm on the mantle. "Robert, I *do*

know him. I served in France with him, and I don't trust him at all. Always in the middle of trouble, he never got caught. Always came out squeaky clean. I suspect that during the war he was involved in some shady deals. His companions were less than desirable." He ran a frustrated hand through his hair. "And I think he's still up to something. Today I stumbled on a meeting between him and three other men."

"Connie's also suspicious, but can't put a finger on anything. Realistically, he's done nothing except make a vague threat while he was drunk. For all we know, he doesn't even remember it."

"Robert, I hear what you're saying, but my gut instinct says otherwise. I'd like to follow him for a while to see what he's up to, but that's impossible. Perhaps it'd be better to keep an eye on Jess."

"And more enjoyable, I'm sure." Robert chuckled. "I'll do what I can to help look after her. Should we say anything to Mrs. McDonald?"

Garth thought before shaking his head. "It'd only worry her. No. We'll keep it between us for now. And above all, we'll pray for guidance and for Jess's safety."

While returning to the boarding house, Garth thought about the meeting between Ian and the unknown men. Something important eluded his memory, and he grew frustrated trying to remember what it was. *Dear Lord, I'm helpless in knowing what to do. Please guide me. And whatever's eluding me, if it truly is important, help me remember.*

Chapter Twenty-Seven

"Hello?" Grandmother answered the ringing telephone.

"Hello, Mrs. Morag." Gwen's sweet Scottish voice came across the line. "How's everyone?"

"Gwen! It's wonderful to hear your voice. We're all fine. How's your sister? Is she well?"

"That she is. It's for that vera reason I'm callin'. The weather's cleared, and I'm comin' home. Me wee train will be arrivin' tomorrow noon. Could Charlie possibly meet it?"

"Of course! He'll be there before noon, in case the train arrives early." They chatted a bit then Grandmother hung up as Jess came in, arms full of folded linens.

"Why are you smiling?"

"Gwen's coming home tomorrow," Grandmother explained. "She wants Charlie to meet her train. It'll be wonderful to have her home."

"It certainly will. I've really missed her cooking."

"Yes, she's spoiled me, I'm afraid." Grandmother reached to lighten Jess's load. "Here, I'll take some of those."

Before they could climb the stairs, Connie walked in, followed by a blast of cold air. Quickly shutting the door, she removed her gloves and hat.

"Connie!" Jess dropped the linens on a nearby chair, putting her arms around her friend. "What are you doing here? You're not here to work, I hope!"

Connie shook her head, smiling. "No, I just stopped by to tell you about Mother's condition."

Dropping her linens next to Jess's, Grandmother pulled Connie toward the couch. "My dear, do come in and sit down."

"Tell us everything." Jess sat beside Connie. "We've heard nothing since Garth took her in."

"She came out of the coma last night. She's talking but is very weak and tired. The doctors say it'll be a long recovery, but Father and I'll see she gets plenty of rest. We've cancelled all of her engagements until spring, so she has no choice. We'll scale down our family Christmas celebration, and Father and I will make the arrangements."

"And what about you?" Jess asked gently. "Have you gotten any rest? You've had a lot happen the last few days."

Connie nodded. "Yes, I know, but after Mother woke, I went home and slept all night. I'm fine."

Jess smiled sheepishly. "Did, uh, Robert come by to see you?"

Nodding, Connie's cheeks flamed. "He came by the hospital yesterday afternoon. We talked for a while, and ... then he proposed."

"Oh, I knew it!" squealed Jess happily, giving Connie another hug. "I just knew it. I'm so happy for you."

"Congratulations!" Grandmother exclaimed. "That's wonderful news!"

Connie laughed happily. "Yes, it is, isn't it? We haven't set a date or discussed plans yet, but for now, just knowing he loves me is enough. In a few days we'll speak to Father together. Robert planned to do it alone, but I wanted to be with him when he approached him."

"Since your father's never really met Robert, it's probably best," agreed Grandmother. "Your father's a good man, and I'm sure he'll see Robert for the good man he is, too. Now we have two weddings to plan. God's brought two more couples together because of their love for Him and for one another. We wish you the best, luv."

"Thank you, but before I can start planning a wedding, I have some unfinished business to attend to."

"What's that?' asked Jess curiously.

"Christmas shopping for the Dale folk, silly! We have Garth's list, and it's less than two weeks until Christmas."

"I'm ready when you are. When do you want to go over the list?"

"Tomorrow morning? Then we can begin shopping Wednesday. We don't want to wait. The closer to Christmas, the more shoppers we'll have to contend with."

"Sounds good!"

Connie stood to leave. "I'm heading back to the hospital now, so I can't stay."

"Has Ian been to see your mother?" asked Jess.

Connie nodded, answering curtly. "Yes, once. Late yesterday afternoon before she woke up. I suppose because he hasn't been home to hear she was ill. He was gone all the night before."

"Connie, luv," Grandmother said gently. "Try not to be bitter. He's a young man of the world with his own plans and ambitions. He's not yet turned his life over to the One who can set him straight. We'll help you pray for him just as we'll continue to pray for your mother."

"Thank you. That means a lot." She shook her head sadly. "I try not to be bitter toward Ian, but it's difficult when he's so self-centered."

"Well, you just concentrate on Christmas shopping and then a wedding." Jess linked her arm through Connie's. "We'll leave Ian to the Lord."

~

As Jess, Grandmother and Claire finished the supper dishes Garth strolled in the back door.

"Hello, ladies." He included all three in his hearty greeting then walking over to Jess, he placed his hands around her waist, pulling her close for a kiss. "Hello, my love," he whispered for her ears only, his eyes capturing hers. "Happy to see me?"

"Always!" she whispered back.

Garth turned to Grandmother, "May I whisk your granddaughter off for a walk? I know it's cold, but if I promise to bundle her up, may I?" he asked with his usual charm.

Grandmother laughed. "Well, I suppose if you bundle her up well...."

Before she could finish the sentence, Garth pulled Jess to the back door, helped her into her coat, and wrapped a scarf around her neck and chin. Then plopping a hat on her head, he held out her gloves. He turned to Grandmother. "Thanks. See you later." Then they were gone.

Grandmother chuckled and spoke to Claire. "You don't think he's in a hurry to be alone with her, now do you?"

~

Jess laughed as Garth tucked her hand into his and plunged them both deep into his overcoat pocket. "What was that all about?"

Slowing their pace Garth steered her around the house and up the lane toward the main road. "Well, I had a busy day and just wanted to relax with you." He paused before continuing in a serious voice. "I also have information that I didn't want anyone at the house to hear."

"What is it?"

"Paul called late this afternoon. They've identified the body of the young woman we found last night. The coroner reports that she recently had a baby. Paul investigated and found a doctor in Wensleydale who said the young girl came to him, seeking his help. She said her husband was away and she had no family to help her. Knowing she'd deliver soon, he and his wife took her in. After the delivery, he overheard her talking to the baby, saying she'd find him a place to live. Her family would never let her bring him home. When the doctor encouraged her to talk about it, she refused. Two days later, she and the baby disappeared." Garth stopped walking and pulled Jess into his arms. "Jess, darling, we believe she was Michael's mother."

Jess stared into the darkness. She certainly hadn't expected this. Michael's mother! Dead? "Garth, how can you be sure?"

Guiding her back to the house, he stopped near the front door where the light shown softly. Reaching into his coat he pulled out a loosely woven scrap of cloth. "This was found on the body. The doctor and his wife identified it as the cloth the baby was wrapped in. Look at these two edges. It looks like it was torn from the corner of something. Unless I'm mistaken, it matches the cloth Michael was wrapped in inside the basket when you found him"

Jess fingered the cloth thoughtfully. "Well, there's one way to find out. Here." She handed it back to him. "I'll be right back."

Moments later she returned, managing to evade detection by anyone in the house. She handed the cloth to Garth. "I saved it for a rag, but haven't used it yet. You're right, Garth."

Finding the torn corner of the larger cloth he held the two pieces together. It fit exactly.

"Garth, did the doctor know her name? Did he have any idea who her family was?"

"No. She said her name was Mary but gave no last name. She needed help so he didn't press for it. He didn't think she was from Wensleydale, though. He knows most of the folk over there and couldn't place her."

"Oh, that poor girl! She must've been terrified, not knowing where to turn. I wonder who Michael's father was."

"Apparently, she took that information with her when she died. And there's no way of knowing where her family is or who they are."

"Well, the least we can do is ensure Michael is raised with plenty of love and care."

Garth held Jess close again. "That we will, my darling. That we will."

~

"How's your mother today?" Jess asked as she sat at the kitchen table across from Connie.

"She's improving. Although she has a long way to go, her spirits are high. Father told her we'd cancelled all her appointments for the next few months. I expected a battle, but was pleased when she accepted it without a fight."

"Maybe she realizes how ill she is."

"I think so, but she's not the type to stay still for long. As she recovers, we may find the battle's still ahead." She reached for a sheet of paper on the table. "Is this the list?"

"Yes. Do you know any of these people?

"Not many. I'm glad Garth gave an approximate age for each one."

As they worked, Grandmother came through the kitchen, so they asked her for suggestions. She knew most of the people and had great ideas. They'd just finished their shopping list when they heard Charlie drive into the back yard.

Moments later Gwen came in followed by Charlie, carrying her bags.

"Welcome home, Gwen!" Grandmother hugged her.

"Aye, tis good to be home." Gwen took a deep breath, sighing happily. "Back in me wee kitchen."

"Didn't you have the run of your sister's kitchen?" Jess released herself from the cook's embrace.

"For a wee time, lass, but when she was better, I had to share it. And ya know what they say about two cooks in the kitchen...."

"Yes, but you needn't worry about this kitchen," Grandmother chuckled. "We happily return it to you."

"Thank ya, much, Mrs. McDonald. I'm glad to hear it. I can't wait to get back to work. And I want to hear all that's happened since I went away."

"Where do we begin?" Jess looked at Grandmother and Connie

Grandmother put an arm around both Connie and Jess. "Well, to begin with, these two young women have both gone and gotten themselves engaged in your absence."

"Well, bless me soul!" exclaimed Gwen, hands pressed against her ample chest. She looked at Jess with a knowing smile.

"And I'm sure it's the handsome doctor that stole your heart away, lass. I knew it from the time ya arrived. It was in his eyes every time he looked at ya."

Jess laughed. "Then you saw more than I did, Gwen. It took me a bit longer."

"And Connie's taken a fancy to a young man as well," continued Grandmother.

"That's right." Jess agreed. "She's going to marry the Reverend Robert Kilpatrick."

"The young minister of the Kirk? The one taking Pastor Wright's place?" Gwen asked, surprised.

"The very same," nodded Grandmother.

"Oh, my!" exclaimed Gwen. "I've been gone too lang!"

~

Jess and Connie spent the following days shopping in Harrogate, Knaresborough, and even York. They purchased an array of gifts and enjoyed themselves, but by the following Monday, they were exhausted. Jess's bedroom looked more like a warehouse than a bedroom.

Having stored their latest purchases with the rest, Connie flopped into the armchair and Jess dropped across the bed.

"I'm glad we're almost finished." Connie removed her hat, laying it on her lap.

"Me too. Now comes the enormous task of wrapping it all," Jess waved an arm toward the huge pile. "Maybe we can enlist Grandmother's and Gwen's help, along with Garth, Robert, and Claire. Maybe even Charlie could pitch in."

Connie laughed. "Somehow I can't picture Charlie wrapping gifts."

"No, I suppose not."

Silence reigned as they rested, unwilling to get up and move again.

"It certainly is quiet," said Connie. "Unusually so."

"Everyone's gone. Charlie and Grandmother took the children to Christmas play practice."

"Well," Connie slowly pulled herself from the chair, "I'd

better be going. Father asked Robert to dinner this evening. When they met for the first time the other night, you'd have thought they'd known each other for years. I'm so pleased Father likes Robert."

Jess sat up on the bed. "Has he met your mother yet?"

"Not yet. Father thinks we should wait until she's back home and stronger."

"He's probably right. Come on, I'll walk you downstairs."

"When will the others return from practice?" Connie pulled on her coat.

"I don't know. I'm sure they ate before they left, so they won't hurry back."

"Why don't you eat then relax in a nice, hot bath."

"I just might do that."

When Connie was gone, Jess found Gwen washing up the supper dishes.

"Hello, lass. You've a plate of food in the warming oven. I'll fetch you some milk."

When Jess was finished eating, she took her plate to the sink. "Gwen, I'm going up to take a hot bath. All this shopping has worn me out."

"What a bonnie idea, lass. Just relax and enjoy it."

While gathering her warm flannel nightgown, robe and a fluffy towel, Jess ran her bath water. Gwen suddenly knocked at the bathroom door, calling Jess. Not yet undressed, she opened the door immediately.

"Lass, there's a young man at the door. Said he needs to speak with ya immediately. Very important it is, he said. Would ya mind comin' to see?"

"Of course not." Jess glanced toward the hot bath. She'd rather ignore this interruption and climb in, but a few more minutes wouldn't matter.

Gwen returned to her room as Jess descended the stairs. The front door stood partially open, a tall, young man standing on the front stoop. His heavy wool coat was pulled up to his ears and chin, while his tweed cap was pulled low over his eyes. An old delivery van sat running in the driveway.

"May I help you?"

"For certain, luv." His voice was gruff. "Someone wants ta see ya real bad."

"Excuse me? What do you mean?"

"I mean this." Before she saw it coming, the man pulled a heavy black sack over her head, yanking her across his shoulder.

Jess tried to scream, but the thick sack muffled the sound. Carried and then dropped onto a hard surface, she heard the van motor rev up then they were moving. Trying to free herself from the sack, she found it tightly secured on the outside.

"Oh, dear God," she prayed, a sob escaping her throat. "What's happening? I need your help!"

Chapter Twenty-Eight

Closing the door behind the last patient, Garth shoved the bolt in place and leaned against the hard wood. What a day! He was tired and hungry. Dad had left earlier to make house calls before going home. He'd annotate his notes in the patient records then head home himself.

At his desk, he pulled the folders toward him. He'd hoped to visit Jess this evening. His intention of keeping an eye on her wasn't as easy as first thought. Between her Christmas shopping and his patient schedule, he wasn't able to spend time with her as he'd planned. Perhaps after supper he'd steal a few minutes with her.

He'd tried remembering what it was about Ian's meeting a week ago that had disturbed him so. Having replayed it over and over in his mind, he still couldn't remember, causing him frustration.

After spending the next half-hour on his notes, he closed the last file, and reached for his coat. As he drove home, he thought back to France. Perhaps he was thinking about it all wrong. Maybe he had to begin in France and not with the meeting a week ago.

Ian had secured a commission through a family friend,

someone high up in the military, and often bragged about it. He'd hung out with some soldiers who were troublemakers. Rumors suggested he was involved in big time gambling, not just the Saturday night card game with the boys. The officials suspected someone of using army supplies as payoffs, but when questioned, Ian claimed to know nothing about it.

Garth remembered some of the men in the company weren't so fortunate. Several were court-martialed. Some of the men who suspected Ian, had attempted to implicate him. One was found dead, apparently a suicide. Garth, as well as others, thought otherwise. But there was no proof.

Parking his car, Garth walked inside, his thoughts still in the past. He'd grab a hot bath before supper, hoping to feel less tired.

As he relaxed in the hot water, letting it ease the tiredness from his body, he suddenly recalled a night in France that he'd forgotten about.

He and a buddy had gone to supper after their duty was over, choosing a little French bistro not far from HQ. They stayed late, relaxing and listening to the live band playing the soldiers favorites. When they left to return to their barracks, they noticed a fellow soldier lying just inside the entrance to a nearby alley. They'd thought he was drunk and had passed out, but as they drew nearer, they found him dead, stabbed through the heart. He was one of the men that had tried to implicate Ian in the gambling and supply rip off. Garth and his buddy summoned the MP's only to find themselves subjected to questioning.

Garth rubbed his face under the hot water. How could he have forgotten that? After finding the soldier dead, two others were found, killed in the same terrible way. He suspected Ian was involved somehow so decided to watch him. One night he spotted Ian returning to the barracks late, followed by three other men, all carrying brown bags.

That's it! The brown bag! The one Ian had carried had a hole in the bottom corner, and even in the dimly lit barracks, Garth saw white cloth sticking out of the corner. Then he recalled the long white robe and belt hanging in Ian's bathroom at Cameron

Hall and the white bundle that Ian had tossed into the back of his car that day in Pateley Bridge. It might've been the same thing in the bag.

He quickly dried himself and dressed then ran downstairs to the phone, his wet hair dripping on his shirt collar.

After dialing, he waited for what seemed forever before Paul Kendall answered.

"Paul, Garth Samuels here. Can we meet? I've something to talk over with you, but not on the phone. I know it's sudden, but it's urgent."

Paul chuckled on the other end of the line. "I'm on my way. Where do you live?"

After giving directions, Garth hung up and hurried back upstairs. He'd forgotten his appearance until he saw his disheveled reflection in the mirror. He made repairs as he waited for Paul's arrival.

~

Gwen went down for a cup of tea and felt a draft of cold air. The front door stood wide open! *Hmmm. That's strange. Jess must not have closed it completely.* Most likely the wind had given it a good push, opening it back up. She closed it, stopping to listen. It certainly was quiet with the children gone. She hoped Jess was enjoying her hot bath. Perhaps she'd leave the teakettle warming in case she wanted a cup afterward. She walked to the kitchen to put the kettle on.

~

Jess couldn't tell how long the van traveled before stopping, but it seemed forever. She'd tried to open the heavy sack, to no avail. A foul smell permeated either the van or the sack; she wasn't sure which. She only knew she needed fresh air soon.

Who had done this? And why? She had no enemies that she knew of. She'd seen very little of her kidnapper's face, and she couldn't place his voice. Was he following someone else's orders?

As the van suddenly stopped, she lay quietly, straining to hear, but all she heard were footsteps approaching the back of the van.

The back doors were flung open and the sack dragged across the floor.

"Who are you? Why are you doing this?"

Hearing a muffled chuckle, she was flung across a broad shoulder and carried a short distance. Then a door squeaked open and she was carried inside a building. She heard distant and unintelligible voices before she was dropped onto a soft surface and left in silence.

Oh, Lord! Help me! As she tried to pray, the foul smell and lack of air took its toll. Within minutes she lost consciousness.

~

"Paul, can't you see the connection?" Garth paced the floor, running a frustrated hand through his hair. "Ian's involved in something sinister here. Those soldiers in France died the same way the victims here have died. The same white robe was in his bathroom closet as he had in the barracks in France."

"Garth, you've no proof of that," Paul responded quietly. "Just because you saw something white sticking out of a bag he carried doesn't mean it's the same thing that's in his room."

"What about his meeting with those men the other day and the fact that he carried a white cloth bundle? All I'm asking is that you investigate him."

"It's not that simple, Garth," Paul said patiently.

Garth paced to the window, his mind racing. He had a bad feeling about the situation, but there were too many missing pieces.

"Paul, why would anyone kill only vagrants and homeless people?"

"What do you mean?"

"Why would the murderer only choose those particular people?"

Paul stared at Garth's back as he stared out the window. "What does this have to do with Ian Cameron?"

Turning from the window, Garth took his chair again. "Please, just help me think. Let's find some answers. Why would they?"

Paul sat thoughtfully for a moment. "Well, possibly someone

just wants to rid the world of vagrants. You know, like a Jack the Ripper. He targeted prostitutes, and since he was never caught, no one knows why. We've also speculated that these are cult ritual murders, but there's not enough evidence to substantiate that. Then there are those who don't have to have a reason. They're just lunatics."

Garth stood again, returning to the window. Cult. He'd had a conversation about that recently. When was it? Unconsciously he drummed his fingers on the windowsill, racking his brain to remember. Jess! They'd talked on the drive back from the hospital after the flax mill accident. They'd talked about human sacrifices performed by druids centuries ago.

"What if a cult is doing this?"

Paul shrugged his shoulders. "Anything's possible, but as I said, there's not enough evidence."

"But you haven't investigated with what I've told you tonight."

"Let me get this straight, Garth." Paul leaned forward, elbows on his knees. "You suspect Ian Cameron, from one of England's richest and most influential families, of wearing a long white robe and being involved in a cult where humans are sacrificed in rituals?"

"Something like that," Garth nodded.

A knock on the door was followed by Mrs. Sixsmith's voice. "Dr. Samuels?"

Garth crossed the room, opening the door.

"Oh, Dr. Samuels," her voice trembled. "There's a call for you. It's Morag McDonald. She says it's urgent."

Without a backward look, he ran downstairs to the phone, Paul right on his heels.

"Mrs. McDonald? What's wrong?"

"Oh, Garth! It's Jess! She's disappeared!" Grandmother spoke franticly. "We returned from Christmas practice to find Gwen upset. She said Jess was tired from shopping and planned to take a long hot bath and retire for the night. But before she could, a young man came to the door asking for her. Gwen assumed Jess knew him so didn't think much about it and went to her room, but later when she came down for some tea, she noticed the front door standing open. She closed it, thinking the wind had opened it. She thought Jess was in the bath, but grew concerned when she never came out of the bathroom. She knocked on the door, but there was no answer. Going in, she found the room empty and Jess's things untouched. She searched the house but couldn't find her anywhere. We came home and found Gwen in tears. Oh, Garth, what do we do?"

As Garth listened, he felt the cold hand of fear grip his heart. He spoke with an assurance he didn't feel. "Try not to worry. Do you remember Paul Kendall? Yes, he's here. I'll explain everything to him as we head over. We'll find her. Just pray! God knew where Billy was, and He knows where Jess is, too."

After hanging up, he grabbed his coat and hat, beckoning Paul to follow him. Having followed half of the conversation, Paul knew something was terribly wrong. In the car, Garth's filled him in. Knowing he was worried, Paul tried to ignore how fast Garth drove.

When they arrived, Grandmother stood by the window wringing her hands and Gwen sat with tears streaming down her cheeks.

"Oh, Garth, Paul!" exclaimed Grandmother. "Thank goodness you're here."

"Oh, Mr. Garth," sobbed Gwen. "I'm so sorry. I feel just awful, but I didn'a know."

Kneeling by her chair, Garth took her work worn hands between his own. "Of course, you didn't, Gwen. How could you? Don't worry. We'll find her. I'm counting on the Lord to help us, and He will."

Paul questioned the women as Garth stood at the window thinking.

"Paul." Garth suddenly motioned him aside. "You should know that recently Jess was threatened indirectly."

"How?"

"Remember Robert Kilpatrick? The chap who helped find

Billy? He told me Ian's sister, Connie, came home one night and found Ian drunk. Apparently he'd asked Jess out again, and she refused him. He told Connie that she'd be 'real sorry'."

"You think this is his revenge for her refusing him?"

"What else do we have to go on? Who else would want to kidnap her except Ian? He's the only one who has even a remote motive."

Paul breathed deeply, letting out a heavy sigh. He searched Garth's strained features. "Alright. What do you suggest?"

Garth spoke quietly. "If Ian's involved in a cult, and he's kidnapped Jess, he may plan to kill her. I wouldn't put anything past him. Perhaps they're meeting up at Megalithic Folly near Ilton. That's the only obvious place where a cult might meet secretly."

"For years there've been rumors that a druid cult meets there, but there's never been a shred of evidence they exist."

"Paul, forget your evidence for once. You said not a half-hour ago that anything is possible. If a cult is meeting there, they'll evade discovery, but we have to investigate. What else can we do?"

"Alright. I'll call for backup." As Garth started to speak, he lifted his hand. "Don't worry, they'll arrive quietly and stay low."

Garth grinned sheepishly then turned to Grandmother. "We're going to search for Jess. All I can say is pray. Perhaps you should call Robert to come over."

She agreed that she would. After Paul called headquarters, he and Garth drove toward Ilton.

"I hope you're right. You realize my job's on the line here, don't you? If we're wrong, and I've called the North Yorkshire Police out on Ian Cameron for nothing, they'll have my badge."

"I realize that, Paul, but as slim as this lead is, it's all we have."

~

When Jess regained consciousness, she couldn't remember where she was. As her eyes focused and she noticed her surroundings, it rushed back to her. The sack was gone, and two women sat by her. She realized they were wiping her arms with warm water from a pan.

"What are you doing?" she asked, frightened. "Who are you?"

Without responding the two women continued their task. Looking down she realized she wore a long white robe, her feet bare. They were in a small, drafty barn of some kind. She felt chilly in spite of the warm water. One woman pulled her into a sitting position then twisted and braided Jess's hair, intertwining it with flowers. The other wiped a faintly sweet smelling ointment over her arms and feet. They worked gently but were intent on accomplishing their task. Jess spoke to them again, but they wouldn't respond.

When finished, they gathered their things and quickly left the room, locking the door behind them. Jess examined the room, but found no other way out. Sitting on the rough cot, not knowing what was happening, she prayed for God's help.

Soon the door was unlocked and an older woman entered carrying a tray of food. Setting the tray in front of Jess, she spoke with eyes downcast. "You must eat." Then she left before Jess could speak.

Jess tried to determine what the food was. A bowl of spicy smelling porridge, a cup of cold water and a slice of grainy bread were all that was on the tray.

Still feeling queasy from the smelly sack, she certainly wasn't hungry. Her mouth was dry, and the water looked refreshing, but what if it was poisoned? You just don't kidnap people, dress them strangely, and then expect them to eat strange food

Leaving the tray untouched, she leaned against the rough wall and prayed. *Lord, I don't have any control over what's happening, but You do. Please deliver me!*

The door again opened and several men in long white robes, their faces hidden by hoods, entered. She struggled to get away, but there was no escape; there were too many of them. Without a word they carried her out and laid her on a stretcher, tying her arms and legs to the poles. Three men on each side, they carried her into the darkness. Jess was terrified. "Oh, Lord! Help me!" she called out, not caring who heard her.

Chapter Twenty-Nine

As Garth parked on the roadside, he spotted vehicles parked in the dirt parking area, no one in sight. Apparently they'd arrived before the backup officers.

"Well? Where are they?"

"They'll be here, don't worry."

They sat silently until Paul spoke, "It's the 20th, you know."

Unsure why this was important, Garth replied, "The 20th? What does that mean?"

"The winter solstice. Hypothetically, druids gather at certain times of the year to worship and sacrifice to their deities. The winter solstice is one of those times. I was taking your thought about a cult one step further as a possible reason for their sacrifices."

"Well, obviously someone's here." He indicated the cars. "Shouldn't we just go down to the stone circle and see what's happening?" Garth looked miserably at his friend. "Paul, I love Jess more than my life, and the thought that something's happening to her, perhaps this very moment, is more than I can bear. I can't just sit and do nothing."

Paul started to speak, but turned as several cars with no

headlights parked behind them. Backup had arrived.

After he issued directions, the men quietly disappeared into the woods surrounding Megalithic Folly. Garth followed Paul as they hurried silently down the wooded path. Expecting to find guards, they were surprised when they met no one.

~

Half frozen, Jess hardly felt her toes and fingers. Twisting to see in the direction they carried her, she saw a bright flickering light through the trees. As they approached a large bonfire cast strange shadows from huge dark objects.

Carried into a clearing in the middle of the woods, she discovered the shapes were huge stones set on end in a neat oval. Renewed fear surfaced as they carried her through the stone entrance. This was the place Garth had brought her! What had he called it? She couldn't remember. Oh, how she wished she was with him now!

Her bearers placed the stretcher on a long flat stone positioned near the center of the circle. Hooded, white-robed figures watched silently from around the perimeter, their quivering, demonic-looking shadows dancing about from the firelight.

A white-hooded figure approached Jess, an unwilling guest to this strange gathering. Terror gripped her as he pulled back the cowled hood, revealing the handsome face of Ian Cameron.

"Ian?" she gasped. "What is this? Why am I here?"

Ian smiled charmingly. "Jessica, my love, I'm happy you could join us. We're celebrating Mean Geimhridh, the winter solstice. See? We've a Yule log burning, just for you." He indicated the bonfire. "You will help us celebrate in our homage to Dagda, patroness of Druids and Bards."

"What do you mean?" Jess no longer felt the cold, her voice quivering with fear.

Ian continued as if she hadn't spoken. "You didn't eat your gruel of barley, linseed and knotwood. It would've been better if you had."

Turning, he took a wooden box from another druid. Terrified,

Jess watched as he opened it and pulled out a dagger, its shiny blade reflecting the firelight.

"Ian! Why are you doing this?"

Looking into her eyes for the first time, he leaned down to whisper in her ear causing her to recoil. "No one rejects me, Jessica, my love. We could've been happy, you know."

Straightening, he spoke loudly. "My friends, witness the ultimate sacrifice. The rest were only in preparation for the sacrifice of one who is pure."

Jess felt her cold face wet with tears. She was going to die. No one would know until they found her body like all the others. If only she could prevent Grandmother's and Garth's sorrow. Her lungs ached from the cold, and she wanted to scream in terror, but no one would help. She wasn't among friends, but she knew her dearest Friend was with her, and He'd comfort Grandmother and Garth.

The 23rd Psalm filled her mind, and she quietly began to recite it aloud. "The Lord is my shepherd, I shall not want."

Ian looked down, hatred filling his gaze.

"He maketh me to lie down in green pastures: He leadeth me beside the still waters."

Gathering the dagger between his hands, Ian slowly lifted it above his head. Jess's voice grew stronger as the meaning of the words became personal. They were no longer just verses of scripture but words meant for her.

"He restoreth my soul: He leadeth me in the paths of righteousness for His name's sake."

Closing her eyes, she heard Ian mumble unintelligible words. "Yea, though I walk through the valley of the shadow of death, I will fear no evil: for thou art with me."

She jumped as a shot rang out. Opening her eyes she saw Ian's surprise as a red stain spread across the front of his white robe before he crumpled to the ground. Ian's fellow worshipers stood in shock as policemen filled the stone oval, handcuffing them.

Jess sobbed in relief! She was still alive! She closed her eyes, thanking God.

"Jess, darling! Can you hear me?" Garth's strong voice came from beside her.

Opening her eyes, she found him leaning over her, face white with fear. "Garth? What? How? I....I don't understand!"

Untying the ropes binding her wrists and ankles, he pulled her into his arms, holding her securely against his chest. "My darling! I was afraid we wouldn't make it in time. Are you alright? Are you hurt?"

"So far, nothing except exposure," she said, teeth chattering.

Removing his overcoat, he wrapped it around her, buttoning it to her chin then lifting her gently into his arms. Jess looked down at Ian, his eyes staring blankly into the clear, starry sky.

"Poor Connie! How will she bear this?"

"With the Lord's and Robert's help."

"And she has us." Jess laid her head on Garth's strong shoulder, weary and sad.

"Is she alright?" Paul approached them.

"She's cold and exhausted."

Paul stooped to examine Ian's body. "Well, old chap," he straightened, clapping Garth's shoulder, "Thanks for following your gut feelings. I had my doubts, but you were right. Undoubtedly you've solved the rest of the murders, too. After questioning these people, I'm sure we'll find the answers we've been looking for."

"I certainly hope so." Garth glanced at the lovely face lying peacefully against his shoulder. Her long lashes lay against her pale cheeks.

"Thank you, Paul. You've helped return all that is precious to me."

Paul nodded. "I thought you'd say something like that. And I'm glad for you." He glanced down at Ian then back to Garth. "Very glad."

~

Jess handed Billy an ornament then lifted him so he could place it on the big tree by the living room window. The children were decorating its long branches. Four days had passed since Jess was kidnapped. Except for a slight cold, she was fine. Garth wouldn't let her go when he, Charlie and the boys selected the tree, but she did help Connie wrap the gifts for the needy, wrapping for two solid days.

Setting Billy on his feet, Jess thought of Connie. Even with her brother's death and the news of what he was, she'd finished what she'd started. Robert surrounded her with love and a shoulder to lean on. Her father had taken the news hard, but was strong for Connie's mother. Home now but still in bed, Mrs. Cameron took the news hard. Ian was gone, but Robert was readily accepted into the family, a solid wall on which they all leaned. The Cameron's would make it through this loss.

Jess glanced around the house. It looked more like Santa's workshop than an orphanage, complete with elves. Even Billy and Katie had jobs. Evergreen boughs and running cedar were twined around the stair banister and placed on the mantel. Big red bows were hung and a wreath placed on the front door. Charlie hung mistletoe in the archway by the stairs. Decorations and candles were placed throughout the house. Gwen even allowed Grandmother and Jess to help with the Christmas baking. The only idle soul was little Michael, but even he sensed the excitement flowing through the house. He laughed gleefully when Jess held him by the lighted Christmas tree. Everyone stood in awe, the younger children clapping and jumping with excitement. Only one more day until Christmas!

That afternoon the truck was packed with gifts, and Garth, Jess, Connie, Robert, Charlie, Grandmother and the children delivered them to the Dale folk. The humble gratitude expressed by the recipients made all the hard work worthwhile. It had been a true labor of love.

After distributing the gifts, they drove to the church for the Christmas Eve service.

The sanctuary filled with children's voices singing the age-old words proclaiming Christ's birth as they performed the Christmas story. Michael played his part as the baby Savior perfectly, cooing and giggling at the children around him.

Garth squeezed Jess's hand. Looking up, she saw his proud smile, as if Michael were already his son.

Robert narrated the precious old story that never loses its power. Even when an angel fell off his hay bale, knocking over a shepherd, Robert's strong voice never missed a word. The little ones were righted and the pageant continued. As everyone left, the children received apples, oranges and peppermint sticks.

~

Grandmother had no trouble getting the children to bed. For once! The quicker they went to sleep the quicker Christmas Day would come. As Grandmother carried Michael upstairs, someone knocked on the door. Opening it, Garth found Paul standing on the front stoop.

"Paul! Come in!"

Stepping inside, Paul removed his hat. Not in his uniform, Jess almost didn't recognize him.

"Evening, Jess, Garth." He handed Jess a brightly wrapped package. "Merry Christmas!"

"Merry Christmas to you, Paul. What is this?" Jess asked, puzzled.

"Nothing really. Just some candy for everyone."

"Then we'll open it in the morning with the rest of the gifts." She walked over, placing it under the tree.

"Have a seat," said Garth.

"I'll get you some hot tea or cider," Jess offered.

"Thank you, no. I stopped by with some information." He twisted his hat between his hands. "Since the other night, an investigation into Ian's cult activities has turned up pay-dirt. Some cult members refused to talk, but others spilled information like water. Ian led the group even before he went to France, but that's where he began taking human lives. It started as nature worship, but when he was investigated for gambling, he used his cult buddies to kill those attempting to expose them.

"After returning home, he continued practicing human sacrifice, killing people with no family or friends who wouldn't be missed. According to some group members, he became obsessed with Jess. He hadn't originally planned to sacrifice her, but when she rejected him, he couldn't accept that. She became his ultimate sacrifice. Her death would serve two purposes. To appease his druid deities and to avenge his pride." He turned to Jess. "One of our investigators who is knowledgeable about cults said the gruel they tried to feed you was to make you acceptable to their goddess. They believe certain grains and herbs have special purposes."

"Thankfully we don't have to rely on such beliefs." Jess shook her head sadly. "God is the only true God, and His ultimate sacrifice was sending His son to die for us. No more sacrifices are needed. Not now. Not ever. It's sad to think so many are deceived."

Paul nodded thoughtfully. "Those are things I haven't thought about for a long time."

Garth clapped his shoulder. "Perhaps you should, my friend."

After Paul left, Jess and Garth found themselves alone in the living room. The distant sound of scurrying feet faded as Garth pulled Jess over to stand in front of him, grinning as he pointed at the ceiling. Looking up she saw they stood directly beneath the mistletoe.

"You know," Garth whispered, gathering her into his arms. "I've waited a long time for this."

Jess lifted her face, prepared for his kiss.

"Uh-uh, not yet," he teased. "First things first."

Jess opened her eyes to find him holding the most beautiful ring she'd ever seen. She gasped, as he slid it onto her finger. Small sparkling diamonds in a gold setting encircled a larger, single diamond. She stared, first at the ring and then at him.

"It was my mother's. A few years ago Dad gave it to me for my future bride. Thank God, I found her."

"Oh, Garth!" Jess gazed at him happily. "It's beautiful! There are no words to describe how I feel right now. I love you so much. I hope and pray I'll be a good wife for you."

"Do I look worried?" he said gruffly, lowering his head to

claim the kiss she eagerly offered.

The End

This is Carol's debut novel

Carol Nemeth has enjoyed making up stories since junior high school, most based in the places she has lived. She served in the US Army where she was stationed in Italy and traveled to over thirteen countries. After marrying the love of her life, who she met while stationed in Italy, they lived in a lot of places, including North Yorkshire, England. They now live in West Virginia, where, in her spare time, Carol enjoys sewing stuffed animals for the local ambulances to give to sick and injured children that they respond to calls for and baby blankets for the Local Birthright organization, a Pro-Life group that provides help to young pregnant woman. Carol and her husband are active in their church and enjoy their two grown children, son-in-law and two grandchildren. A third is expected soon and Carol looks forward to spoiling that one, too.